ALAINA T. LEE

Insatiable

First edition

ISBN: 979-8-21-845376-3

Editing by Hannah G. Scheffer-Wentz, English Proper Editing Services
Cover art by Alexis Hooper
Proofreading by Hannah G. Scheffer-Wentz, English Proper Editing Services

This book was professionally typeset on Reedsy.
Find out more at reedsy.com

This is for all my fellow good girls who just wants someone to burn the fucking city down for them and then take you home, wrap their hands around your throat, and fuck you senseless. Damn, we love it here.

Contents

Trigger Warnings

As usual, before proceeding it is important that you know that this book contains degradation, BDSM, water play, breath play, murder, gun violence, trafficking, child abuse/rape (mentioned, not on page), miscarriage (mentioned, not on page), birth control tampering, gun play, knife play, breeding kink, spanking, and CNC.

If any of these could be triggering to you, I strongly recommend you do not move forward with reading this. Your mental health is important to me and I trust you know your limits. Read at your own risk.

Xoxo,

Alaina T. Lee

Playlist

Hold Me While You Wait- Lewis Capaldi
Crazy in love (remix)- Beyoncé
Call Out My Name- The Weeknd
Wicked Games- The Weeknd
I Feel Like I'm Drowning- Two Feet
Never Say Never-The Fray
Haunted- Beyoncé
What Was I Made For?- Billie Eilish
I Put A Spell On You- Annie Lennox
Those Eyes-New West
Lose Control- Teddy Swims
I See Red- Everybody Loves an Outlaw
Gonna Love You-Parmalee
River-Bishop Briggs
Pretty Little Poison-Warren Zeiders
Beautiful Things- Benson Boone
Love Is a Bitch- Two Feet
Pointless- Lewis Capaldi

Spotify link: https://open.spotify.com/playlist/3wtuKJBlbkVo
iCJX8JRC4H?si=aKI_HgEyRj6gdrBlDY_4tw&pi=u-SiOtjp-9R
b2O

1

Liza

"Was that a gunshot?" Alicia cries. I jolt up and head for the door, punching in the code to open it.

"Mr. Salando said to stay here, ma'am. I think we should wait for him or for his team," Martin sputters out as a group of men in all black barrels through the doors, going directly to the stairs. I'm assuming that's the team he was talking about, but all I can wonder is who the fuck they are.

"I am not waiting around to see who that gunshot was for." I bolt for the elevator, not wanting to get in the way of the team using the stairs. I take a deep breath and gather my thoughts.

What if Graham's hurt? This is my fault. This is all my fault. I step out of the elevator and run towards my apartment. My door is wide open and I can hear men yelling in their walkies-talkies for emergency services to get up here immediately. I push past the officers who are blocking my view as I desperately try to reach Graham.

"Ms. Crambell, I need you to wait" someone yells, but I push them out of the way. My heart stops and my face pales at what I see. *Blood.* Blood everywhere. Brains? Are those fucking *brains* on my wall? *Graham.* Where is Graham? Suddenly, my vision becomes blurry and everything goes black.

* * *

"She's coming to. She'll be fine, she was just in shock. Give her some water and tell her to breathe." I blink my eyes open to see a petite lady dressed in a pantsuit with her hair pulled back into a tight, low bun.

"Ms. Crambell, you fainted. Paramedics say you'll be alright, though." I sit up on the couch and grab my head. Fuck, that hurts.

"Graham, where is Graham? I heard gunshots. Is he hurt?" She comes and sits beside me, turning to me.

"The paramedics are downstairs checking him out. I need you to tell me what happened here today." Tears immediately filled my eyes.

"Graham and I argued in the elevator; he usually walks me in and stays, but this time he didn't." I cringe at the memory of our argument. "When I got in here, Tim was here with a gun pointed at me. He told me that if I didn't do exactly what he said, he would shoot me. He used his gun to touch me...sexually. I tried to fight him...I tried," I croaked.

"It's ok," she soothes.

"He tied me up and tried...tried." I start to cry and she rests her hand on my shoulder.

"Take your time; he tried to do what? Did he try to perform sexual encounters on you?" I acknowledge her accusation with a nod.

"Ok and then what?"

"I headbutted him and rammed my knee into his groin. But when he took his dick out I threw up all over him. He got upset and hit me on the head with the gun, which caused him to tie me up and gag me. Then he left to make a phone call. That's when Graham got here, set me free, and told me to go to the safe room." I wipe the tears from my face and remember all the blood. "Is Tim..."

"Dead? Yes. That man of yours though is a hell of a lot luckier than your father was. Tim had every intention of coming here to kill him. We found his journal; he had a list of 'threats' he needed to eliminate to keep you for himself. Mr. Salando was at the top of that list."

"What will happen to Graham?"

"Nothing. The cops turn a blind eye to anything the Salandos do. They own a lot of things in this city. Mr. Salando does a lot for the police department and in return they help him when things *happen*. Besides, this was clearly self-defense. But don't focus on that, focus on knowing that Tim will not be a problem for you again." She smiles softly.

"Can I see Graham now?"

"I'll take you to him." She leads me to the elevator and escorts me in. Once the doors shut, she turns to me and warns.

"When you see him, just brace yourself."

"Brace myself for what?" *Ding.*

The doors open and I see Graham sitting in the back of a black SUV past the lobby. His shirt is soaked in blood as he holds an ice pack up to the side of his face.

"Graham!" I croak out. He drops the ice pack and runs towards me. I reach him in record time, jumping into his arms. He wraps me tightly in his arms and lifts me off the ground.

"Angel, I'm ok." I sob into his arms and he kisses my forehead. "Come on, let's sit." He puts me down and directs me to sit in the back of the SUV. He wipes my tears from my face and inspects the gash on the side of my forehead from the gun. He puts his head down and takes a deep breath.

"This is my fault," he claims in a faint voice.

I frown. This wasn't anyone's fault but Tim's. We were only attacked the first time a few days ago—no one could have known he'd come back so soon. I wrap my arms around Graham's neck and nestle into him.

"This isn't your fault."

"I should have walked you in your apartment. I *always* walk you in. If I had walked you in then..."

"Then he would've shot you and took me anyway." I lean back and look him in the eyes. "The lady told me that he was planning on killing you."

"Yeah, I figured that much." The lady comes over to us and extends her hand out to Graham.

"I'm Aggie Jones. We've been watching Tim under Brant's orders for years, but he recently went off the grid. We knew his target was most likely Ms. Crambell. I'm glad you got here when you did. Based on the journal we found, there's no telling what he would've done to her if you hadn't come back."

Graham pulls me into his side, running his fingers through my hair. I lean into him and sigh. "You two should go home and get some rest. Ms. Crambell, if you need anything, Mr. Salando has my phone number. We'll keep this as quiet as we can." She walks off and I look up at Graham. I can still see the anger pouring off him.

"Can we go?" I ask. He kisses my head and nods, directing

me to his car.

The ride to Graham's house is silent again, but this time for different reasons. We both replay the series of events in our heads. Graham holds my hand so tightly during the drive that I start to feel my fingers go numb.

He carries me upstairs when we get to his house and starts the shower. I turn to him and look at his blood-splattered shirt. I approach him, running my hand over his cheek and down his arms. Tears fill my eyes and he shakes his head.

"No more tears over me. If you're going to cry, cry because someone breached your privacy. Cry because you were afraid of what would happen to you, but *do not* cry for me."

"But your shirt—you could've been hurt."

"It's not my blood, baby. I'm ok." I reach for the shirt and pull it over his head. I kiss his chest and then the bruise on his jaw.

"You can't do that again. What am I supposed to do if you die? What am I supposed to do if you get hurt?" I weep uncontrollably at the thought. "You can't leave me, Graham."

He lifts me and I wrap my legs around him as he walks into the bathroom, sitting me on the counter. He lifts my shirt over my head and carefully removes my bra, pants, and panties. I hop down and unbutton his pants, pulling them down for him to step out of before I remove his boxer briefs.

He lifts me again and walks us into the hot water. He sits on the bench inside the shower and nuzzles into my hair. He kisses my hair then my neck as he whispers in my ear, "I'm never leaving you." I look up at him and plant a soft kiss on his lips, holding back tears. I've cried enough and needed to soak up this intimate, passionate moment with the man I love.

"I love you."

"I love you." He kisses me again. This time it's with more urgency, plunging his tongue into my mouth. I kiss him back with the same force, tugging his hair and kissing his neck. He pulls my breast into his mouth and sucks as I let out a low moan.

"Hold onto me." I wrap myself around him as he guides himself inside me. I sink myself further onto his cock and we both moan at the intrusion.

"I'm never letting go," I tell him.

Because God as my witness, I never plan to.

2

Graham

After giving Liza several rounds of deserved orgasms, we kept searching for excuses to touch each other. It was like today was the wakeup call neither of us knew we needed. I knew that I could be ruthless. I knew that I would do whatever necessary for the people I love. But what I didn't know was how boundaries truly don't exist when it comes to Elizabeth. Any human being that brings her pain, I want to annihilate. The thought of someone, *anyone,* touching her makes me see red. It's a height of anger I never knew I could reach, but for her? It's still not enough.

"Are you hungry?" I ask her, pulling on sweatpants. She slips on one of my t-shirts and I stare a second too long before I'm caught.

"What?" She shrugs. "This is my favorite t-shirt of yours... It smells like you." I pull her into my body and hug her tight. "I like seeing you in my clothes." She stands on her tiptoes and kisses me, tugging on my lip with her teeth.

"You need to eat first, angel."

"I don't want to go anywhere. Can we order in?"

"Actually, I'm going to cook for you." She raises her eyebrow and tilts her head at me.

"Really, now?"

"Yes, really," I say to her confidently. I'm a good cook. Our childhood chef taught both Selle and I how to cook growing up. "We need to talk about earlier as well, pretty girl." She rubs the back of her neck.

"I know." I kiss her cheek and guide her downstairs. I pull out two ribeye steaks and two lobsters, pointing to the chair for her to sit.

"Sit. We'll talk while I cook."

"You're cooking steak and lobster? What's the occasion?"

"The occasion is you being safe and here. With me."

Soon enough, she'd be with me every day. She leans over the kitchen island and I meet her halfway. I place a soft kiss on her lips, our foreheads resting on each other.

"Did he touch you?" The words are out of my mouth before I have a thought to stop and consider my delivery for this conversation. She sighs and even her exhale cracks. "It's ok. We don't have to talk about it right now. Let's just focus on you being safe," I reassure her.

She plays with a piece of her hair, her tears dissipating in the rim of her eyes.

"I'm sorry about earlier," I whisper. She closes her eyes. "Look at me."

She turns to me, looking at me with those bright, brown eyes.

"I'm sorry, too. I wasn't trying to hurt you," she says quietly.

"I know you weren't, but I wanted to talk to you about something and that just kind of derailed me."

"Ok?" she pries, raising her eyebrow. "What is it?"

"I think we should wait until after dinner for that conversation."

"Oh, come on. You can't do that," she groans. I turn and tilt my head, giving her a wicked grin.

"Oh yeah?" She sticks her lip out and starts to pout, frowning. "Don't frown, you'll put wrinkles on that beautiful face of yours." I wink at her and look at the clock: 5:15 p.m.

"Alright, dinner should be ready by 6:00 p.m. Want some wine?" She nods her head and smiles.

"After my day—hell, after my week—I think I'll have a whole bottle."

"I can't have you drunk tonight, angel."

"Why? Then you can take advantage of me." She gives me a wink. I grab the wine to pour her a glass, shaking my head and letting out a chuckle.

"What am I going to do with you, woman?" She giggles and takes a sip.

"I'm sure you'll find something." I pour myself a glass and take a sip, too.

"That I will."

3

Liza

The dinner Graham made was exceptional and the wine was even better. But my favorite part was laying in his arms being safe, warm, and happy. I planned to tell him I was staying here in Seattle with him, but for some reason, I wanted to do it in a unique way. I know he second-guesses whether we will be together, always thinking I will leave him. I want to tell him in a way that he has no reservations about us; that there is no doubt that I'll stay with him through everything.

I also know I need to tell him what happened with Tim. I need to tell him that he touched me, but not how he thinks...

I look up at him as he sleeps peacefully despite giving me yet another one of the best orgasms of my life. I kiss his chest and watch it rise and fall. I start to join him when my phone rings. *Eli.*

"Hi, Eli."

"Hey, sis."

"What's up?" The other end of the call goes silent. I pull the phone from my ear to check if it is still connected.

"Eli?"

"Yeah, I'm here...I just...I wanted to ask you something."

"You know you can ask me anything. What is it?" Silence again. "Damn it, Elias, spit it out."

"I want to move to Seattle and I was wondering if I could stay with you in your apartment. I've already started the paperwork to transfer to UW and will still be on track to graduate next May." My eyes widen in surprise.

"You love being in California."

"Yeah, but I love being with Selle more." My heart flutters.

"You love her, don't you?"

Silence. Eli lets out a long sigh. "I know it's fast. I know you think I'm stupid."

"I don't at all." I look up at a sleeping Graham and smile. "When you know, you just know. The heart wants what the heart wants. You love her and that's all that matters."

"I haven't told her yet."

"She knows, trust me."

"Yeah...I hope so. So, is that a yes?" I laugh at his question.

"Yes, of course, it's a yes. I'm so happy for you."

"Thanks, sis. I love you."

"Love you." I hang up the phone and smile at my conversation with my brother. Graham flutters his eyes open and I kiss him on the cheek.

"What has you smiling so much?" he asks in a groggy voice.

"My brother. He surprised me just now, that's all." Graham raises his eyebrow and I wink at him.

"I don't even want to know." I laugh and he pulls me towards him.

"You feeling ok?" I ask. He runs his fingers through my hair and nods.

"I am. Have you heard from that Jones lady?"

"Nope. Not yet. I umm, I want to tell you what he did…to me." Just then, my phone rings.

"Hello?"

"Ms. Crambell, this is Aggie Jones." I quickly put the phone on speaker.

"Hi, Ms. Jones."

"I just wanted to be the first to tell you that Tim had photos of your entire family as well as Mr. Salando's. He was planning something very big. We found bomb parts and surveillance videos of your brother and parents' house. Mr. Salando's reputation doesn't give him justice—make sure you hug him a bit tighter tonight. He didn't just save your life; he saved your family's, too." My breathing quickens and Graham's body tenses. He puts a hand over mine and tightly squeezes it.

"He was watching them?" I ask.

"Yes, it looks that way." I wipe away the tears that start falling on my face. "Anyways, I want you to forget this happened. I sent you information on a therapist if you need one. But I want you to understand that this happened because you were protecting yourself. I encourage you to move on with your life. You deserve it."

"Thank you, Ms. Jones. Have a nice night."

"You as well." I hang up and my hands start to shake.

"Don't cry." Graham says. I wipe my tears again and look up at him. My protective Graham. I should be terrified that he seems fine after killing a man. I should wonder how many he's killed before right? Why don't I care?

Because he protected me.

I cup his face and look him in the eyes.

"You protected me. I'm still here because you protected me. I'm forever grateful for you and want you to remember that. But I have to ask you, are you ok?" He inhales deeply and briefly glances away from me.

"Baby...talk to me," I plead.

"I don't want you to think differently of me."

"Nothing would make me think any different of you, " I encourage.

"This isn't the first time I've taken someone's life, Elizabeth. You know I'm dangerous. You know I stop at no lengths to protect my family and those I love. There have been many times where my life and theirs have been threatened. I've had to do things a human being my age should never have to do." He pauses. "When Selle and I were taken...I...I killed two of them; it was the first time I'd done it. I didn't think twice, I had to save Selle. It was the same thing with Tim, I had to protect you. But angel, I felt *nothing* when I did it."

"I don't care about that. When you were taken circumstances changed, you had to adapt to that change. You're the same person to me." I run my finger over his cheek as he kisses the inside of my palm.

"When I realized Tim's goal was to kill me and take you, something lethal came over me. It was different than those other times. All I could think about was you. Protecting you. Making sure you were safe. I'll never have remorse for taking someone's life who thought they could take yours." I wrap my arms around his neck and climb into his lap.

"He can never hurt me now. I'm not crying because I'm upset; I'm crying because I'm happy. I know that sounds bad. I shouldn't be happy that someone is dead. But I'm happy that it was him and not you." He wraps his arms around me.

"Me too, angel. Me too." I take a breath and steady myself to say the words I'd never thought would come out of my mouth.

"He gun fucked me. He used a knife, too...and tied me up with bondage rope to leave marks..." Graham is silent. Too silent. I can't make myself look at him. I wonder what he's thinking, what's going through his mind.

I finally muster the courage to look up at him. His jaw is clenched and he has a look in his eye that I have never seen before.

"I—I was afraid I wouldn't want you to touch me," I continued. "I felt violated, sick, degraded. I hated it and I can't get it out of my head. It's like it's on repeat."

It's silent for a moment before he responds.

"That fucker is lucky that he is already dead. I need you to look at me," he commands gently. I peer up behind my lashes and reach his gaze. "There is nothing that can happen that will change my desire for you. We're going to try something. If it's too much for you, I want you to think of a safe word. Ok?"

"*Lilies*," I say instantly.

"*Lilies?*"

"Yes, it's what you gave me to convince me to go out with you. So, *lilies*."

"If it becomes too much, you say *lilies* and it's over. Got it?"
"Got it."

He slides out from under me and leans over, pulling out a gun from the drawer next to his bed. He stands and goes into the closet, returning with a bladed knife. My breath hitches and I shoot up into a sitting position. He watches me as I watch him. "We're going to erase that memory of that piece of shit ever touching you. The only man you'll remember gun fucking you, *knife* fucking you, will be me." He cocks the gun and pulls me to him by my hair. I don't know how it happened, but I'm wet. Like, puddles of water dripping down my fucking legs, wet. He slides his hands into my underwear, cursing under his breath before he slides his finger inside of me.

"Fuck, you're soaked. Does this turn you on, angel?

"Only when it's with you," I moan. He slowly inserts the barrel of the gun into my pussy and I gasp.

He moves the gun in and out of my pussy, watching my every reaction. "You look like a perfect little slut riding my gun, coating it with your juices. I can smell you from here, baby."

When he turns it to the side and spreads my leg open more, I feel the handle of the knife being added. I fall backwards onto the bed, moaning his name. He pushes the handle deeper into my pussy. His hand is wrapped around the blade and there's blood dripping down his wrist. I gasp and he squeezes it tighter, not showing a slither of pain. My pussy is sore from the four rounds we'd had earlier, but yet I want more. What kind of person wants to be fucked by a gun after her kidnapper did it to her? What kind of person wishes it was the sharp end of the knife instead?

Me, apparently.

My body is tensing and I'm squeezing my legs tight. I'm praying this gun isn't fucking loaded, because I'm sure the orgasm that's about to tear through me will be enough to make him pull the fucking trigger.

"Graham...baby...I'm coming."

"Come, pretty girl. Come all over my gun. Coat my knife with your juices and forget that waste of space ever fucking touched you. *You're mine.*"

"Yours," I agree.

I come with such a force my body is stuck in a frenzy, trying to catch up with my mind. The gun and knife are gone and it's suddenly over. Graham pulls me to face him. He runs his hand through my folds and licks the taste of me off his fingers.

"I will erase any man who's touched you, tasted you, or even thought about you," he swears.

"Thank you," I say, breathless. As fucked up as it sounds, this was what I needed to move on from what happened to me. He cared enough to recreate what happened to me, to make me forget about how awful it was, and replace it with a memory I welcome. One I'll probably be asking him to do again.

I bring his hand up to my face and inspect it. There's a gash and blood is still coming out of it. I lift his hand and smear his blood over my chest as he watches in astonishment.

"Yours," I say, planting a kiss on his hand.

After showering for what feels like the twentieth time, I decide to make the dreadful phone calls to my parents to update them on my day. They got the doctors to release my dad immediately and are flying home tonight. My mom is distraught and my dad is pissed. Brant, the glue who keeps them together, was glad I was alright.

"About that talk," Graham mumbles into my hair. I roll over to face him.

"I'm listening."

"I want you to move in with me."

Finally.

This is the perfect way to tell him I'm staying here in Seattle and show him my home is wherever he is.

"Why?" I ask, knowing it's eating him alive that I haven't already said yes.

"Because I don't want to be away from you. Because I don't

want to sleep without you. Because I don't want to ever have to worry about your safety again."

"Can I think about it?" I know I'm going to say yes, but I also know that I want it to be in a special way. It won't hurt for him to wait for my answer. He's waited for me his whole life. What's a little more waiting?

"Just don't make me wait too long, I'll go crazy," he says in a low tone. I kiss him and smile.

"I know."

4

Graham

Two days have passed since I asked Liza to move in with me. She still hasn't given me an answer, which is driving me fucking insane. Is she really ok with being away from me? Is she not as tormented as I am? Does she not feel how I to be around her, wanting to constantly protect her? It's tantalizing. It keeps me up at night with the unobtainable urge and need to keep her within arm's reach at all fucking times.

I crave her constantly. Even when I'm around her, it's still not enough. I could never get enough of the desire, the want, the heat she makes me feel.

I'm pulled out of my daze when the door to my gym opens.

"Hiiiiiiiii, I need you to get dressed, please," Selle orders, handing me a towel. I raise my eyebrow at her. "Don't look at me like that, go."

"And where exactly am I going?"

"That's for me to know and you to find out." I take the towel from her and wipe my face.

"Giselle, I am not playing your little games," I say, heading for the door.

"Please, just this once, listen to your little sister. You won't regret it." I tussle her hair and she groans. "Thank you. And please, for the love of God, take a fucking shower."

I shower and dress in a black button-up and black jeans. Since Selle won't tell me where we're going and I don't know what to wear, I know I need to be ready for anything with her. She's given me no clue, but you can never go wrong with all black.

"Is this fine? Or is this a fucking black-tie event or something?" She looks me up and down.

"Nope, you look perfect." She approaches me and sniffs the air around me. "Perfect, you wore your good cologne." I tilt my head.

"I only have good cologne, you creep." She waves me off and heads for the door.

"Let's go, let's go. We can't be late." We walk out and Ellis is waiting at the Audi Q7.

"Graham."

"El?"

"Strict orders to tell you nothing."

"Oh, they pay you now?" He ignores me as I get into the backseat after Selle, who is giddy and beaming from ear to ear.

"What the fuck is going on? Why are you so happy right now?" She pinches my cheek and I nudge her hand away.

"Just happy to see my big brother, is all." I know that's complete bullshit. About ten minutes pass and we arrive at an old dock my family owns. My dad's boat is on the water and I can see my parents, Brant, Bethany, Eli, Hogan, and Axel in his wheelchair. They are all mingling with each other. Where is my Liza? Where has she been these last two days?

"Where's Liza?"

Selle looks down at her phone, responding to a text.

"She'll be here. Dinner isn't for another thirty minutes." She looks over at me and I raise an eyebrow in question. "I wanted our families to have dinner together. Is that a problem?"

"No, no problem, but why was it secret?"

"Because I knew you'd find a way out of it and keep Liza to yourself."

She's right about that. Liza hasn't answered her phone more than once a day, twice if I'm lucky.

"Well, I haven't talked to her much these last two days." Selle reaches for the door handle and climbs out.

"I know."

"*You* know? How do *you* know?" She doesn't acknowledge my question at all. I follow after her.

"Hi, darling," Mom greets, bringing me in for a hug. I kiss her on the cheek.

"Mother." She swats at me.

"Stop it with the *Mother*," she snips, yet still smirks. I grin at her and say hello to everyone. I stop at Eli and narrow my eyes at him. I glance at Selle, smiling as she talks to our mom.

"She's happy, I can see that. As long as that smile stays there, you'll have no problems with me," I say. He gives me a low grin and stares at her. I recognize that stare. That's the look of a man in love. It's the same way I look at Liza. "Hurt her and you'll be six feet under," I say in a low tone.

Eli nods his head. "If I hurt her, I'll hand you the shovel myself." Just then, the atmosphere changes and I know *she's* here. I am always warped by her. My desire and fire never change, she instantly brings it out of me.

She walks down the dock in a red cocktail dress that stops

mid-thigh. Her long hair tumbles over her shoulder in big, loose curls.

There's my girl. Beautiful as ever. Breathtaking.

She gives her mother a hug and kisses her father on the cheek as she quickly starts greeting everyone else. I stand back, hands in my pockets, gazing at her. She stands in front of me and tilts her head.

"Something wrong?" she asks, standing next to me.

"Besides the fact that I haven't seen you in two days, and when I do, you're wearing a dress that's too damn short?" I pull her in and kiss her forehead. "I missed you, angel. Two days is too long."

"I missed you more." My lips find hers and I almost forget that we're surrounded by our families. Leave it to Selle to be quick on her feet and make sure I'm more than aware.

"Once again, get a room." Selle nudges. "You look so damn good! I want your dress," she says to Liza.

"It kind of looks like yours," Liza tells her. I look between the dresses. My sister's is almost identical, except hers is blue and *much* shorter. Eli comes over and wraps his arm's around Selle. "Except hers is too fucking short," he growls out, kissing her cheek.

"I fucking agree," I mutter.

"Boys! Language." My mother peeks over at us, giving us her deathly glare.

"If everyone wants to head onto *Madeline*, dinner should be just about ready," my dad announces, gesturing towards the boat. My mom and Bethany walk before him and we follow closely behind.

"Can I steal you for a second? I have something I want to give you," Liza whispers to me once we board. I grab her hand

and pull her into one of the bunks. I catch Selle watching us. She tries to look away before she's caught, but she isn't quick enough. I don't know what the fuck is up with my sister tonight, but I'll be damned sure to find out.

"Is everything ok? You and Selle are both making my wheels spin tonight." Her face looks different—she seems nervous. She reaches into her purse and pulls out a small, black box tied with a red bow. "What's this?" I ask.

"Open it."

I untie the bow and open the box to find a piece of paper that's folded into a small square. I look at her and raise an eyebrow. She looks down as I unfold the paper. It's the lease to her apartment and a check for the next two months of rent. I search her face. "According to one of your clauses in our rental agreement, if I break my lease I have to pay the next two months of rent," she explains.

I chuckle at her confidence. I tear up the check, followed by the lease. "None of your parents' checks were cashed for rent. What makes you think yours will be?" I stalk towards her and she puts her hand out to stop me.

"You're telling me I've been living there for free?" she asks incredulously.

I ignore her question and move her hand, pulling her up to me. "You're serious? You'll move in with me?"

"If you still want me to." I kiss her, seeking entrance with my tongue. She opens for me, as she always does. Our tongues glide against each other and I guide her to the wall. I slip my hand under her dress and move her panties to the side, plunging my fingers into her.

"I told you this dress was too short." She moans into my ear. "I'm going to do this to you every night in *our home*." I squeeze my hand around her throat, slightly cutting off her air supply. "I'll tell you when to breathe." I tug a little harder around her throat and run my tongue up the side of her neck. She groans and I tighten my grip more. "Goddamn, this is a fucking sight to see. Your lips are turning blue, but yet you're still riding my fingers like you're my desperate little slut." I squeeze once more before loosening my hold from her neck. "Breathe, angel." She gasps for breath. I bite her lip as I say, "Mine." She kisses me and bites my lip back. I squeeze her neck again as I dig my fingers deeper into her pussy. "You have ten seconds to come, otherwise you'll have to wait until I get you *home.*"

"Graham..."

"Ten...nine...eight...seven...six..." The sounds her pussy makes is music to my ears. I love the feeling of her dripping all over my hand. I know she can barely breathe, but instead of chasing air, she's chasing her orgasm. *Dirty girl.* I speed up my fingers, counting a little faster when I feel her pussy start to clamp around my fingers.

"Almost there, angel. Five...four...three...two...Come, now." She explodes. It's like her body is connected to me. It does exactly what I say when I say it. I've learned every inch of her body, every tick that sets her off. It's become my favorite fucking thing to do. She digs her nails into my shoulder and bites down on her hand to muffle her screams. I continue to finger fuck her until she stops shuddering. She tries to push my fingers away when her legs start to shake. I release my hand off her neck and place a kiss where my hand was.

"I liked that," she tells me, trailing off and staring at my hand still inside of her. I raise my eyebrow and yank her to me again.

"We have to stop. Our families are right outside that door and I'm not so sure I'll be able to stay quiet this time," she whispers. I reluctantly pull my fingers out of her and she whines at the emptiness.

"For the record, my home is wherever you are, Graham. I love you so much that I can't think straight most of the time— so much that even after having you, it's still not enough for me." She's saying the very words that invaded my thoughts mere hours ago.

"Angel, you have no idea...Let's get this dinner over with so I can fuck you in every inch of *our* house."

"Mmm, I can't wait."

5

Liza

Selle comes up behind Graham and me, clearing her throat. "Do I even want to know where you two went? Our parents were especially curious." I try my best to keep a poker face, but I think not answering was equivalent to shouting that Graham just made me come from fucking me with his fingers only minutes ago.

She pats me on the back. "Don't worry. I covered for you, but both of you owe me," she says as she walks towards Eli. He looks away from Hogan and pulls her to his side.

"He loves her," I say, staring at them. Graham looks at me and follows my gaze, slipping an arm around my waist.

"Yes, he does," he agrees, staring down at me. I lean into him and look at both of our families together. This is what life is supposed to feel like—the happiness, the love, and the memories.

"Alright, everyone, let's eat!" Madeline bellows with a smile. We all gather around the table as a few servers come out with trays of appetizers and salads.

"A toast," Joe states, standing up. He looks around the

table and smiles—a smile I've never seen before. "To family, our children, and to them always being safe." We all lift our glasses.

Halfway through dinner, Graham asks me, "Should we tell them?" I sip my champagne trying to mask my fear.

"I'm nervous. What if they don't approve? We're not married."

"Then we'll get married," he says without hesitation. I roll my eyes.

"I'm serious."

"I am, too." I can't help how high my eyebrow raises. He's *impossible*.

"You don't even have a ring, Casanova."

"Who says I don't?" My eyes widen and he winks at me. "We're adults—we make our own decisions. If they have a problem with it, they can deal with it themselves."

"Ok..." I say hesitantly. He kisses my cheek and turns to everyone.

"We have something to tell everyone." All eyes turn to us and he looks at me and smiles. "Liza and I are..."

"Engaged?!?" our mothers enthusiastically ask in sync.

"No, we're moving in together," I say. My mom smiles and Madeline clasps her hands together in happiness. I look over at my dad and he gives me his signature look of approval. Having his support is so important to me. It means the world to me.

"Does that mean I can I have your apartment?" Eli cuts in.

"Oh, honey, why on Earth would you need an apartment here in Seattle?" Mom asks.

"Yeah, Elias, why could you *possibly* need an apartment here?" I tease as he narrows his eyes.

"I'm transferring to UW this semester."

"What about graduation?" my father asks.

"I'll still graduate on time." Selle looks at Eli in complete shock. I guess he hadn't told her about his plan yet.

"I take it you knew something about this, sweetheart?" Madeline questions. Selle shakes her head and swallows, looking up at him.

"No, I wasn't...aware."

"I've already started the transfer paperwork and packed my things at Dad's." Hogan pats him on the back.

"You mean our stuff. You started packing *our* stuff." We all laugh at him and he turns around and shrugs. "What? There's no way he's leaving me in California. Sorry, Selle, you get two for one."

She playfully pushes him and I down the rest of my champagne.

"So, no objections?" Eli asks, looking at our parents.

"I trust your judgment, son," my dad says. "You and your sister are both adults and seem very happy." He glances at Selle and smiles. "That's all we care about." He looks at my mother and she nods.

"Of course, I'd be happier if you all were in New York, but I'll take what I can get," she jokes, winking. That's my mother—constantly pushing for more. Eli looks at me and raises his eyebrow.

"So, about that apartment?" I look up at Graham and he shrugs. I reach into my purse and throw him the keys.

"Consider this a late birthday present."

"Love you, sis."

I wink at him and Selle silently thanks me.

After dinner we danced and had drinks. Everyone is enjoying

themselves and it brings me joy to see them all together.

"How are you feeling?" I ask my dad. He pats his lap and I sit down gently.

"Your old man's perfectly fine. How are you? Moving in together, that's a big step."

"Yeah. I know. But I can't imagine it being anyone else. I can't explain it."

"I'm having a hard time grasping the idea of you replacing me, Lizzie." I kiss my dad's cheek.

"I wouldn't dream of it. You'll always be my favorite man."

Graham clears his throat as he approaches. "Ahh, there's my competition," he says.

"What can I say? She's been tied to my hip since she was born," Dad says triumphantly.

Graham holds his hand out to me and gently lifts me from my father's lap.

"Doing ok, Axel? How's the shoulder?" Graham asks.

"Oh, it feels fine. I don't know why they insist on a fucking wheelchair. I can walk perfectly fine."

"The medications you're on are strong, Dad." He waves me on and I fold my arms.

"Yeah, yeah. Go dance with your Prince Charming and leave me be, will you?" I kiss his cheek.

"Love you, old man."

"Love you, Lizzie."

The music is soft and slow while the weather tonight is perfect. Our families are taking photos with each other and enjoying each other's company, but Graham's father is barely present for any of it.

"Where does your dad keep ducking off to?" I ask, searching around us.

"I'm not sure, but he's been off all night. He's practically glued to his phone."

"Hopefully everything is ok."

"Is it ever, angel?" I nudge him and he spins me to the music.

"Is it bad that I'm ready to get out of here?"

"No, not at all. In fact, I was thinking the same thing." He kisses my cheek. "Let's go home."

6

Graham

Ellis drops us off at home and I give him the rest of the weekend off. A driver won't be needed for what I have planned for Liza. I planned to keep her here, to myself, and explore every piece of her body.

"Ugh, my feet hurt," she whines, walking into the house. I scoop her up into my arms and carry her to the couch. Pulling off her Louboutin heels, I start to massage her feet. She leans her head back and closes her eyes with a moan. "You're too good to me."

"Not possible." She relaxes as I work my magic on her sore feet. "Are you tired?"

"Hm?" That answers my question. I lift her and take her upstairs to our room. She catches my hand when I lay her on the bed. "Come here."

I push a strand of her hair out of her face.

"You're tired, get some rest."

"I'm not too tired for you to fuck me," she says suggestively. My lips start to curl up, but I fight the urge.

"Angel—" She pulls my hand under her dress and pushes

my fingers against her slick pussy. The moment I feel her wetness I close my eyes and swear under my breath.

"I need you," she begs.

"Fuck." I don't fight it as I push my finger deeper into her. She throws her head back and moans. I pull her panties off and move in between her legs. I can't help myself but to lick all over her pussy like a man possessed, tasting her sweetness.

"Please," she groans.

"Please, what, my little slut? What do you want?"

"You. I want you. Please." I insert my tongue inside of her and she jerks her body up. I place my hand on her stomach and push her back down as I continue to devour her.

"You're going to come, just like this, and then again from me fucking you. Understand?" She nods eagerly as I continue to tongue her pussy until her body tenses and she releases her cum. I lick and suck every drop she offers my mouth.

She balances herself on her elbows and watches me undress as she unzips the side of her dress. I growl in satisfaction, sliding her dress down her body. She lays there, her brown eyes focused entirely on me. Her body is on full display for me as I tease her opening with the tip of my cock.

"Please. Please, Graham."

"So impatient," I say, sliding inside her. I move in and out slowly, torturing her as she whimpers. I play with her a little more and finally give her what she wants. Slamming into her body she screams out, digging her fingers into my back. "Is this what you want?" I grunt.

"Yes. *God, yes.*" I pick up my pace, pushing myself deeper and deeper into her. She wraps her arms around me. When her body tenses, I know she's right there. I bury my face into her neck, giving her a rough, animalistic bite.

"Come, angel. I'm right there with you."

On my command, she lets go and my body tenses as I release inside of her. "Fuuuck. *So good*," I growl.

I'll never be tired of this woman.

An hour later, we are still wrapped in each other's arms when my phone rings—unknown number. I look at the clock; it's 11:00 p.m. I hit the ignore button and wrap my arms back around Liza.

"Who was it?"

"Unknown number." She lays her head back down on my chest and her stomach growls. "Someone hungry?"

"Cereal, I want cereal," she mumbles. I pull the covers off us and we go downstairs as I fix us both a bowl of cereal. "Thank you, baby." She shoves a spoonful in her mouth and my phone rings again.

"Unknown number, again."

"Maybe you should just answer it. How many times have they called?" She swallows, taking another spoonful.

"This is the second time...Hello?" The other end of the call is silent. Just as I am about to hang up, I hear breathing. "Who is this?" I ask.

"The person that's going to kill every fucking member of your family, starting with your father."

"Who the fuck is this?" Silence again.

"Oh, and Graham, that little bitch that's sitting across from you...I'm killing her next." *Click.* What the *fuck?*

I jump up and check the doors, closing the curtains over the windows. Reaching under the coffee table, I pull out the hidden Glock and cock it. Liza turns and looks at me in confusion and fear.

"What is it?" I ignore her and pick up my phone. "Graham!

Damnit! What?"

The call to my father goes to voicemail. I call again—voicemail. *Fuck.* I call my mom and she picks up immediately.

"Honey? What's wrong?" "Where's Dad?"

"In his study. Would you like me to get him? Is everything okay?" I hear her get up and can hear her walking down the stairs.

"Just get there, Mom. Something's wrong. Quickly." I hear her pick up the pace until she swings the door open.

"Joe, sweetheart, it's Graham. He wants to—" Silence. Her breathe catches.

"Mom...Mom, what is it?!" After what feels like an eternity, she finally speaks.

"He's gone. And there's blood everywhere."

7

Graham

It's been two days since I received a phone call threatening my family and the woman I love. We still haven't found my father and my mother is growing increasingly worried. My father has a lot of skeletons in his closet and now it's up to me to figure out which one had he completely fucked over. No way in hell is anyone getting to my family.

"Graham," Liza says, laying a hand on my shoulder. I look out the window in my mother's living room. She wraps her arms around me, turning me towards her. "Are you ok?" I nod at her and she rubs my cheek with her soft, small fingers.

I take a deep breath, leaning into her touch. "I'm ok. Just running through the list of people that my father could've fucked over. It's a pretty fucking long list." The doorbell rings and startles us as my mom goes to answer it. "I got it," I say, stopping her in her tracks.

When I open the door, there's a box laying there addressed to my mother. *Something doesn't feel right.* I step outside and look around, finding no one there. How the fuck did it get here with no one else in sight?

"What is it, darling?" Mom asks, peeking outside of the door. Her eyes land on the box and she reaches down to pick it up.

"Mom, don't open that." She pulls the card out to read it. Her face goes pale and she quickly opens the box. Her screams take over the whole house. The box drops along with my mother.

I flip over the overturned box and see my father's wedding band—with his finger still attached. Gathering my mom in my arms, I hug her tight.

"I'm here. I've got you," I whisper as she tightens her arms around me.

"Mom! What is it?" Selle pulls her out of my arms, engulfing her. She glances at the box and I shake my head at her.

"Do not look inside, Giselle. I mean it." She frowns at me, but nods, tugging my mother back inside of the house. Liza searches my face for answers and I put my head down, reaching for the card.

He isn't dead yet...but he will be. I'll be in touch.

I tuck the note in my pocket and grab the box, closing it up. I look at Liza as she wraps herself in her own arms.

"Go inside and stay there. I need to call Ellis," I say.

"What's inside the box, Graham?" I shake my head at her and pick my phone up, quickly pulling Ellis' name up. "Tell me!" she shrieks.

"His finger! It's his fucking finger. Now go!" She jumps when my voice raises and quickly turns for the house, shutting the door behind her. I don't have time to be gentle—I'll apologize later. I start walking towards the front gate; the guards should remember who the fuck they let in.

* * *

Both guards had been knocked unconscious and the cameras were busted. Neither of them remembers what happened, just that they had been hit in the back of their heads. Ellis is already on his way with my team. None of my family will be left alone from here on out.

Our family doctor examines the bodyguards while Ellis' team checks the perimeter.

"They'll be fine, probably should take the rest of the day off. The size of the knots on the back of their heads will require ice and rest," the doctor says. I nod, but the guards shake their heads.

"I don't need to rest, I need to get back to doing my job," a guard groans out. I raise my hand, silencing him.

"You heard the doctor. You both are off for the rest of the day. Now get out of here." Once they leave, I reach into the black bag I've been holding.

"This is what they sent my mother," I say to Ellis. He looks down and opens the box, not even flinching at its contents. That was El, though. Tough as fucking nails. Nothing rattled him. Ever.

"Have they reached out yet?" he asked.

"Not yet. But if they start with his finger, El, what the fuck is next? They addressed it directly to Mom, she nearly had a heart attack."

"Your mother is strong. You know I'll do whatever I have to do to protect you and your family."

"No, El, *we* will do whatever we have to do to protect them."

8

Liza

A finger. Joe's finger. In a box. What the fuck.

It keeps repeating in my head as I watch Madeline pour herself a glass of wine. Despite the fact that it's 12:00 in the afternoon, I don't blame her. Actually, I could use one myself. Reading my mind, she steps into the living room where Selle and I sit.

"Wine?" We both nod and she hands us our glasses, sitting next to me on the couch. I rest my hand on her knee, giving her a squeeze. She looks at me and smiles.

"I'm ok, honey. I promise." She tips her glass back, swallowing the wine in one gulp and quickly refilling it with the bottle that sits on the table.

"So, his finger?" Selle asks. Madeline nods. "With his wedding ring still on?" She nods again. "What type of sick fuck—"

"*GISELLE*. Language." Selle shrugs her shoulders. Our heads snap towards the door as it opens. I let out a sigh of relief when I see Graham and Ellis stroll through.

Graham walks over to us and puts his hands in his pockets.

"Drinking at noon, are we?"

"With the last forty-eight hours I've had, sweetheart, you're damn right I am. I should've started a long time ago." Graham nods.

"You are absolutely right, excuse me." Graham walks over to the bar and fixes himself a Jameson on the rocks. He quickly throws the drink back and turns to me. "A moment, please?" I nod and get up.

"Excuse me," I say to Selle and Madeline. They both nod and start talking amongst themselves. It seems like Madeline wants to talk about any and everything other than the situation at hand. I can't say I blame her, though.

I follow Graham into his old room. He shuts the door behind us, and when I hear him lock it, I turn to face him with my eyebrows drawn together.

"Everything ok?" I ask.

"It will be. After I fuck you."

He yanks me to him and crushes his mouth over mine. Even though I know this isn't the time, I still open for him. My body always responds to Graham, even when we are in the middle of trying to make sure his father stays alive.

When I break the kiss, I stare at him, seeing the sadness fill his eyes. I also see the need—the need to take control.

"What do you need?" I whisper. He rests his forehead against mine.

"You, just you."

"Take what you need, Graham." He wraps his arms around my neck and kisses my cheek, then my neck.

"Take your clothes off."

He steps back and my hand quickly goes to my shirt, pulling it slowly over my head. He sits on the bed, watching me closely.

I unbutton my pants and shimmy them off. I begin to hook my finger under the seam of my underwear.

"Stop," he commands. I freeze and look at him. He stands and walks over to me.

"You know what I wonder?" My breathing quickens and I shake my head. "I wonder just how quickly I can make you come, without me being inside you, without my tongue, fingers, or touch…I wonder…can I get you off with just my words?" I swallow and immediately my pussy responds. I know he could, I know within a matter of minutes I could come from just his words. "I think we're going to try that," he drawls.

"Now?" I ask breathless.

"Yes, right now. See that mirror right there?" He points to the full-length mirror that hangs on his wall. I nod. "We're going to watch you come to *nothing* but my words, then I'm going to fuck you until you scream my name. Do you understand, pretty girl?" I lift my head to nod again, but he shakes his head. "Words."

"Yes, I understand."

"Good girl." He walks me over to the mirror and stands behind me, making sure not to touch me. He brings his mouth to my ear, whispering, "Ready?" Chills cover my body.

"Yes."

"Have you ever wanted someone so bad that you only see *them* every time they walk into a room? That's what happened to me when I first saw you, Liza. I wanted you." He looks into the mirror and watches me as I lick my lips and shift my stance, my pussy already getting wet at the sound of his voice.

"It took everything in me not to follow you into that bathroom. I wanted to, so bad. I wanted to bend you over the sink and fuck you. I wanted to kiss those sweet, plump lips into oblivion. Then Emily left...but what you don't know is, I told her to." I frowned. "Don't look at me like that, angel, it was her idea. And I thank her every day for it. She wanted the room to herself and I wanted you to myself."

I settled because I didn't care if he told her to leave me. I wanted him from the moment I saw him, too, and I want him even more right now. "When you got to my house, the only thing that was going through my mind was the different places I could fuck you. The different ways I could make you come." He tilts his head and looks at me. "I think I'm going to tell you the ways I thought about making you come. Would you like that?"

My legs feel like noodles, I'm pretty sure I'm going to bite a hole through my lip. I can't speak. "I asked you a question, Elizabeth." I nod quickly and his lip tips up a fraction.

"My first thought was to eat that sweet pussy of yours, to push my tongue in and out of you, insert my fingers and milk you over and over again. Then I thought about simply laying you on the counter and pushing my cock so far inside of you, slow and gentle at first, leaving you so close to the edge, you thought you'd die if you didn't come." I close my eyes and moan as he continues. "I think you would've liked both of those options. Wouldn't you?" I nod.

"Yes, please." I need to be touched, I need to come. I reach for my pussy, but he grabs my hand.

"No touching." I groan in frustration. "You want to come? Don't you, angel?"

"Yes, yes, I want to come. Please, let me." He lets out a small, evil chuckle.

"Don't you want to hear the rest of my story?" I nod. If

it'll help me come, I need to hear it like I need my next breath. "My shower was my next idea. You were going to straddle me and take every inch of my cock. You were going to ride me like you owned me. I was going to suck those perfect tits and massage your pussy as you rode me *up and down* to your own rhythm." I moan and at that moment my legs became weightless. I was coming, I was coming from Graham telling me how he planned on fucking me the first night he met me. In the middle of my climax, I felt Graham pushing my underwear down my legs. Within seconds, his hand was grabbing my pussy, circling his thumb over my clit. My breath hitches and I brace my hands against the mirror.

"I knew you could do it, baby. Now I'm going to fuck you." He pulls his pants down and lifts me. "Wrap your arms around me and spread those legs." I oblige and he plunges into me. Pushing my back against the mirror, he sinks his teeth into my shoulder and I claw at his back.

"Oh, God," I moan as he pushes in and out of me, harder and harder with each thrust, tangling his hand in my hair. I wasn't sure how much longer I'd last. "I have to come again."

"You will wait for me. I'm almost there. You come when I say you can." He thrusts harder and yanks my hair, pulling my face toward him. He kisses me roughly, pushing his tongue in my mouth. "Fuck, angel. Come, come right now. I need to feel you tighten around my cock." I let go immediately. "My name," he growls. "You say *my name*. Only my name when you're coming."

"Graham!" I scream out. He throws his head back.

"Fuck, yes," he grunts, completely unphased with his family being in the house with us. He needed this. He needed me. I'd never tell him no. Whenever he needs me, I'll be there.

9

Graham

I sit Liza down on her feet and withdraw from her, suddenly annoyed by seeing my cum drip down her leg. For some reason, it bothers me that it's escaping her body. She runs her finger over her pussy and brings it to her mouth. If she sucks that finger, I'm done for. I will have to fuck her all over again.

She looks me in the eye and smiles, sticking her finger in her mouth and sucking my juices off. My cock stands up immediately; I never knew I could get hard again so fast. But that's what she does to me. I groan and yank her to me, crushing my mouth over hers.

"Why'd you do that?" I demand.

"I wanted to see how we tasted together," she says coyly.

"And?" She licks her lips and pushes her fingers between her legs again. She goes to put them in her mouth again, but I grab them. "If you do that, I'm going to have to fuck you again."

I let go of her fingers and watch her as she battles with her choice. She pushes her fingers into her mouth and I smile. "Now it's my turn."

I lift her and toss her on the bed, crawling between her legs. I lick every inch of her, tasting both of our juices together—something I never fucking thought I'd do. The last thing I wanted to do was taste myself, but fuck, she drives me so fucking wild that I'd do anything to feel close to her. I eat her pussy with a vengeance, fucking her until she begs me to stop. I make sure to push every ounce of my cum back into her. Right where it belongs.

* * *

Liza fixes her hair in the mirror as I stare at her. "You're beautiful." She looks at me and smiles.

"You're beautiful."

"Are men beautiful?"

She walks over to me, standing in between my legs. "The man I'm staring at right now damn sure is."

I rest my head on her stomach and wrap my arms around her waist. She wraps her arms around me and pushes her hands through my hair. Before I know it, tears fall uncontrollably down my face.

"Hey, it's ok. We'll find him."

"If I can't protect the people I love, I've failed." She squeezes my chin, tilting it up to her.

"You haven't failed at anything. You put a lot of weight on your shoulders to carry alone. We're safe. Your father will be, too." She wipes my tears and stands me up, planting a long, soft kiss on my lips. "I love you."

"I love you. More than you know." I indulge in the moment, trying to control my breathing. When my phone rings. Liza gives me a nervous look and squeezes my hand. "Unknown number. It's them," I confirm. I stare down at the phone, walking downstairs to where my mother, Ellis, and Selle sit. "It's them, they're calling me," I say.

"Alright, you know the routine, Graham. Keep them on the phone and we can trace it," Ellis says. I clear my throat, waiting for El to set up his equipment. My finger hovers over the answer button as the phone stops ringing.

"We missed it, they're going to kill him," my mom says. I reach for her and kiss her cheek.

"They'll call back. Relax." God knows I hope I'm right. Five minutes later, I'm put out of my misery with another phone call. I look at El and he nods.

"Ready when you are," he says. I take a deep breath and Liza grabs my hand.

"You got this," she says. Selle slides next to her on the edge of the couch and watches me closely, giving me a small smile.

"Get him back, G."

I answer the phone aggressively because I'm done with this shit.

"What?" I demand, my tone sharp.

"Ahh, there you are. I was beginning to think you didn't care about your old man."

"Cut the shit and tell me what you want."

"Your entire family dead."

"Not happening." I'm cocky with my responses. I know what my family and I are capable of.

"Maybe, maybe not. But I can promise you that someone is going to die. Whether or not it's your father is up to you. Here's what's going to happen. You are going to wire five million dollars to the account number I'm going to text you.

Once you do that, we can *discuss* letting your father go. If the money is not there by tomorrow at 12:00 p.m., I'll send your mother another piece of her waste-of-space husband. You understand?"

"I understand," I grit out through my teeth. I'm going to slice this fucker's throat the moment I lay eyes on him. The only thing I can think is how perfect it'll look when he's choking on his own blood.

"Good, we'll be in touch." *Click.* Moments later my phone dings with a text message containing an account and routing number. I look at El, but he shakes his head. *Fuck.*

"Must be using an untraceable phone."

"We need to call the police, honey." Mom says, I look at my mother and shrug—I know there's nothing I'll be able to do to change her mind about that. She picks up the phone and makes the call none of us wants to make.

The call that would officially broadcast my father as *kidnapped.*

Thirty minutes later cops were everywhere. I hadn't expected anything less; my father was an important person and he owned over half of the fucking town. Of course they'd give it their all.

"The FBI will be here shortly, Mr. Salando. We've made it our number one priority to find your father. We have one of the top hackers tagging along. If anyone can figure out who that account belongs to, it's this guy," one of the cops tells me.

My mom smiles sadly at Liza, holding her in an embrace. "I hate what's happening, but I'm so glad you two are here," she says.

"We wouldn't be anywhere else," Liza replies. Selle raises

her eyebrows at that as my mom turns around, conversing with a police officer who is asking her questions.

"Anywhere other than G's room fucking like rabbits..." Selle mutters. Liza's eyes widen and her cheeks turn red.

I slide my arm around Liza's waist and scowl at Selle.

"You're embarrassing her, Giselle. Besides, you should *not* have been listening."

"I wasn't, trust me," Selle quips.

If there's one thing about Liza, she cannot fucking be quiet. The only time she can be quiet is when I have my hand wrapped around her throat or my cock gagging her mouth.

"I...I didn't know you could..." Liza says, tucking herself against me.

"Hear you Neanderthals? Yes, I absolutely could." Selle turns and walks away, laughing. I turn Liza to me and she flushes.

"If she heard me, then your mom..."

"Elizabeth, I am a grown man. I can fuck whomever I want, wherever I want. I'd fuck you on that kitchen table while my mother was in her room thirty feet away if I wanted to." She gulps down a loud swallow. "Hearing me talk like that turns you on, my little slut?" I grin. She slowly bounces her head up and down. "Later, angel," I say, nipping her earlobe with my teeth.

10

Liza

The next five hours went by in a blur; there were FBI agents everywhere. People asked question after question, but Graham and his family handled it without a sweat. I hadn't expected anything else, though. This was a twenty-five-year-old man who ran a multi-billion-dollar company. One who didn't flinch when a gun was going off towards him. Someone who could take anything that came his way. This was *my* man.

"Do you need anything?" I ask him once he's finally alone. He shakes his head, looking down at his phone. "I'm going to check on your mom and sister," I continue. He nods again, not bothering to look up at me.

This isn't about you, Liza.

"You guys ok? Need anything?" I ask, walking over to Selle and Madeline.

"I'm fine, sweetheart. Tell me you both are staying here tonight? I couldn't bear the thought of being alone in this big house tonight," Madeline says as she pats my shoulder.

"Of course, we'll stay, Mom." Selle had just moved out and gotten her own place. She was excited and happy to finally be on her own, but I knew there was no way she'd leave her mom while this was happening.

"I keep thinking who would want to hurt your father. And the list is so damn long, I can't narrow it down."

"You don't think it could be the cartel again?" Selle asks. Her mom's face suddenly whitened. "Mom...Mom?"

"The note, where's the note?" she asks frantically, looking around the kitchen. Graham appears next to us.

"What's wrong?" he asks.

"I mentioned the cartel and she freaked, saying that she needs to see the note," Selle provides. He reaches into his wallet and stares at the card. He looks at Selle and his jaw tenses.

"G, what is it?" He ignores Selle and hands the card to his mother. She flips it and stops her antics, sitting at the kitchen table.

"That's impossible," she says her voice barely a whisper. Selle sits by her, reaching for her hand. Graham begins to pace the kitchen floor, back and forth. Back and forth.

"Graham, stop fucking pacing. You're making my head spin," Selle says. "What is it, Mom?"

"This card. It's the same card we got when..."

"When what?" Selle asks. Madeline puts her head down and Graham pales. "When what, goddamnit?!"

"It was the card your father and I received when you and Graham were taken, Giselle. I don't know how I missed it. It looked familiar, but I wasn't thinking straight," Madeline whispers. Selle sits back against her chair, her eyes filling with tears.

"So, I'm right? It's the cartel...again..."

"Your father...he was supposed to handle it. He *said* he

handled it."

Handle it? Was she talking about killing them? What the fuck is going on in my life right now? I thought the Tim situation was fucked up, but for fuck's sake, my family had nothing on this.

"He was supposed to kill them," Graham grits out. "We've got to get these fucking cops out of here. Now." Graham moves with swiftness, heading for Ellis and giving him the rundown. Ellis moves toward the police and moments later they all leave except for two men. They seem familiar with Graham and his family, like they knew each other.

Ellis moves to stand beside me.

"Who are they? Why'd they stay?" I ask Madeline, nodding towards the two guys who are standing next to the door.

"That's the hacker and the agent that helped us when Graham and Giselle were taken."

"It's nearly 1:00 a.m., I'm going to get some rest. Graham, I trust that you'll wake me with any news?" Madeline asks. Graham hugs his mom and kisses her on the cheek.

"Yes, Mother. Get some rest, love you." Selle brings her in for a hug, giving her a kiss on the cheek as well.

"Love you, Mom."

"Love you both." She turns to me and hugs me, whispering in my ear, "I'm so glad you're here, I'm so glad he has you." She turns and Ellis walks her to her room.

"Let me know if you need anything, as usual I'll be right down the hall," she says over her shoulder, disappearing into her room.

"Fuck this, I'm going out," Selle says. Graham turns to her, his eyes dark and full of anger.

"Like hell, you are. It's one in the morning, Giselle, and our fucking father was just kidnapped."

"I need a drink. The town bar is open until two. I'll be quick."

"What part of *a hit on our fucking family*, don't you under-stand? You want a drink? Go to the fully stocked bar directly behind you."

He's being harsh, rude, and mean. He never talks to her that way—his sister is his best friend. He's stressed about his father, and Selle knows that, but she still winces at his words.

She grabs her coat and Graham yanks it out of her hands. "I am a fucking adult, give me my coat!"

"You aren't leaving, Giselle." She pushes him, but she may as well have pushed against a wall because he doesn't fucking budge. Tears fill her eyes as she glares at him, pointing her finger into his chest.

"I am not letting this fucking cartel ruin my life again. I will not live my life in fear, *again*. I refuse." Her entire body starts to shake, releasing the tears that she was trying so desperately to hold back. Graham drops her jacket and pulls her into his embrace.

"No one is going to touch you again. Nothing will happen to you. I swear." She sobs into his arms, speaking unintelligible words. Graham strokes her hair as tears stream down his face.

"I hate him. This is all *his* fault. It's always his fault. What they did to me, what they did to *you*, and what they're doing now." He continues holding her as Ellis clears his throat and walks into the kitchen. I take the hint and follow. This felt personal; too personal to witness.

"I hate seeing her this way. This shouldn't be the way their lives are," Ellis says, sitting at the table.

"I thought my life was insane..." We both chuckle at my comment. It was nice to laugh, even if it was only briefly.

Moments later, Selle comes in, kissing me and El on the cheek.

"I'm going to bed. Goodnight."

"I'm here if you need me, Selle," I whisper to her as I hug her.

"Angel...ready for bed?" Graham appears.

"Yeah. See you in the morning, El." He nods and walks into his room that's not too far from Madeline's. We head up the stairs into Graham's room where he fucked me just hours before.

I turn to Graham and look at him. His under eyes are dark and he looks tired. He shuts the door and lets out a long, dragged-out sigh.

11

Graham

"Baby, you're tired," she says, running her hand over my cheek. She's right, this fucking day needs to end. I'm losing the ability to think, to be level headed. What I truly want to do is start a fucking blood bath, but I know it'd make everything worse.

I lean into her touch and place my hand over hers.

"Thank you for being here with me."

"I'm always going to be here for you, Graham. You know that." I sit on the bed and she bends down, pulling my shoes off for me, one by one. My pants and shirt follow as she looks to me and says, "Come on, take a shower so you can rest. You've had a rough day."

"Yeah, to say the least." I reluctantly stand and trot into the bathroom. She turns the shower on and the room quickly fills with steam.

I step into the shower directly under the water. The water rolls over my head and down my back. I put my head against the wall and close my eyes.

I rack my brain over and over on what the fuck the cartel

could want with us again. I personally knew that my father had them killed. I overheard the entire conversation he had with the personal hitman he hired. At least, I thought I had...

Before I knew it, tears pooled out and down my face, mixing with the water. My palm slammed against the wall.

"Graham!"

I continue to cry, letting out every emotion I've held in for the last forty-eight hours. Liza steps in behind me fully dressed, not caring about her clothes getting wet. She pulls me into her and hugs me.

"It's ok. It's ok to be scared." She reaches up to shut the water off. I sink my head, gathering myself when she lifts my face to meet her gaze. She's right—it's ok to be scared, except I'm not scared. I'm livid.

"I'm here, I'm right here. Whatever happens, I'm with you. Whatever you want to do tomorrow, I'm with you. You want to burn the world down? I'll hand you the match. I've got you, always." I rest my forehead against hers and kiss her. She smiles against my kiss and tugs me out of the shower. "Let's get to bed."

Liza snuggles against my chest, her fingers trailing up and down my arm, while my other drapes over her as we lie in bed.

"If he had them killed...how are they back?" she asks, snuggling closer to me.

I sigh. "My father told us he had them killed, I thought I even overheard a conversation he had discussing that. But now, I'm not sure if he said that just to please my mother or not. I never...I never told you details about Selle and I getting taken. I wasn't sure it was something I could relive without wanting to kill my father myself." She kisses my chest and looks up at me, resting her head on her hands. "He was responsible...Selle and

I had been followed the day before leaving school. We knew it had something to do with my father because Selle had seen the man at his office before. What we didn't know is that our father was helping the cartel traffic women and children. A part of me wonders if that's where he met my birth mother. But I never figured that out. When she left she killed herself not long after. He never admitted it, and when he realized we were putting the pieces together, he tried to pull out. That didn't go over well with the cartel, so they took us. He told my mom it was a ransom kidnapping, but really, he sold Selle and I to give himself a out with the cartel. That was the deal I overheard the cartel offer to him when they called. Selle never knew. Dad fed her lies when Ellis got us back himself; told her he'd been doing everything he could, but I knew the truth. If it weren't for Ellis, we would have never made it out. My dad made his decision that day. It took me so long to be able to look at him, to be able to stomach being around him. He was a liar in my eyes, but I couldn't prove it. So finding out that he never followed through on his promise to handle them, doesn't fucking surprise me."

"He *sold* you?"

"Both of us."

"I'm sorry...and your mother, you never got any closure... you deserved closure. I'm—I'm sorry."

"Don't be. I've recovered. I never missed my birth mom. Selle is older and dealt with our kidnapping in her own way. I wish she didn't have to deal with this again."

"Are you afraid?"

"I am for Selle, for my mother, and for you. Not for myself." A crease forms above her eyebrow.

"For me?" Fuck, that's right. I never told her about them

threatening her.

"Yes, for you. You're a target because of what you mean to me." She looks away and I smooth her hair behind her ear. "Don't look away from me. I'd never let anything happen to you. I'm just as dangerous as they are, angel." She is still looking away, so I turn her face to me. "Tell me you know that..."

She looks at me and after a few silent moments she utters, "I know."

"Come here." She sits up and straddles me, wrapping her arms around my neck. "I love you."

"I love you," she says, planting a kiss on my lips. "And you don't have to be afraid for me...I'm pretty tough." I grin at her, rubbing my hands up and down her back.

"I don't doubt that for a second, angel." I tuck her into my side and moments later she drifts into a deep sleep. I follow suit not even a minute later.

* * *

The next morning came quicker than I wanted it to. Was today the day I was going to get my father back alive? Or was it the day he'd be delivered to us dead?

I look down and watch as Liza sleeps, bending down to kiss her forehead. I slowly slide from under her, careful not to wake her. I shower quickly and go downstairs to see El and my mother sitting in the kitchen, smiling at each other.

My mother and Ellis have always been friendly and polite to each other, but Ellis is in love with my mother. He always has been. It wasn't a secret he hid well, at least not from me and Selle. When he found us at the compound of the cartel, he was feral. All he cared about was finding us and putting a smile back on my mother's face. In some ways, Ellis has been more of a father figure to us than our own father. The thing is, my mother is in love with Ellis, too. Everyone else, including my dad, thankfully, was oblivious to it, but my sister and I knew. We always knew. When we were young and Dad first cheated on Mom, Ellis was there for her. She doesn't believe in divorce, even though she hasn't been happy in years. Even though she wishes she could be with Ellis instead.

I walk in and clear my throat, making Ellis stand quickly.

"If you two think I don't know about this," I gesture back and forth between them, "you both are *seriously* mistaken."

"Honey, I'm not sure I know what you're talking about," my mother says dismissively. El just looks away. If there's one thing he won't do, it's lie to me. Avoid admitting it? Yes. But lie? No.

I grunt as I pull two coffee mugs out for Liza and me, being sure to put more creamer than coffee in hers. I turn toward them, raising the mugs to them. "Please, continue whatever this *isn't*."

"Sweetheart, one second." My mom follows behind me, placing her hand on my back. "Has the money been transferred?"

"No, I need to know Dad's alive for sure first."

"Well, if I know your father, he's probably making it really hard for them *not* to kill him." I know that she's trying to make light of the situation to make herself feel better. But the truth of the matter is, a part of me wonders if she'll truly care if he doesn't make it out.

"Mom, he'll be fine...We will all be fine." I hope to hell I'm right.

12

Liza

I wake up to Graham biting on my nipple before he pushes himself inside of me. He plants a kiss on the side of my neck as he pushes deeper into me. I moan, my eyes still closed from recent sleep.

"Give me those eyes, pretty girl." He lifts my leg on his shoulder, pushing himself further inside me. I practically feel his cock in my throat with how deep he is. "Being inside you is the highlight of every fucking day." I jerk my eyes open when he wraps my hair in his hand and yanks. "Mmm, there she is," he coos. He slams his lips over mine as he increases his speed, fucking me harder like an animal. My pussy struggles to keep up. I'm so close to coming that my body no longer feels like my own. "Someone's about to come," he taunts.

"Graham…"

"Mmm, good girl. Say my name. Always have my name on your lips. Give it to me." And I do. My head thrashes back and he buries his face into my chest as he pumps me full of his cum. I can feel its warmth dripping out of me. He looks down and frowns, pushing his cum back into me.

"Can't waste a drop," he says, smearing the leftover cum over my lips, which I eagerly clean off with my tongue.

"You know I'm on birth control, right?"

"So?" He rolls his lips together.

"*So* that statement contradicts itself." I laugh as we both get dressed. Although, now that I think of it, I can't seem to find my pills. "Speaking of, have you seen my pill pack?"

"Can't say I have," he says, kissing my cheek. I don't believe him, but there's also no way he'd hide my pills from me. He leans over and grabs a mug off the nightstand, handing it to me. "Just how you like it."

I sit up and take the warm cup in my hands, inhaling the scent of the coffee. I take a sip and let out a low moan, closing my eyes. "Mmm, I love you."

"I love you, too, angel." I pop open my eyes and look at him.

"Oh, I was talking to the coffee." I wink at him and we laugh. He sits next to me in his pajama pants with his chest bare. I rest my head on his shoulder and he tucks his arm around my waist. "It will all be over today, angel...then we can get back to our lives."

He takes the mug out of my hand, setting it beside his. "In the meantime, I think I know how I want to spend the next thirty minutes of my morning." He grabs me and smashes his lips to mine. I gasp, losing air as he sucks in more.

"*Again*? We don't have time."

"We *do* have time." I bite my lip. He stands and walks to his closet, returning with a black silk tie. "Lie back."

"What?"

"Do you want to use your safe word?" he offers.

"Well, no, but—"

"Then lie. Back. Elizabeth."

"Don't call me that." He raises his eyebrow as he stalks toward the bed.

"Do as I say and lay back." I slid down, laying back on the bed. He climbs over me and puts my hands above my head, taking the tie and wrapping it around my hands. "Stay there." I bite my lip and sigh, but I don't move.

Graham lifts my shirt up and plants kisses on my stomach, licking around my belly button. I shift a little and he looks up, eyeing my hands. He slides my pajama shorts down, taking my panties with them. He pushes his hand between my legs and swears under his breath. "Always wet for me."

"I can't help it," I croak out. He trails his fingers down my legs and brings his tongue to my clit. Swiping once, he looks up at me.

"Good, I don't want you to." He devours me furiously and I need to touch him. I pull my arms down and he stops, wiping his mouth and looking at me. I whimper at the emptiness I feel from the loss of his tongue on my pussy.

"Please. Keep going," I beg. He climbs over me and grabs my arms, pushing them back above my head.

"What did I say? Don't. Move. Move again and you don't get to come." I need to come right now. I need him to lick me, to suck me. I *need* him to fuck me. I nod in agreement and he smirks at me. He pulls my shirt over my head and brings my breast into his mouth, switching them off one at a time.

"I need you, please. Please, Graham," I plead. Within seconds he pushes into me, plunging deep, rocking forward and holding onto my hands with each thrust. He kisses me and I open my mouth for him. His tongue sweeps in and out as mine does the same. I love kissing Graham. I love his taste. I love his mouth on mine, how his lips feel fighting for dominance against mine.

I love everything about being with Graham. "I need to touch you," I whine.

"Not this time."

He fucks me harder and I wish I could dig my nails into his back. I wish I could give him marks he'd wear for weeks, adding to his collection. He moans in my ear as I push my hips up to him, matching his force and movement. "Fuck, I can't get enough of you," he whispers into my ear. My body tenses and I know I can't take much more.

"I'm going to come. Please, Graham, come with me."

"I'm with you, angel." The moment the words leave his mouth, my pussy tightens around him and my legs shake. The orgasm takes over my body and my breathing quickens. Graham's body tenses as he pumps in and out of me in short, hard thrusts.

"*Fuuuck.* So good, always so good." He lays on top of me, kissing my neck as he releases my hands. Sweat beads on his forehead. We slow our breathing as I run my fingers up and down his back. Silence fills the room, but silence with Graham doesn't feel awkward. It feels normal, natural, and real.

He loosens the tie and slides it off my wrist.

"We have to get this over with..." he says eventually.

"What are you going to do?"

"I'm going to wire the five million to the account they gave and hope they're good on their word. Then after I get my father, I'm killing every last one of them."

"I'm going to choose to ignore the fact that you just told me you plan on killing people and focus instead on the fact that you just have five million dollars laying around." I nudge him.

"Angel, you'll have to learn how rich I am one day. And I

told you from the beginning...I'm a dangerous man." He gets up and walks into the bathroom. I follow behind him, playfully grabbing his ass. "Hey, cut that out," he warns with a smile as I laugh.

"I'm going to shower, I'll meet you downstairs." He kisses my forehead and nods.

I shower and dress quickly, coming downstairs to join the others. Everyone is here, including the hacker and agent who helped them during the first cartel kidnapping. I look around and notice Selle isn't down yet.

I knock on her door and she opens it. "Hey," she says, leaving it open for me to walk in.

I shut the door behind me and sit in her vanity chair. "You ok?"

"I'm fine, just tired as shit and a little hungover." I raise my eyebrows at her. "No, I didn't go out. But I did go downstairs and get shitfaced." I chuckle at her and she starts getting dressed.

"I just wanted to check on you, see how you were holding up."

"It'll be over today. Graham told me he's paying the ransom. Men like that, all they want is money. Well...usually." She looks away as she says it, but I don't push her. Instead I stand, walking over and give her a hug.

"I don't know exactly what happened to you when you were taken, but your brother won't let anything happen to you now." She hugs me back, tighter than I expected.

"You know," she says, pulling back and looking at me. "You're not just good for him, you're good for this entire family. Somehow, some way, you are helping us all. We love you so much for it." I smile at her and she smiles back. Her eyes begin to fill with tears.

"No tears, Giselle. Finish getting ready and I'll meet you downstairs."

In that moment, I knew that this is the family I'd be a part of. No matter what, I'd have their backs and I knew they'd have mine.

13

Graham

Liza sits beside me and I entwine our hands, bringing it up to my mouth. I plant a soft kiss on her hand and she smiles.

"Graham, the wire is set for transfer. We also installed an encryption to track them when they accept it and withdraw," El says. *Good.* This shit was ending today and I was getting back to my life.

At 11:45 a.m., my phone rings.

"Do you have my money?" the voice asks.

"I need to know that my father is still alive before I send it. And I don't want to just talk to him, I'm not stupid. I know you'll kill him the moment you get the transfer." I'm met with silence on the other end.

"Meet me in fifteen minutes, I'll text you the location. But if I see one cop, I'll blow his fucking brains out and kill the rest of your fucking family."

"Fifteen minutes," I growl, ending the call. I turn to Liza. "Time to go."

"Please don't," she says, her eyes filling with tears. I palm her face in my hand and kiss her.

"I have to go. You'll be fine. I'll be fine." She wraps her arms around me so tight that I gasp for air. I hug her back, equally as tight. I look at her and kiss her again. "Don't worry," I reassure her.

"Sweetheart, please be careful. Don't let them fool you," my mother says, then she looks at Ellis. "You, either. Stay ahead of them. Protect my son and bring him back to me." Ellis nods as my mom gives us each a hug and a kiss on the cheek. Selle stands at the door, her arms wrapped tightly around her body. I pull her into a hug and kiss her forehead.

"I'll be ok, I'm going to bring Dad back. *And* I'm personally going to kill those fuckers for what they did to us." She stays still in my arms.

"Love you. Please, hurry back, G."

"Love you, too, Selly." I look at Liza whose tears are now streaming down her face. I wipe her tears away with my thumb.

"I love you, angel." When she smiles this time I quickly take a picture of it with my mind.

"I love you, Graham." As Ellis and I walk out the door, I turn around and see all three of my girls looking at us with fear in their eyes and worry on their faces. I turn to Ellis.

"Let's end this shit." I mean every word of it. I have to end this quickly. I have to get back to my family.

* * *

Fifteen minutes later, Ellis and I pull into an old, abandoned storage unit building that my father used to own. I read the text that gave the number of the unit to meet at. *Unit 666. How fitting.* Fucking evil piece of shit. I get out and look around. He said no cops, but I'm not stupid enough to not inform them about what the hell is going on. There are two trucks full of ex-marines waiting for my signal to come in and kill these fuckers.

I stand in front of the storage unit, the unit that probably contains my father. My phone rings as I reach for the handle.

"Right on time. Open the unit," the voice instructs. I cautiously reach for the handle and lift the storage door. Ellis stands close behind me. My father sits there, blindfolded and tied to a chair. Blood drips out of the side of his ear.

"He's alive. Now transfer the money or he dies."

"Dad!" I yell. He tries to lift his head and speak. "How do I know that once you get the money you won't kill him anyway?" I demand. "Do you honestly care?" the voice retorts. "After all the lies he told you. For fuck's sake, he told you he had us *killed*, when in reality, he paid us to let him out of the business. Your father helped us traffic those women and kids. He helped us smuggle those drugs, he did it all; as long as he got his cut out of it." I look at my father whose head is dangling again. He needs a doctor and fast.

"If you were business partners, then why are you trying to kill him?"

"Your father was a piece of shit; only thought of himself. He got too greedy, wanted more than he was owed. He fucked everything up and had my brother killed," the voice growls.

"You kidnapped his kids and had us both *raped* numerous times. What the fuck did you expect him to do?" I grit out. I see Ellis flinch at my words, his fists curling until his knuckles turn white. If the relationship he had with our family motivated him to search the ends of the Earth for us, then the rage of him finding Selle and I in that state was enough for him to slaughter everyone in that hostage compound. To this day, I have never seen Ellis quite like that. Or myself, for that matter. That was the day the beast came out.

I promised Selle no one would ever hurt her again. That she would never be forced like we were, day in and day out, as they lined up out the doors for their turn. The guilt alone over the fact that I couldn't keep that promise when we were both kidnapped could kill me, but I'll be damned if anyone so much as lays a finger on my sister again. This isn't just about freeing my dad, this is an overdue sentence.

A sentence that will cost every fucking life in the cartel. There was a pause on the other end of the line for a moment.

"That was unfortunate...my men weren't supposed to touch either of you in that way. They were just supposed to slap you both around a bit until your old man settled his dues. I do a lot of shit, but raping women and men ain't my type of business."

How nice. You just sell them to the bastards that do it instead.

"I'll wire it right now, but give me your word that you won't kill him."

"Are you bargaining with me?"

"If you want this five million dollars wired to your fucking account, then I suggest you give me your word."

"Fuck off, you have it." I look at Ellis and give him a nod. He transfers the money and I hear a chuckle on the other end of the phone.

"Pleasure doing business with you. Much smarter than your old man. The code to the bomb attached to your father is 0154. You might want to hurry, I believe it's set to go off *any* second now." *Click.*

Bomb? He's attached to a *fucking bomb?* I run towards my

dad, quickly pulling the blindfold off him. I look around his body. *Where the fuck is the bomb? Where do I put the code in?*

"Graham?" my dad asks as he tries to lift his head.

"I'm here, I'll get you out."

"It's the cartel, they're back. I didn't have them killed...I'm sorry. I lied."

"Save your breath. I have to disable this fucking bomb... Where the hell is the entry point to key the fucking code in!" My dad's head hangs low again and he slowly starts shaking it side to side.

"They'll get away, leave me here. I deserve to die, I did this."

"They aren't getting away, Dad. I have a team set up to stop them the moment they fucking leave this place." Within seconds I hear gunshots firing and footsteps running towards us.

"Graham, leave me, son. Go, take care of your mother and sister..." He looks at me straight in my eyes. "And marry that girl. She's perfect for you. Have lots of children, give them and her the world. This was always my fate. I've accepted it. Your mother should be happy. She needs to move on. I not only cheated on her, but I betrayed her so many times since then. Made a fool of her countless times. The drug cartel, the fake investments, the trafficking."

"Trafficking?" I question, hoping he'll finally admit what I've known since I was seventeen.

"Yeah...trafficking. You were right, I'm not proud of it. The women, the children that I helped them take...You and your sister were *never* supposed to happen. I hope you know that." What he is saying may be true, but he still sold us out when it was *his* life on the line. "This will never end unless you kill them all, son. Your mother, she only knew some of the skeletons in my closet; she knew I helped the cartel with drugs. I tried to prepare her for what was coming. I tried to get out of it. I never had the heart to tell her I was sick enough to extend my greed into trafficking."

My eyes fill with tears as I look at the clock that reads ninety seconds on it. The numbers tick down. I search his body quickly, pausing when I see the keypad tucked behind wires. I quickly punch the code in. The timer freezes and turns red, then the numbers speed up.

He lied to me.

Of course, he lied. My father is responsible for his brother's death, this was his plan all along. I look at my father, whose face is calm. For the first time I realize that I could forgive him, despite everything. I wish I did it sooner, but I don't have time.

"Go. Run. I'm ready. I had a good life. I love you, son, and I'm proud of you. I've always been proud of you. Remember that. I'm always here."

"I love you, Dad. I'll—I'll make you proud." I look at the clock, forty-two seconds. I run as fast as I can. I pull the gun out of my waistband, stopping and shooting a man who runs towards me with his gun raised. I see Ellis lift his gun and shoot, hearing the sound of a body dropping behind me.

"BOMB, EL, RUN!" I continue to run when I hear the explosion around me. Then blackness surrounded me.

14

Liza

Thirteen times. I've called Graham's phone thirteen times. Why? I have no clue. I knew what he was doing. I knew where he was going. But I still called.

"You have to calm down, they will all be fine," Madeline says. I look at her and shove my finger into my mouth, chewing my nail bed. I stand at the window, looking out over the driveway willing the car to come back.

Moments later, my heart leaps when I see the black SUV coming up the driveway.

"They're back," I whisper, my voice barely there. Madeline and Selle look out the window and I run to open the door. Graham pushes the door open and climbs out as I run to him. Right into his arms, I wrap myself tightly around him and cry.

"You're back," I sob as he kisses my hair and strokes my back. "Everything's ok. I need to talk to my mom and sister. I have to put you down, ok?"

He places my feet on the ground and I look at Ellis.
Where is Joe?

"Graham, where's your father?" He looks at me, his mouth

open when his mom barges out.

"Oh, sweetheart, thank God you're ok." Madeline mimics me. "Where's Joe?" Graham briefly puts his head down before looking back to his mom.

"Where's Dad, G? Just tell us. What happened?" Selle asks, standing next to Madeline. Graham reaches for his mother's hands.

"He's gone, Mom. I'm sorry. I tried. I couldn't save him. And even if I could, he had already made the decision to die today." Madeline's face was blank. She said nothing. She didn't move, she didn't cry, she didn't ask questions; she just stood there. Her hands gripped Graham's tighter.

"He's really gone?"

"Yes, Mom, he's gone." Selle starts to cry and I reach her side and pull her into my arms.

"The cartel?" she croaks out. "They did this? Did they get away?"

"No. They're all dead." When I look at Graham I see what I missed before, he has blood on his shirt, hands, and face. I don't know how I missed it when he got out of the SUV. I frown, turning my attention back to the conversation; I'd look more closely at him later.

"You're sure?"

"Yes, Giselle, I'm sure."

Something is happening between the two of them. It's like they are having a silent sibling communication about something else, but no words aren't being used. I see Selle release a breath like she had been holding it for years, like it had a chokehold on her up until now.

We walk into the house and sit on the couch. Graham's father is dead. And Graham had to witness it. Graham hands his mother a glass of wine and sits beside her with Giselle on the other side.

"We have to plan his funeral," Madeline speaks for the first time since hearing the news.

"Mother, he just died. I don't think you have to do that right now," Graham says.

"Graham, listen to me. He was your father and I loved him for giving me you two. There are things you don't know about your father, there are things that you *think* I don't know about your father." I watch Graham shift around after her last sentence. *What is going on?*

"I loved him," Madeline continues, "but stopped a long time ago. I'm sad that he's dead. I'm sad that you two no longer have your father, but I am not sad that he can no longer torture me. I am not sad that he can no longer keep me unhappy. I want this funeral done as soon as possible so I can be free of him." She stands up and walks away, wine in hand and her head held high. "I'm going to the wine cellar; I'll be right back."

We all watch her as she walks out of the room. Graham looks at Selle and she raises her eyebrows at him.

"What the fuck?" Selle asks. "I've never heard Mom say anything like that. Especially not about Dad. I mean, we all knew she was unhappy, but fuck's sake, that was brutal." Graham's eyes are full of pity as he looks at Selle.

"I can't blame her, Selle. The things he told me before he died would've been enough for Mom to leave years ago. But she stayed because of us. He told me he wanted her free of him, that he wanted her to finally be happy. Maybe now she can be." Graham looks at Ellis from the corner of his eye and Ellis puts his head down. *What was that about?*

I quickly give a confusing look at Graham and he shakes his head. I make a mental note of all the things we need to talk about tonight.

Selle gets up and pours herself a glass of wine when, right on que, Madeline returns with two bottles of wine herself. She sets them on the counter and turns to me. "Would you like a glass, sweetheart?" I give her a curt nod as she pours me a hefty glass and hands it to me.

The wine is smooth on my tongue. It's sweet and smells of white grapes with a hint of cinnamon. They discuss funeral arrangements, which wasn't much because Madeline said that Joe started planning his funeral about four months ago.

"Why was Dad planning his funeral?" Selle asks. Madeline shrugs her shoulders.

"He told me that he knew that things were coming to a head. That his skeletons were catching up to him. He said that he didn't care to fight them anymore if he kept us safe and happy." She finishes her glass of wine.

"He's never cared about our happiness before. Why now?" Selle asks.

"He cared. He had a hard way of showing it, and he's made decisions that have seemed unforgivable, but he cared. He told me tonight he was proud of me, that he loved me. That he wanted us all happy and to move on," Graham says, looking at his feet. Selle looked at Graham for a moment, as if she was milling around what he said in her head before speaking.

"We'll all be ok, it's all over now. It sucks that Dad is gone, but at least he tried to face his demons. We'll celebrate his life." Graham picks up his whiskey and raises his glass. "To Dad." We all follow, the sounds of glass clinking against each other.

"Well, if you all will excuse me, I'm going to walk the grounds before it gets dark out. I'll see you all at dinner," Madeline says. Ellis abruptly stands up after her.

"I think I'll join you, Madeline, if you don't mind. I know it's over, but I still don't feel ok with you trotting around alone."

"Maybe they'll finally fuck and get it over with..." Selle mutters, downing her glass of wine.

"Giselle! Our father just fucking died," Graham scolds.

"I'm just saying..." For the first time since this shitshow started, we laughed. I knew then that they would both be alright.

* * *

A week later, Joe's funeral was full to maximum capacity with friends and family—my parents, brothers, and Brant—coming to celebrate his life. Madeline, Graham, and Selle spoke, all saying kind words and telling stories about him. When they spoke of him they cried, but they laughed some, too. They promised each other that they would remember the good times with him. That they wouldn't be sad that he was gone, but happy that he lived a good life.

After hours of watching Graham, Selle, and Madeline hug people and shake numerous hands at the burial site, we headed back to his mom's house. There were a few people who came over to give Madeline some company and comfort. What they didn't know was that she probably didn't need it. She was sad, but not that he was dead. She was sad that her kids no longer had a father. I guess that's something to grieve...

I couldn't blame or judge her. There are things that women

should never have to endure and she endured more than a few of them. She stuck around, honored her vows, and put her kid's happiness over her own.

"When will they leave? I want to get drunk..." Selle says, plopping down next to me on the couch with Eli and Hogan trailing behind her.

"I was thinking the same thing..." Graham says, sitting on the other side of me, pulling me into him. "I say we ditch them and go to the basement." Selle raises her eyebrow. Graham looks down at me and I shrug my shoulder.

"Whatever you want to do." He bends down, his mouth brushing over my ear.

"I want to tie you up to my bed and feast on you like it's my last meal." My breath hitches and I elbow him.

"Stop it," I whisper and he chuckles at me.

We all head for the basement with Selle grabbing a few bottles of wine while Graham and Eli grab bottles of whiskey. Hogan carries the ice and I carry the cups. I turned to look at him and smile.

"So, I hear you're still seeing that girl from my school. How's that going?" I ask him.

"We stopped talking about a month ago. She was... different." Hogan runs his fingers through his hair and shrugs his shoulders.

"Oh...I'm sorry."

"Don't be. Selle introduced me to one of her friends last week. Her name's Samantha, you'd like her. We've gone out a few times. I have a good feeling about it." He pauses. "I'm happy for you two, Lizzie. I'm glad you both found love, you deserve it."

"You'll find it, too."

15

Graham

I slowly follow everyone downstairs, I'm still sore as fuck from everything that happened. It's been a week and I still don't feel like myself. That bomb killed a lot of the cartel before we came in to finish the job, and honestly? I'm surprised it didn't kill me. My bruises are fresh and the cuts from the windows busting haven't begun to heal yet. Liza hasn't badgered me about them, but I know it's coming soon. She stares at them when she thinks I'm not looking. When we're in the shower, she's gentle with me. When we're in bed, she doesn't look anywhere other than at my face. It's almost like seeing me in pain hurts her. Which is why I refuse to show it, no matter how much of bitch it actually does *hurt*.

After the shitshow with my father, I brought in another security guard, Ralph. He will be used more for Liza. He's ex-military and on his shit. Always. I like him. I know that between Ralph and Ellis, my family and Liza are protected.

Always.

The funeral wasn't as bad as I thought it'd be to handle. I was more upset that Travis and Emily's flight got canceled last minute then I was about the actual funeral. I think it's because I finally made peace with it. I made peace with the wrongs my father did in his life, and instead of hating him, I chose to celebrate him and move on. They say everyone grieves differently, but they have no idea how much of a small relief it is to know he's not fighting his way out of things anymore.

"Shots!!" Selle yells, pulling out a bottle of Bulleit from under the cabinet.

"So, you're the one hiding all the good shit," I say, yanking it out of her hands. She ignores me and sets up the shot glasses. I pour an equal amount into each glass and distribute them out.

"What should we toast to?" Selle asks.

"To Dad." Everyone raises their shot glasses and tips it back into their mouths. The smooth burn travels down my throat and I watch Liza as she tips hers back with ease. She licks her bottom lip and looks at me, tilting her head. I walk over to her and pull her into my arms.

"You've been too far away from me today. I haven't been able to touch you as much as I want," I growl.

"I thought *I* was your needy slut?" she whispers, wrapping her arms around my neck. I dip my head down and brush my lips across hers, tasting the whiskey from her shot. "Don't tease me...kiss me if you want to kiss me," she says. I raise my eyebrow at her and chuckle.

"I always want to kiss you and you *are* my needy slut. I bet you're soaking wet for me right now, aren't you, pretty girl?"

I smash my lips onto hers, pushing my hands through her hair. She opens for me, plunging her tongue into my mouth. One shot and she was already showing her tipsiness. "Don't forget we aren't alone down here," I groan into her mouth.

She giggles and shrugs.

"Jesus, I didn't think you two could breathe," Eli says. We turn and look at the three of them staring at us and we all laugh. Selle cues some music on as she and Liza start dancing. We are all enjoying ourselves. Some may say under the circumstances we should be sad, down, and upset. But instead, we're drinking, dancing, and laughing. My father wasn't the best man, but he did have a good life. He made it clear that we were to continue on with our lives.

I look at two of the most important women in my life, smiling and dancing with each other. I turn to Eli and Hogan, pouring myself another whiskey.

"I hear you and Samantha have been spending a lot of time together," I say to Hogan. He grins, picking up his cup.

"Yeah, she's cool, man. I like her." Samantha and Selle had been friends since high school, but she always, like Selle, picked men who were no good. Hogan would be good for her and I think she'd be good for Hogan.

"Yeah? Good." I looked at Eli. He's watching Selle just like I watch Liza. He loves her; it shows. I finally learned to accept the fact that they would probably never leave each other. After all, he is a good guy and my sister could do a lot worse. I throw back the rest of my drink and walk towards Selle and Liza.

"Dance with me?" Liza asks, swaying her hips in my direction. I grin at her and pull her into my grasp.

"Can't ever tell you no." She smiles at my response and wraps her arms around my neck.

"I like dancing with you."

"I like dancing with you, angel."

"I think I'm drunk..."

"I think you're drunk, too." She giggles and puts her head

down. She looks up quickly and bites her lip. "What are you thinking?" I ask.

"That I'm extremely horny right now and I wish we were home in our bed." My eyes level with hers and my body responds immediately.

"We're leaving." I grab her hand into mine and head towards the stairs. She quickly waves to the others, giggling.

I race Liza upstairs to my room. "Pack quickly, angel."

"We live so farrrrrrr...."

"The lake house is forty-five minutes away."

"Oh, I forgot you own seventy-two houses." I laugh at her and she smiles. "I like it when you laugh," she says. I walk over to her and kiss her on her nose.

"Hurry up. I'll get Ellis." She nods and starts packing.

I walk downstairs to see the crowd finally thinning out. "Mom, we're heading out in a few moments."

"Oh? You two aren't staying another night?" I shake my head.

"We're going to the lake house."

"Well, alright, honey. Thank you for staying so long." I kiss her cheek.

"Of course, Mom." I pick up my phone and call Ellis.

"G, everything alright?"

"Yeah, El, we're going to head out. Going to the lake house."

"I'll pull the car around." I end the call and go to get Liza. She has everything packed and is walking out of the door when I get up the stairs.

"Where are you two going?!" Selle asks, stumbling behind me. I steady her and shake my head.

"To the lake house."

"We're about to head out, too."

"Where's Hogan and Eli?" Liza asks, looking behind her as she rolls the suitcase down the hall.

"He walked Hogan out, he's going to meet Samantha tonight." Liza smiles and nods. Selle walks over to me and hugs me. I kiss her cheek and ruffle the top of her hair.

"Love you."

"Love you, too, G."

When we pulled up to the lake house, El pulled our bags out and put them into the house for us.

"Go inside, angel, I'll be right there." She nods and gets out of the car.

"I want you to stay with my mother tonight..." I say to El as he closes the trunk door. He turns to me and raises his eyebrows.

"Why?"

"Because I don't want her in that big fucking house alone tonight. She needs you and I trust you."

"Graham, I don't think that's appropriate."

"El, you don't have to admit it, but I know you are in love with her. And because of that, I know that the next person I can count on to keep her safe is you." He looks away and nods. I give a slight smirk in satisfaction as he climbs into the car. I watch him drive off and walk into the house.

The lights are dimmed and it is quiet.

"Liza?" Silence. "Liza, where are you?" I hear a giggle.

"Come find me."

"Seriously?" *The fucking shit you do for love.* I climb the stairs and search in the movie room for her, looking under the rows of seats. Then I check the guestroom—nothing. I push open the door to the master bedroom and can instantly feel her. I know she's in here and I smile.

I walk into the bathroom and the feeling gets stronger. I turn the light on and hear her giggle again. She's hiding in the bathtub. I sit on the edge and smile at her, shaking my head.

"You want to play, pretty girl?"

I lift her out of the tub and throw her over my shoulder. She squeals and I slap her butt. I toss her onto the bed and hover over top of her. She looks up at me and smiles. My world stops every time that smile appears on her face.

"You're cute." She giggles and touches the tip of my nose with her finger. I smile at her and shake my head.

"And you're drunk." She shakes her head in denial. "Yes, you are." I lean down and kiss her softly. She wraps her arms around my neck, pulling me down to her. I groan into her mouth. "I'm glad you're here with me," I whisper into her mouth.

"There's nowhere else I'd rather be." She deepens the kiss. Her hands travel down to my pants, tugging on the button and the zipper. I quickly strip off my pants and pull my shirt over my head. I look down at her as she watches me closely. She bites her lip and my dick twitches.

"You have too many clothes on," I declare.

"What should we do about that?" she asks, her voice barely over a whisper. I raise my eyebrow at her and stalk towards the bed. I pull her to the edge by her feet and she squeals. I lift her foot, kissing her red-painted toenails. I slide my hand up her leg and she shifts her body. I unbutton her pants, sliding them down her legs. I dip my head down to her legs, running my tongue up until I reach her lace panties. Her breathing hitches as I kiss her pussy. I grin at her reaction.

I hook my finger in her panties and slowly tug them down. I push her legs open and place myself between them. I eat her with a vengeance. She pushes her hands into my hair, moaning uncontrollably. I push my tongue in and out of her pussy, adding my fingers.

"Fuck...oh God." She starts to unravel; I know she can't take much more. Her back arches and she digs her feet into the bed. I put my hand over her belly, holding her down as I continue to eat her out. "I can't, I have to come."

I look up at her as I continue to devour her. I stop briefly and she whines from the absence of my tongue. "You come when I say you can," I growl as I push my fingers inside of her. She throws her head back and I watch her as she fights every desire to come. I suck her clit and swirl my tongue in and out of her.

"Please, please let me."

"I said you'll wait." Her back arches as I lap her pussy slowly now. I'm torturing her. I want to see how long I can drag her out. I want her to disobey me so I can punish her.

"Graham! I can't. I have to!" She releases without command, grabbing the sheets next to her. Her climax is violent and hard. Her body shakes and her breathing quickens. I climb over her and push my dick into her as she wraps her legs around me instinctively.

I push in and out of her, watching her as her eyes close. "Eyes on me, always. You didn't listen to me, so now after I fuck you, I'm going to punish you, too." She opens them and I unwrap her legs, pushing them apart and allowing me to fill her deeper.

"Fuuuck, you feel good. You always feel so good," I groan into her ear. She can't talk, only moan. Louder and louder. The pleasure takes over her body, her shakes become uncontrollable. I slid out of her and flip her onto her stomach. "Hands on the headboard." She rests her hands on the headboard and braces herself. I push inside of her hard and fast, wrapping her hair in my hand and tugging.

"Graham, please."

"More?" She nods quickly, so I fuck her harder and deeper, giving her everything I have. My body tenses and I know I'm at the end. I flip her over again and wrap my hand under her neck, pulling her to me. "I'm going to come and you're going to come with me." I put one hand on the middle of her back, the other still around the back of her neck. I push into her slow and deep, savoring her in these last few moments. "Come. Now." She kisses me and our tongues clash as we both come together, our juices slapping together.

We stay like that for a few minutes with me still inside of her. I kiss her softly and pull out of her. My body saddens immediately. I walk into the bathroom, wet a cloth, and clean her up. She's exhausted and I am, too. But, she's still getting that punishment.

"Turn over. Ass in the air." Her eyes widen and she staggers. "Now." She scrambles to get into position. I wet my lips at the sight before me, her waiting for me to punish her.

"Do you know why you're going to be spanked?" She bobs her head and I yank her head back by her hair. "Words, angel."

"Because I came before you said I could."

"Mhm. And that makes you a bad girl, right?"

"Yes."

"Yes, what?"

"Yes, sir."

"Good girl." I release her hair and her head falls down. Her breath hitches the moment my hand makes contact with her ass. She yelps as the next smack comes quickly.

"Fuck, you always turn so red for me." Her hands tangle in the sheets and her knuckles turn white. "Four more."

Smack. Smack. Smack. I run my hand over her ass cheeks, massaging them. "Last one, pretty girl." *Smack.* I slide my fingers through her pussy folds for good measure. "I can smell you from here, you filthy fucking girl." I push my fingers in and out of her, bringing her to her climax. "Give me one more."

"I—I can't."

"Yes, you can. Your pussy is already squeezing my fingers. Give me one more."

"Graham—" My hand comes down on her ass again.

"Unless it's *yes, sir, I'm coming*, don't fucking speak." She groans as I add another finger. When I hit that one spot that always sends her revving, she screams out. She claws at my hands, pushing them away. I increase the speed of my fingers and she clenches around me.

"I'm coming," she gasps. I remove my fingers and push my tongue inside of her as she comes. Her cum explodes in my mouth, her juices saturating my face. Her taste is so fucking sweet and it keeps coming and coming. The more she screams, the tighter she clenches. "Fuuuuuck."

When her body relaxes, I kiss the inside of her thighs and praise her.

"Good fucking girl."

16

Liza

By morning my body was sore. I didn't mind it; it reminded me of the intimacy of last night, the rawness. I appreciated the soreness, I appreciated the memory. Graham woke me up to the best orgasm of my life and I welcomed it.

We lay in bed, tangled in each other's limbs. I study his face while he watches TV, examining the scratches and bruises he had. "I'm fine, Elizabeth," he says, never looking at me. "I feel you staring and I am fine."

"But you were hurt." It had been a week and we hadn't talked about how he got those marks. We hadn't discussed how he watched his father die.

"I know you want to understand why I'm ok, if you can handle it; I'd like to tell you." He says running his hand down my cheek. I nod, sitting up to face him as he speaks.

"When I realized that Selle and I were taken because of my father I felt empty, I didn't want to fight anymore. There were always three men that came to give us water and bread. But after a while I guess they got bored, so they started raping us. They'd take turns with my sister; she always got it worse than me. Only one of the men would touch me, while all three lined up and waited their turn with her. The first time they did it, I was tied up and gagged. I couldn't help her. It broke me watching what they did to her. I felt like I failed her. After the second time, two of the men got greedy and started coming back twice a day. One day, they were rushing, almost like they were afraid they'd get caught this time, and forgot to tie my hands as tight as they usually do. I let them rape me and stayed still, keeping my hands behind my back. But when they moved on to my sister, that's when I picked up the brick they had holding the door open and hit the first guy over his head with it. When he dropped, a gun fell from his waistband. The other guy was still fumbling with putting his dick back in his pants that I had enough time to grab the gun and fire a shot directly at his head. Selle was so young, so impressionable. She wasn't even a teenager yet but had been raped numerous times, all because her father was a piece of fucking shit. That day, all the times they'd violated us made me lethal. I was prepared to kill anyone that got in my way of getting Selle and me out of there that day."

"And did you? Have to hurt anyone else that day?"

"No, that was the day Ellis found us. He was already close and the gunshot I fired lead him straight to us."

"But your father, how'd you face him that day?"

"I was a slither of myself we when got back home. No one mattered except Selle. That's why we're so close. She started sleeping with me at night because she started having nightmares. I knew that I couldn't risk her hearing or seeing me confront my father. She had way more healing to do than me. So instead of confronting him, I started defying him, questioning him, and honestly, hating him. As time passed, it got easier to not tell her that he was the reason we were taken. It got easier telling myself that I was protecting her from hurt. And it got easier to believe that my father wouldn't turn a blind eye to his fucking kids being sold."

"Graham..." I say, tears gathering in my eyes. They didn't deserve this. Their lives were destroyed and they were so fucking young. How do you go on your entire life staring at the man that caused you so much pain? I reach for him and he gives me a small grin.

"Angel, I'm okay. I know you think it's odd, but he gave me the closure I needed before he died." He turned his attention to me. "I'm fine, I promise."

"I hate him. I hate what he let happen to you. To Selle." He pulls me to him and kisses my forehead.

"No need in hating someone I already forgave, pretty girl. We're ok, let it go." I nod into his chest and he runs his hands through my hair.

"I'm sorry you didn't get to see Em. I know you were excited to see her," he says, changing the subject.

"It was for your father's funeral. Yes, I would've loved seeing her, but the circumstances weren't the best. I'm sorry you didn't see Trav. She said they're planning for Spain and will be there for three or four weeks." He nods and I lay my head on his chest.

"Maybe we'll go to Spain, then," he suggests. I shrug.

"I start work on Monday." He entwines our fingers together, planting kisses on each finger.

"I know. Are you excited?"

"I guess."

"You know there's no rush to work. You can spend time with your parents."

"No, I want to work. You know that."

"Yes, but I'm telling you the option is always there." My phone rings and I reach for it.

"Hi, Mama."

"Hi, sweetheart. How's Graham doing?" I glance at him and he climbs out of the bed. He walks over to the closet, pulling a shirt over his head.

"He's ok. We're heading back home tomorrow, possibly tonight. I'm not sure."

"Well, our plane leaves in an hour or two. Your brothers are coming back with Giselle. Graham asked your father and I if we could have dinner next Friday." I pause and frown. "Honey? You there?"

"Yes...I'm here, Mama. I'm sorry, I didn't know."

"Maybe it was a surprise. I hope I didn't ruin anything." I smile.

"Mom, it's ok...I have to go, though, I'll call you later."

"Ok, love you, sweetheart."

"Love you, too, Mama." I end the call and walk into the bathroom, opening the shower door. Graham's back is facing me. I take in all of his glory before stepping in behind him.

I wrap my arms around his waist and kiss his back. He puts his hands over mine and gives them a squeeze.

"We're going to New York next Friday?" He stills and turns to me, water beading down his back.

"We are. But you weren't supposed to know that yet."

"Why not?"

"Because there are some things I wanted to talk to you about first before mentioning New York." I raise my eyebrow in curiosity.

"Ok, what things?" He pulls me into his embrace and kisses

my forehead. I smile at his affection. Even after all of the kisses he gives me, it never gets old. It gives me chills and butterflies.

"Wash up, angel. We'll talk later." I pout and he grins at me as he gets out of the shower.

Graham is sitting at the counter with his laptop in front of him and his phone to his ear. He's in business mode, one that I'll be seeing a lot more of now that we've graduated. He looks up at me and motions toward a cup of coffee sitting next to him. I smile at him and grab the coffee mug, taking a big sip. I climb atop the counter and sit on it watching him tentatively, occasionally taking a sip of my coffee.

"Andrew, you live to make my life hell." I smirk and he shakes his head. "Yes, I see it. I'll look over it more at the office on Monday. There's no reason why it can't wait." I can't hear what Andrew is saying on the other line, but Graham's eyes whip to me, studying me. "Monday at noon." Then he ends the call and slides me down the counter, planting me in front of him.

"Coffee good?" He rubs the side of my legs.

"Yes, so good."

"So, New York. Your mom couldn't keep quiet, huh?"

"She never can..."

17

Graham

"So, do you want to go? I know you start your job Monday." I rub my hand up and down her thigh and she takes another sip of her coffee.

"Of course, I'd love to go. I enjoy New York. I didn't at first, but I do now." She peeks over her coffee mug at me.

"And you're wondering why I didn't tell you…" She takes another sip of her coffee.

I've been so nervous to talk to Liza about what had been on my mind since I left my dad's side. *Marry that girl.* My dad's words had been replaying in my mind every day. I never thought I'd want marriage or that I'd find someone who made me feel how Liza did. But it was quick, many will think it's too quick. Will Liza think that, too?

"Graham, hey. Did you hear me?" She taps my nose and I grin at her. "Tell me."

"How do you feel about marriage?" Her eyes widen at the question.

"I like the thought of it."

"The thought?"

"Yes, the thought of being a wife, having someone feel like they can't live without me."

"Someone already feels like that..." I stand and push myself between her legs. She inhales at my response. I grab her coffee out of her hand, setting it on the counter next to her. "I do...every day, every moment I'm not with you, every second I'm not around you, I can't fucking breathe. Even when I am around you, I still can't get enough of you. You are fucking *insatiable*, Elizabeth."

"So are you," she whispers, I dip my head and place a tender kiss on her soft lips. She rolls her lips and looks down.

"What is it?"

"I...just...why'd you ask me that?"

"Curiosity...Come on, let's head to my mom's so we can get the hell out of here."

When we get to my mother's house, Giselle and Elias are outside.

"Hey, G," she says, hugging me. I embrace her tightly back.

"Hey, Selly."

"When are y'all leaving?

"Within the next hour. We're going to New York next Friday."

"Why?" I shoot a quick glance to Elizabeth; she's wrapped up in a conversation with Elias. Was I seriously going to go to New York and buy a ring for her? Was I really going to ask her parent's permission to marry her? Am I ready for marriage? Is she?

"G, why?"

"I'm going to ask her parents for their permission to marry her." Selle freezes. Seconds later a smile spreads across her face.

"You are? Oh my fucking God," she squeaks. I push my hand over her mouth as Liza and Eli look at us both. "Sorry," she whispers. I drop my hand and she's still smiling.

"What is up with you two?" Liza asks. Selle smiles at her, shakes her head, and walks into the house. "Crazies," she mutters. Liza grabs my hand and we follow behind Selle and Eli.

My mom is sitting at the kitchen table with El. She looks up and smiles when she sees us all.

"There they are. Where's Hogan?" she asks, hugging Selle and Eli.

"He's with Samantha," Selle says as she smiles and raises her eyebrow.

"Sweetheart, I'm glad you stopped by before leaving." She holds her arms out for a hug. She smiles at Liza before giving her a tight hug.

"Do we have time to eat or is everyone on their way out?"

I personally planned on leaving this fucking house within the next forty-five minutes. I wanted to get Liza home and keep her there for the next three days before she started her new job.

"We were actually getting on the road, but I wanted to talk to you first about something." She loops her hand through my arm.

"Of course, let's go talk." She pats my arm. "Is everything ok?"

We get into the den and she closes the sliding door. "Yes, everything is fine. I, umm, I'm going to New York on Friday..."

"For business?"

"No, not exactly...we're having dinner with Brant, Axel, and Bethany...I'm going to..."

"Going to...what, honey?" I take a deep breath and my mom lets out a small laugh. I look up and she's wearing a knowing smile.

"You want to marry her, don't you?" I nod my head and she walks over to me, putting my face in her hands. "And you should, she is amazing. She gave me my boy back."

"You don't think it's too soon?" She passively waves her hand.

"Oh, honey. When you know, you know. You love her, right?"

"Yes."

"You want to spend the rest of your life with her, right?"

"Yes."

"Then marry her and give me lots and lots of grandchildren to spoil." I kiss her cheek.

"Thank you, Mom."

"I want both of my children to have happy lives with people they love. This brings me so much joy. Now, let's get you back before your sister gets curious."

"She already knows."

"Even worse. Let's go before she spills the news."

My mom made it even more clear to me.

Elizabeth is destined to be my wife.

18

Liza

"Finally, home," I say, dropping my bag at the door. Graham stretches behind me and closes the door.

We had *lived* together for a week and we still hadn't spent a single night in our house. With everything that happened with his father, it was impossible to be home. There was no way Graham would leave his mother alone so soon and I didn't blame him. I enjoyed being around his family and he seemed to be getting more enjoyment out of it.

"Order some food. We are not leaving this house for the next three days." I smile at the thought of that idea. He picks up the bags and logs them upstairs. I decide to go with Thai food, ordering both of our favorites.

We watch a movie as we eat our food. Graham opens a bottle of red wine that goes perfect with it. I look over at him and smile, thinking about our conversation earlier.

How do you feel about marriage?

I wasn't lying with my response. I was done pretending that I didn't want happiness, that I was against love. That all went out of the window when I met Graham. He knocked down every wall I had, every fear I had, and replaced them with love and hope.

"What are you smiling at over there?"

"You," I say honestly.

"Me?"

"Yes. Our conversation earlier...about marriage." He raises his eyebrow.

"What about it?"

"Just, you're the reason I even believe in it again. The reason I think that love truly exists." He pulls me onto his lap. "You made me strong again and I can't repay you enough for that," I say. Unshed tears form into my eyes and he shakes his head.

"You don't owe me anything, just keep letting me love you," he says, planting a kiss on my neck.

"As long as you want."

"Forever?"

"If that's what you want."

"That's not long enough."

"Tell me about it." He smiles into my mouth.

"You excited to start your new job?" I nod my head. It was still surreal to me that I'd be starting my job as a psychologist right out of college.

"Luke's a smart man, most of the time, so you should enjoy working for him." I raise my eyebrow at him referring to him as *Luke*.

"Luke? I take it you know him?"

"Grew up together, he is a year older than me."

"Tell me you didn't have anything to do with me getting this job, Graham..."

"I absolutely did not. You, angel, did that all on your own." He stands and extends his hand out. I slide my hand into his.

"Now, if it's ok with you, I'd like to *finally* spend a night with you in our home." I smile at hearing him call it *our home*.

Graham shuts the door to our room and stares at me. "You know what?"

I tilt my head at him and walk toward him. "Nope, what?"

"I'm going to do many, many, *many* things to you."

"Oh, yeah?"

"Mhm, starting with you kneeling by the bed and waiting for me. Can you do that?" My breathing hitches. *Kneel?* I'd never knelt for anyone. I'd read about it, watched movies with it, but never done it.

"What's your safe word, angel?"

"Lilies," I breathe.

"Do you want to use your safe word?" he offers. "It's important that you know you can use it at any time; it's ok."

"No." I shake my head.

"Arms up," he commands.

He pulls my shirt over my head and quickly discards my bra. He kisses my shoulder and neck as I let out a low, slow moan.

"Now, get on your knees. Palms flat on your thighs." I slowly sink down onto my knees and he walks around me.

"Perfect, Now wait there for me." My palms grow a little sweaty and my breathing starts to quicken. A moment later, Graham comes back with a black flogger and a blindfold. "Remember, anytime you want to stop, you say your safe word. You understand?" I nod.

"Words, angel."

"Yes, I understand." He pulls my hair back from my shoulders and lets it spiral down my back.

"Get on all fours, I'm going to blindfold you now." I shudder at his touch on my neck. He slips the blindfold over my eyes and darkness falls upon me. I feel the flogger running down my back and I heat instantly. "Breathe, baby."

I exhale and feel the flogger come down on my ass. I let out a low moan and feel it again, this time harder. My pussy starts throbbing and before I realize it, I'm craving another blow. When it comes, my body gyrates and I dig my nails into the carpet. "Last one," he promises. I let out a satisfying groan of his name, wanting to beg for more, but holding out for what would come next.

"You're going to feel something cold. It's just lubricant, ok?"

"Ok," I whisper out. A moment later there is a cool sensation over the rim of my asshole.

Oh my fuck.

I arch up and Graham places his hand on my back, pushing me back down.

"Ok?" he asks.

"Yes. Keep going." I hear his feet pad away. Seconds feel like hours pass when I feel him push something into my asshole. I inhale sharply at the sting, then I hear Graham's voice and settle.

"Take a deep breath. You'll enjoy it, I promise." He kisses my shoulder and pushes what feels like a plug into me. "Turn over onto your back." I flip myself onto my back, feeling another cool sensation. I grip it a little and realize it's a blanket.

"Open your legs, angel." He pushes inside of me, deep and hard, making me gasp for whatever air I have left. My body shutters at his pace, at his roughness. "Fuck, you feel good," he grunts.

I moan or maybe squeal; I'm not sure. I can't keep up with

my body's feelings, it's too overwhelming. I dig my fingers into his back and will myself to breathe. His mouth covers mine and I plunge my tongue inside.

He's torturing me.

"Fuck. I'm not going to last." As if those were the words I was waiting for, my body convulses under his. I'm shaking uncontrollably. I wrap my legs around him and bring him in as deep as I can. It feels too good to speak, to moan, to breathe. He doesn't stop; he speeds up, pushing deeper, toying with the plug that pushes into my ass.

"Harder," I yelp. He grunts and flips me over, taking me from behind. I'm coming again, not even thirty seconds later. *Fuck me.* I can't take much more.

He gives me one last thrust that takes me over and I cry out his name. His body stills as he comes inside of me. He rips the blindfold off, turning me over and gently removing the plug. My body is limp; there's no way moving is an option. Graham must read my mind because seconds later, he's lifting me and placing me into a warm shower. My breathing is ragged, but my body is craving more. I know I can't handle more, but it doesn't stop me.

I push Graham down to the shower bench and seat myself onto his cock. A thrilling sensation rolls through my body as he pushes his fingers through my hair, pulling my mouth to his. "I love you," he whispers. I open my mouth to say it back, but nothing comes out. He lifts and drops me harder and harder, water suctioning in and out around us. "I can't get enough of you, it's never enough," he continues. I feel my pussy tightening and I explode over him, wrapping my arms around his neck. He nuzzles into my neck and kisses my earlobe.

"You ok?" he whispers. I nod and look at him. "Come on, let's get cleaned up."

The weekend passes in a blur. Graham kept his word and we stayed in the entire weekend—making love to each other and blocking out the outside world. Monday came quickly and so did my 6:00 a.m. alarm clock.

19

Graham

Liza's alarm wakes us both up three hours after we finally decided that it would probably be a good idea to stop having sex and get enough sleep for the workday. Her first day is today and she seems excited. Luke hired her on the spot. I hope it was for her impressive resume and not because of me. Our friendship drifted apart over the years, but we still wanted what was best for each other. If he ever needed me, I'd be there. But the last thing I wanted was for Liza to feel like she can't do things on her own. That's part of why she left me the first time.

I'm making her coffee when she wraps her arms around my midsection. "All set?" she asks as she kisses my back and I turn towards her. "Coffee?" I offer.

"Thank you." She takes the thermos and tilts it up to her mouth, smiling at the taste of more creamer than coffee. "Perfect."

Yes. You are.

"Ellis will drive us today."

"Sounds good." She grabs her purse while I grab my

briefcase and we head out the door.

We're about five minutes from Liza's building when she starts fidgeting. I look over from my laptop to her. "Nervous?" I ask.

"Yes. Fuck yes. What if I do something wrong?"

"Angel, this is your first day. I don't think he's expecting you to cure PTSD by lunch." She rolls her eyes and smiles. "You'll do great. Don't worry," I assure her. She rolls her lips and gives me a kiss on my cheek.

Moments later the car stops and she peeks out the window. "Well, here it goes," she says.

I grab her hand and give it a reassuring squeeze. "You've got this." I pull her face into my hands and kiss her gently.

"Have a good day, Graham."

"We'll be here at the same spot by 4:30 p.m. to pick you up."

"I love you," she says, smiling at me. I kiss her again.

"I love you, too."

Walking into the office this morning, I feel all eyes on me. I'm used to it, except today I know it's because of my father's death. I know they're pity stares, stares of shock that I'm even here at work so soon. I climb off the elevator and let out the breath I didn't know I was holding in.

"Good morning, Graham," Angie says, smiling at me. I smile back at her. "Angie," I greet.

"Ready to tackle this day, I hope? It's full, of course."

"Fuck, I hate Mondays." She swats my arm and follows me into my office, glaring at me. "Is there something you want?" I ask.

"Just want to make sure you're ok. You don't need to be here, you know." Just as I'm about to answer, Andrew strolls in.

"Yeah, I could've handled it for a few more days. You sure you want to deal with this shitshow of a Monday we have?" Andrew asks.

"While I appreciate both of your concerns, I'm fine. I *need* to get back to work, and Andrew, for the love of God, learn to knock." He rolls his eyes and plops into my seat.

"Do either of you need breakfast?" Angie asks. We both shake our heads.

"We're good to go, Ang, thank you."

"Meeting in thirty minutes," she says as she leaves. Andrew leans forward, placing his elbows on his knees.

"You really ready to be back?" he asks. I pull up my laptop and review my schedule for the day.

"I told you I was, didn't I?"

"Just want to make sure." he says as he stands and heads for the door. "If you change your mind, let me know." I give him a curt nod, never looking away from my screen.

Fuck off.

Maybe I should've worked from home if I knew they'd be breathing down my fucking neck all day. I take out my phone and text Liza.

20

Liza

Graham: *How's it going?*

    Liza: *So far so good, I've seen two patients on my own.*

    Graham: *Atta girl. Have lunch with me?*

    Liza: *Of course. Are we going to actually eat this time?*

The last time I met Graham for lunch, I ended up getting fucked on his couch. Food was the last thing I cared about.

    Graham: *Depends on my mood.*

I roll my eyes and smile, tucking my phone away.

"Knock. Knock." I look up and see Dr. Cinkade at the door. I smile and wave him in. "I hear you had your first two patients today," he says.

"I did, the last one just left, actually." He smiles at me and leans on the edge of my desk.

"How are you feeling? Is your office ok?" he asks me.

"Yes, everything is perfect. Thank you so much for this opportunity," I say. He waves me off.

"You were an excellent intern, Elizabeth. It was never a question of whether or not we'd offer you a full-time position. The clients loved you, the staff loved having you around, and *I* loved having you around, picking my brain. It was a win-win for us all."

"Well, still, thank you." He migrates toward the door, grasping the handle.

"Let me know if you need anything."

"I will, Dr. Cinkade."

"Again, call me Luke. I'm not that much older than you, Elizabeth." I give him a small smile and nod.

Weird.

It was 12:00 p.m. exactly when my phone dinged.

Graham: *Outside.*

Liza: *Be right down.*

I shut down my computer and grab my clutch. I nearly run into Dr. Cinkade—I mean, *Luke*—on the way out, tripping as I try to avoid colliding with him.

"I'm sorry! I didn't see you!" He catches me, cradling me against his chest tighter and longer than needed. I gently push against him and regain my composure. A wave of nausea comes over me when he tightens his hold briefly before letting go.

"That's ok, I was just heading out. Unless you need anything from me?" I try to keep my face from turning up as the words come out of my mouth.

Please say no.

"No, not all. Enjoy your lunch." I hurriedly walk towards the staircase, quickly catching my breath. *That was weird.* I ignore my conscience and push out of the front door.

"Ms. Crambell," Ellis says. I roll my eyes at his formality.

"One day, Ellis, you will *not* call me that. I can't wait for that day." He doesn't acknowledge anything I say, his face staying the same as I climb into the back seat.

Graham has his phone to his ear. I slide up next to him and kiss his cheek.

"Andrew, I gotta go. I'll see you after lunch." He pulls me to him and kisses me gently. "Missed you," he groans in my ear.

"It was only a couple of hours..."

"A couple of hours too long." He rakes his eyes over me and I raise my eyebrow at him. I roll my lips into my mouth and can hear the privacy screen sliding up, dividing us from Ellis.

"On your knees, pretty girl. I'm going to stuff your mouth with my cock."

I sink to my knees in front of him without reservation because that's the effect he has on me. I'm always in the mood to have a mouth full of his cock. I'm always in the mood to make him feel good.

"Good girl." He runs his hand over my head as I pull out his cock. "Make me come," he commands.

"Yes, sir," I answer before teasing the tip of his cock with my tongue.

I push his cock further into my mouth, making myself take every inch of him. He takes control quickly, jerking his hips into my mouth. I gag, but I don't dare stop. I'll never stop, not until his cum is trickling down my throat.

"Mmm, you love when I fuck this pretty face. You love when you get face fucked like a good little slut, don't you?"

I bob my head up and down, slurping as I go. His hands tighten in my hair and I know it'll be fucking ruined by the time this blowjob is over.

"I'm going to come down your throat and you'll swallow every drop." I brace myself and wait for his explosion. He puts his palms on each side of my face, pushing himself deeper and deeper until I feel him in the back of my throat. Not even seconds later, the warmth and saltiness of his cum shoots in my mouth. I swallow and swallow, making sure to drink all of him in.

I lean back on my heels and run my tongue over my lips. He wraps his hand around my neck and yanks me on top of him. He swipes his thumb over the edge of my mouth and pushes it inside. "Missed a drop." I suck the remainder of cum off his finger.

"Good girl, now ride my cock." I wore a dress, so it doesn't take long before I embed myself on his still semi-hard dick.

"Graham..." He pushes his hands into my hair and tugs as he thrusts inside of my pussy. I grind back and forth as he kisses all over my neck. This man will be the death of me. The way he fucks me, the way he caresses me. It's too much.

He lifts my ass and slams it back down, the force making me yelp. He puts his hand over my mouth. "Filthy fucking girl. Unless you want me to cut off Ellis' ears because he had the luxury of hearing you come, you better keep fucking quiet."

"I can't, I'm coming," I mumble under his hand. He tightens his hand over my mouth, covering my screams as he pumps in and out of me. The man is a machine. He just came yet I can feel him coming again. The warmth of him fills me. The sound of his groans and thrusts fill the back seat. I slap my handover his mouth as he continues to come. I yank my face away from his hold and whisper in his ear, "No one gets the fucking *luxury* of hearing *you* come, either."

He kisses me as I climb off him, his cum streaking down my leg. Like always, he runs his finger up and pushes it back inside of my pussy.

"You know that's how babies are made, right?"

"Hmm. You didn't find your pills yet?" he asks. After his father was taken, my pills went missing. I got them refilled and fuck all if I misplaced those, too. I told him we needed to use condoms until I found them, but instead of listening to me, he's taking every opportunity to pump me full of his cum.

"You probably have them hostage somewhere," I accuse. He tilts his head as I pull my panties back into place and lean my head on his shoulder.

"Maybe I do." I smack his leg, hoping that he's kidding.

"How's it been going today?" he asks, changing the subject. I think back to Luke and how nice he'd been this morning.

"Good so far. Luke is accommodating and very sweet."

"Not too sweet, I hope," he mutters. I nudge Graham playfully.

"Hungry?" I ask.

"Starved. I shouldn't have skipped breakfast."

The privacy divider rolls down. "There's a roadblock taking us the long way," Ellis says. Graham nods and his phone dings.

His face hardens and his jaw tenses, a look I know all too well. "What's wrong?" He turns around and looks out the back window.

"Ellis, you see that black truck?" Ellis nods, looking in his mirror. "Lose them. Now." I frown and turn around to see the truck.

"Graham, what is going on? Who is that?"

"Elizabeth..."

"Don't fucking *Elizabeth* me, who's following us?"

"The cartel." I suddenly feel like the air in my lungs have been sucked from my body.

"I thought they were gone." Graham turns to speak when we get hit by another car, sending the Audi crashing into the back of another truck. My head jerks forward and smashes into the back of the passenger seat.

"Elizabeth!" Graham yells, reaching for me. I can't reach him, my leg is stuck. I tug on my leg in an attempt to get it free.

Pop. Pop. Pop.

21

Graham

I lunge toward Liza and yank her leg free.

"Give me your hand!"

She shoves her hand in mine and I pull her out of the wrecked car, shielding her with my body. We find a building close to the wreck and I deposit her next to it. "Stay here. I'll be back for you."

She grabs me when I turn to walk away. I cup her face and force her eyes to me. "Elizabeth, I am coming back for you. Do *not* move. If someone comes for you, fucking shoot them." As I push a gun into her shaky hands, something in her eyes changes and I know she'll protect herself. "You got this, pretty girl."

A man in all black with a ski mask spots us. I'm quicker than he is, managing to pull my gun out and taking him down before he can fire. I crouch down by the car, take aim, and shoot. Ellis is next to me, firing a shot and taking another one down. The police get there quickly, taking aim at the cartel. They're always on the Salando side. Even though my father did illegal shit, he was a huge benefactor for the police force.

That favor carries onto me.

"Graham!" Ellis yells.

"I'm good."

"Let's move, I'll cover you." I stand and run toward the car that took us out. A police officer takes aim at one of the men shooting our way, but gets hit by another bullet. He drops. *Fuck, this is messy.* The shooting stops and I see the remainder of the cartel fleeing the street.

"FUCK!" I push my hands through my hair. My phone dings.

Unknown: *You know where your sister is?*

My heart skips a beat and another text comes through.

Unknown: *I do.*

"El!" I bellow.

"I'm here."

"Giselle."

His eyes darken and he speaks with another one of our men. I pick up my phone and call my sister.

"Graham?"

"Where are you?"

"The apartment. Everything ok?"

"Is Elias with you?"

"Yes, you're scaring me..."

"Listen to me, this shit with the cartel isn't over. They just tried to take me out in the middle of a fucking street. They're getting desperate. I'm on my way to you. Stay there."

"But—"

"Let me speak with Elias." I hear her trying to explain, but she gets caught by a sob instead.

"G, what's going on?" Elias asks.

"I need you to listen. In your sister's old room there's a stand next to the bed. There's a sensor on the side of it."

"Going right now." Seconds pass and I grow impatient.

"You there?"

"I'm here."

"Good, now press it. The top of the dresser is going to pop open. Take one of the guns and wait there. I'm on my fucking way."

I hang up and shove the phone into my pocket. If he knows where she is, that means he was already there. Or he had someone there watching her.

"Graham!" I turn and see Liza running down the street towards me. She wraps herself around me and takes in the scene around her.

"What the *fuck* is going on?" she asks.

"We have to go. Now."

"I'm going to your mom," El says. "Ralph will drive you to your sister. But if they know where she is...your mom—" Ellis' voice cracks a bit. He never flinches in a gun fight, never backs down from any fight. But when it comes to my mother, his heart is out of his fucking chest.

"Is alone. *Fuck.* Ok, get her back here with us." He stuffs us into the back of a black SUV. Ralph pulls out, not bothering to wait until we're buckled in. I turn to Elizabeth and pull her seat belt across her chest. She flinches and I frown at her, just now noticing the gash on her head. I take off my suit jacket and press it against the wound. She turns away from me, taking the jacket herself.

"I've got it," she says without looking at me.

"Elizabeth, look at me." She doesn't at first. She takes a deep breath then turns those pretty, brown eyes to me. "I won't let anything happen to you, do you understand?" The tear she was trying so hard to hold back falls down her face.

I unbuckle her seatbelt and pull her into my side. Again, she flinches.

"What is it, are you hurt?" I ask, rushed.

"No, no, just a little sore. There was a guy after you left, he hit me."

"Hit you? Where?" She shakes her head when I start looking over her body. Then my phone rings, distracting me from pushing her further.

"Salando," Ellis' voice echoes through the other end. "I got in touch with your mother. She's packed and I'll be there within the hour. I'll use the plane then we will head back to you."

"Does she know?"

"She knows. She isn't surprised, she is worried about you all."

"Just get her here."

"I won't let anything happen to her." I let out a sigh as we pulled into the apartment complex.

"I know. Call me when you get her." I hang up and step out of the car, Liza quickly on my heels.

"I'll check the premises and get a team ready," Ralph says as I grab Liza's hand, walking into the building.

22

Liza

"Alicia," Graham says, approaching the front desk. "Has anyone been here who isn't a resident?"

"Yes, sir. Someone asked for a tour, said they were interested in leasing. I told him we didn't have any available units and he left."

"What did he look like?"

"He was tall, had extremely blue eyes, and was wearing a suit. He had a hat on, so I couldn't really see his hair." Graham nods at her and we heads for the elevator.

My stomach coils into a knot and the pain from my ribs starts to intensify. I know that they are probably broken, but there is no time to worry about that. When Graham left me in that alley, another man found me. Before I got to fire my gun, he pistol whipped my temple and began kicking me in the ribs. The moment he stopped I gathered the last of my energy and shot him in the chest.

I killed a man.

I struggle to stand straight up, ultimately losing the battle and deciding to lean on Graham for support. The elevator opens and I try to move, but my legs feel weak. I know if I move, I'll hit the ground. Graham grabs my hand and starts walking off the elevator. Just as I guessed, my knees buckle and my pain grows worse.

My knees hit the ground and I grab my side. "Elizabeth!" Graham kneels beside me, trying to lift me up. The door to my old apartment flies open and I see Eli running towards us.

"Lizzie! What happened to her?"

"I don't know, she just dropped." Graham looks over my body and at my hand over my stomach, moving it. He lifts up my shirt and his face hardens. "What the fuck happened to you, Elizabeth?"

I cough and wince in pain. He swoops me in his arms and carries me into the apartment. Selle stands up immediately when she sees me.

"Is she ok?"

"Her fucking ribs are broken. Call the doctor, tell him to get here. *Now.*"

"I'm ok, I just need a bath." I try to sit up, but Eli pushes me back down.

"Lizzie, keep still." I open my mouth to protest, but Graham glares at me.

"Elizabeth," he growls. I lay my head back onto the couch. There's no way to talk either of them out of this.

"He said he'll be here in fifteen minutes," Selle informs. Graham clenches his fist and sits next to me as Selle sits in front of us.

"What happened? You said someone hit you?" he asks.

"Yes. The guy in the alley...he found me. I—" I start to hyperventilate and Graham rubs my back.

"What the fuck did he look like? Tattoos? Eye color? Height?

Weight? Give me something to go on here."

"He's still there…" I croak out and Graham stills. "I killed him." I break out in a sob and Eli rounds to the other side of me.

"Lizzie, who gives a fuck?" he says softly before his voice hardens. "He probably would've killed you, too, after he did whatever the fuck he wanted to do to you," Eli spits.

Graham grinds his teeth at the thought. He tilts my face up to look at him.

"You're ok. Breathe. I've got you. You did the right thing." He kisses me and I focus on my breathing. Once I've calmed down, I feel him gently tuck me into his side.

Moments pass before Selle lets out a sigh, turning to Graham.

"So, what is going on? The cartel is back? How is that possible?" she asks.

"I don't know. It doesn't make any sense. No one from that family is alive."

"Graham, you know that's not true…"

"Giselle, don't," Graham snaps. I look at him in confusion.

"He may not claim them, but he is a part of their family," she argues.

"Who?" Eli asks. They both remain quiet.

"Is anyone going to answer?" I ask, annoyed.

"Luke…" Selle says. Graham gives her a death glare.

"Luke who?" I ask, confused.

"Your boss, Elizabeth." My blood freezes and I try to wrap my head around what they are saying.

"I don't understand…you said you grew up with him."

"I did, we both did. He was a year ahead of me. My father was best friends with his father, they were in business together.

Turns out Luke's father ran the cartel. We didn't know that at the time—we were kids. When Selle and I got taken, that's when it came out who his father was. When I learned about what my father was into, I assumed his father was in on it, too. It was confirmed when Ellis got us back; we saw their father fleeing the building. Luke found out, left, and disowned them. He said he didn't want anything to do with his family. Then a week or so later, my father had Luke's father killed."

"So, he knows you were taken?"

"Yes, and he was a big help in helping get us back, as well. After Luke's dad was killed, his uncle took over. That's who I killed when I went to get my father back. Anyway, after Ellis got us back, we never talked again after that. I'd see him here and there at events, but that was it. Our friendship shifted a lot the day his father took us. I never blamed him, but he kind of disappeared after that."

"So, he lost his father and his friend at the same time?" Eli asks. Graham shrugs his shoulders and settles back into the couch, rubbing my arm.

"Essentially, yes. But why did you mention him, Selle?" Graham asks. She takes a deep breath.

"Back then, he disowned them because of what they did to us. But when he found out our father had his father killed... you should've seen his face that day. I was a kid and I still remember it. His eyes...they were raw, filled with emotion, rage, pain. But his actions...it was weird."

"How did they know where you were today?" Elias asks.

"I don't know. I had just picked Elizabeth up from her job to take her to lunch," Graham says.

"Did you tell anyone where you were going before you left? Do you think they could've just followed us from home this morning?" I ask.

"No, you saw what they were driving, I would've noticed it," Graham replies.

"Did you tell Luke where you were going?" Selle asks. I frown at the question before answering.

"Just that I was going out for lunch."

"Did he ask with whom?" she continues.

"No, he's never asked me personal questions."

"So, he's never mentioned the fact that he knows Graham?"

"No, Selle. Now that I think about it, he's never given any kind of signs that he knows I'm with anyone at all." Graham looks at me and tilts his head.

"What do you mean?" he asks with an edge.

"He's never said anything about you. He's never said your name. I didn't know you two even knew each other until you told me a few days ago." Just then my phone rings. Speak of the devil. "He's probably wondering why I'm not back from lunch," I say.

"Answer it, put it on speaker," Graham says. Eli sits on the other side of me and folds his arms.

"Hello?"

"Elizabeth? Everything ok?" Luke asks.

"Oh, yes, I'm sorry. I ran into some lady issues and had to run home and change." I shrug my shoulders at the lie and look at Graham. He's grinding his teeth so hard that I can't focus on anything other than the sound of it.

"I wanted to call and tell you not to come back to the office, anyway. Apparently, there was a shooting right down the street and they've shut our entire strip down."

"Oh, really? A shooting?"

"Right after you left, actually. Well, I'm glad you're safe.

I wanted to apologize again for almost mauling you in the hallway. I tend to walk without looking often, so I can't promise it won't happen again," he chuckles.

"No worries, Dr. Cinkade."

"Elizabeth..."

"Sorry, I mean, Luke...well, I've gotta run. I need to prep for tomorrow's patients."

"Oh, before you go, I wanted to see if you were interested in having dinner with me." Graham stiffens beside me and Eli rolls his eyes.

"I'm sorry?" I croak out.

"Tonight, maybe? I don't think they'll let us back in the building tomorrow either, so you're off the hook for chart prepping."

"Uhhh, I have a boyfriend." He is silent for a moment.

"I see. My apologies. I will text you when the building is open again." I hang up and look at Graham.

"He's lying," he says getting up from the couch. "He knows you're with me."

"He said he didn't."

"Elizabeth, you've been photographed in damn near every magazine there is with me."

"Yeah, Lizzie, come on. It's impossible for him not to know," Eli says.

"But why would he lie about it?" I ask.

"Because he's playing a game and we're the star fucking players," Selle says, standing up to answer the knock at the door. My body starts shivering as I think about what they are insinuating. Was Luke responsible for me almost being killed?

23

Graham

Two hours later, the doctor gave me bandages for Liza's ribs and gave her a prescription for pain.

"Have her soak in a bath, wrap this around her after, give her one of those pills, and make her get some rest," the doctor says.

"Selle, call Ellis. Let him know we're all staying at the house tonight and to take Mom there. I'm going to get Liza home. Grab your stuff and head straight to the house. I'll have a car follow you."

"G, do you really think he'd do this?" Selle asks. I run through the person I know Luke to be and I can't see him doing this. He hated his father just as much as we did.

"No, I don't," I reply.

"Then who?"

"I don't know. But we're going to find out." I help Elizabeth with her stuff and we head home.

I lift Liza out of the car and carefully take her upstairs, sitting her on the bed.

"I'll run your bath, just stay put." She leans her head back on the pillow. I start her bath, putting in a cinnamon and lavender bath salt. I rack my brain on who would do this. We made sure to end this cartel bullshit when my father died. My phone dings and a message from Selle appears.

Selle: *We're here. Mom's a nervous wreck, just a heads up.*

Graham: *I'll be down after Liza's bath. Tell her to calm down, we don't need the extra fucking stress.*

Selle: *How am I supposed to calm her? You're her favorite.*

Graham: *Give her wine. I'll be down later.*

Selle: *Fine.*

I lift Liza up and she squirms. "I can walk," she protests.

"No, actually, you can't. Let me help you."

"I said I can walk."

"Will you please stop fighting me? It's my fault you're like this. Let me fucking help you. Jesus." I raise my voice as I run my hands through my hair and she softens. I take a deep breath and turn to her. "Can I help you or not?" She sags her shoulders, but lets me lift her and take her into the bathroom. I gently undress her and help her climb into the tub. She sinks into it and closes her eyes.

I watch her, examining her injuries. My eyes burn with tears. This is not the life I want for her. This is not the life she deserves.

"Stop staring. This isn't your fault," she says, her eyes still closed. I prepare myself for what I know I need to say. She opens her eyes when I don't respond and slowly sits up.

"Elizabeth..."

"Don't, I'm fine."

"You're not fine. *This* is not fine. None of this is fine. This isn't the life you deserve."

"What are you talking about, Graham?"

"You shouldn't be with me. You should be with someone who doesn't have so much *baggage*. Someone who can give you happiness and safety."

"Graham, did you forget that you *killed* a man for me? Did you forget that you saved me from a *stalker*? Shut up. I am with someone that gives me happiness and safety."

"Elizabeth, you need to go to your parents. It's not safe anymore. Us being together isn't safe." She nearly jumps out of the bathtub, her injuries slowing her down. I grab her arm and help her out. She yanks away from me, throwing daggers with her glare.

"Have you lost your fucking mind? We are stronger together; you cannot just send me away!"

"I don't want to."

"Then why would you say that? Why would you do that to us, put us through that *again*?" She screams as tears run down her face.

"Stop. Don't cry. I'm sorry, I just don't know any other way to protect you."

"It's not me that needs protecting...it's you."

"It's not your job to take care of me, Elizabeth." She walks away from me, quickly wrapping her ribs and getting dressed. "Let me help you."

"Don't touch me," she says with a trembling voice. She grabs a bag and starts throwing things into it.

"What are you doing?"

"I'm tired of telling you that we take care of each other. That we are a team. That we are here for each other. That your problems are my problems." She goes to the closet and pulls a few shirts off the hangers. "You want me to leave? Sure fucking thing." She stops and turns to me, zipping her bag.

"But understand this, when I walk out of that door, when you figure out that you cannot do this without me, your groveling better be damn good. Because *nothing* will fix this." She pushes her finger into my chest, harder with each word.

"Liza, don't be mad. I am trying to protect you the best I can."

"By sending me away? Whatever. Good luck. We're fucking *done*." She slams the door and my heart shatters.

Why the fuck did I just send her to New York? And why the *fuck* did I get chills when she said *we're done*?

24

Liza

I quickly call Luke's number, but it goes straight to voicemail. I opt for a text in the meantime.

Liza: *Hey, Luke, I have to fly to New York for a few days for a family matter. I will be back in a few days. Please call me when you get this text. I am happy to work from home.*

I pack my stuff in the cab waiting outside when my phone dings.

Luke: *Fly with me. I have a business meeting in New York tomorrow morning, remember?*

Liza: *I must've forgotten, sounds perfect.*

Luke: *I'll send the address to the landing strip.*

Liza: *See you then.*

I know I shouldn't be flying with Luke; it's insensitive, irresponsible, and utterly stupid. But I'm going to, anyway. I want to hear for myself if he was lying about knowing about me and Graham. I also need to know if he is a part of the reason that I could have been killed today. I look at my phone, hovering over my mom's name. I have to call and tell her what was going on.

"Hi, honey!"

"Hi, Mama. I have to tell you all something."

"Let me put you on speaker."

"Lizzie…what's going on?" my dad asks. As I let out a sigh, I tell them everything that had happened in the last twenty-four hours.

"What the *fuck*?" Brant said. "I knew Joe was into illegal stuff. He had been for years, but said he stopped. I never knew it was this deep."

"And Graham? Is he involved?" my father asks.

"No, he's just the target now since he's the one that practically put an end to it all." My mom is quiet on the other end of the line. Too quiet.

"Mom?"

"I'm sorry, honey. I just, I don't understand how you didn't tell us any of this when Joe passed away."

"It wasn't my story to tell. Anyway, I'll be there soon. Love you."

"We love you, too, honey."

* * *

I climb out of the cab and Luke is standing by the plane waiting for me.

"Elizabeth, good evening. You look beautiful."

"Thank you."

Once we were seated, I realized how wrong it was to be here, but I needed to know the truth and I didn't have time to waste and pretend that I didn't come with an agenda. The stewardess hands us both a glass of wine and a tray of grapes and cheese. I nod at her and give her a small smile.

"I need to ask you something," I say. He looks over at me, setting his glass of wine down.

"You can ask me anything."

"Earlier, you said you didn't know I had a boyfriend...was that the truth?" He clears his throat.

"No, Elizabeth, that wasn't the truth."

"So, why'd you lie?" He looks out the window before answering.

"Because I don't stand a chance against that man. I never have."

"What do you mean you never have?"

"Growing up, we were inseparable. Two alpha males who were used to getting what they wanted. My brother was the one who wanted to do his own thing, so Graham and I always did things together." *A brother?* "Anyway, even then, the girls I wanted, wanted him instead. He'd do what he wanted with them and then throw them to the side when he was finished. He doesn't deserve to do that to you. You're too good for him."

"You're wrong. That's not him anymore."

"That may be true, but do you think that I don't know that the shooting today was because of him? He's not good for you."

"Did you have anything to do with that?" He frowns at me.

"You think I'd go after him while *you're* with him? I'd never put you in harm's way, Elizabeth. And I'd never hurt someone that helped me through my shit of a childhood. My father put them through enough..." Relief floods through me.

"But..." he starts.

"But what, Luke?"

"I know who would..."

25

Graham

Twenty-four hours later and my mom and sister were still pissed with me. Elizabeth wasn't answering her phone, the cartel was suddenly radio silent, and I was quickly realizing that I couldn't protect her if she wasn't with me.

"Sweetheart, please help me understand why you told her to leave?" my mom asks.

"I don't know, Mom. I thought she'd be safer away from me. If they thought I didn't care about her, maybe she wouldn't be a target." She smiles at that and I raise my eyebrow. "What?"

"It's no secret that there's more between Ellis and I. Being with him has always been something that felt unattainable, now there's a window and I want you to know first that we are taking the opportunity. With that being said, there's no reason in hiding this. He told me the same thing you told Elizabeth years ago. Before your father and I started dating, Ellis and I were best friends. We always wanted more, though. He told me he wasn't good for me, that I needed to be someone who kept me safe." She shakes her head and looks at me before continuing. "The problem with that, is that I didn't wait for him. I married your father and it nearly ripped him into two when he realized he let me walk out of his life and into another man's. He stuck around because of our friendship and his relationship with your father. He'd rather be in my life with the bare minimum than to not be in it at all."

"Why are you telling me this, Mom?" She sits next to me and rests her hand on mine.

"Sweetheart, you barely survived being without her for a week. What makes you think you'll survive the rest of your life without her? You don't know how long this will go on. You sent her away, but what happens if this is still happening six months or a year from now? So protect her. It's what you're good at. But you can't protect her by sending her away. Ellis has everything clear here. Take Ralph with you and go.

"I don't know, Mom. I fucked up." She kisses my cheek and grins.

"Then fix it, sweetheart."

* * *

Four hours later I was at the door of Brant and Bethany's home. I stood there for what felt like an eternity, my nerves taking over. *Why the fuck did I think I could do this without her?*

I lift my hand to ring the doorbell and within seconds Brant opens the door. "We all thought you were going to sleep out there. Took you long enough to ring the doorbell." He smirks at me and Bethany smiles as I walk in.

"Graham. Hi, honey." She pulls me in for a hug and Axel nods his head at me.

"Where is she?" I ask, feeling her absence.

"She went out with... a friend. She flew in with him last

night," Bethany says.

"A friend?" *Him? Who the fuck is him?*

"Yes, I'm sure she'll be back anytime now."

"I want you to tell me what is going on," Axel says, motioning for me to sit down at the table. I sit down and let out a long, dragged-out sigh. I tell them everything from beginning to end. From how I thought she wasn't safe if we were together to how I told her she needed to come here for a while until everything was over.

"I was wrong. The moment she walked out that door I lost every sense of confidence I had to put an end to this shit."

"Then fix it," Axel says simply. "I know my daughter. The moment she sees you she'll forget the problems, the arguments, and the fear."

"I was going to ask for your blessing to marry her when we came this weekend...I don't know how we got here instead." Bethany's breath hitches and Axel and Brant look at each other.

"And now?" Brant asks.

"Now it's all I've been thinking about since she left. She said we were done. She has no clue that's not an option." I smirk and rub the back of my neck.

"You'll love her with every piece of you. Keep her safe and keep her happy?" Brant asks.

"Of course. There's nothing more I want to do."

"Then you have our blessing," Axel chimes in. Bethany smiles at me and I smile back.

"I have to fix it first." The sound of a car door shutting outside stops us mid-conversation. I stand and head for the door. I open the front door, only to see Luke holding his hand out to Elizabeth, helping her out of his fucking car.

26

Liza

"I've got it. Thank you, though," I said, bypassing Luke's hand and sliding out of the car. "Would you like to come in? We can brainstorm more about what you told me."

"I don't think he'd like that," Luke says, looking over my shoulder.

"Who?" I ask, turning to look at the front door. Graham is standing there leaning against the door frame, one hand in his pocket and the other balled into a fist at his side. He looks relaxed until you land on his face. He's *pissed*. When did he get here?

"He doesn't dictate who I spend my time with. Besides, if what you say is true, then he needs to hear it from you."

"You're mad at each other, aren't you?"

"That obvious, huh?" Graham starts towards us and my pulse quickens.

"Elizabeth," he growls

"What are you doing here?" I quip.

"Well, I came to *grovel*, but it doesn't seem needed any-more," he says, looking between Luke and me.

"Oh, please. Spare me the jealousy act."

"G, good to see you. I'm sorry about what's going on," Luke offers.

"Are you?" Graham scoffs.

"I am. I hope you get it worked out and put to an end," Luke says evenly.

"I will," Graham says, responding to Luke, but never taking his eyes off me.

"Tell him Luke…" I urge.

"Tell me what?" Graham questions.

"He thinks he knows who's behind this." Graham raises his eyebrow and looks at Luke.

"I'm wrong," Luke says suddenly. "I've got to get going, you two be safe. Elizabeth, come back to work when this is all sorted out. Don't worry about your patients, I'll transfer them onto my schedule." *What?* Is he fucking kidding me?

"What? But you said—"

"I know what I said, but it's impossible. I'll see you back at the office." He climbs into his car and pulls off in the blink of an eye.

What the fuck just happened? We spent the last four hours discussing who was behind this. He told me yesterday at dinner and was convinced it was impossible. Then today we decided to put the puzzle pieces together. It all made perfect sense, now he didn't want to believe it? Something's not adding up.

I rub my temples. I thought after Tim, my life was finally on track to being normal. The irony of how wrong I was is actually amusing. I let out a small laugh at the thought. Leave it to me to fall in love with a man who not only will kill someone for touching me or looking at me wrong, but has ties to a fucking cartel. What type of voodoo doll does someone have on me?

"Did that make you feel better?" Graham asks, his voice low and dangerous. "Going out with him?" He moves closer to me.

"Go home," I say, trying to walk by him. I'm not dealing with him or his jealousy right now. He's the one that pushed me away and now he's mad at *me*? I had to figure out a way to prove this theory right, which included talking to Luke. Arguing with Graham about me having dinner with someone who actually helped me put this theory in motion wasn't going to give me any answers.

"Answer me," he demands, blocking my way and wrapping his hand around my neck. I look up at him and his eyes change from anger, to fear, to sadness. I'm not going to be sucked into this with him right now.

"It was just dinner," I force out as he tightens his hold on my neck.

"And a flight with another man."

"With my boss."

"Who wants you."

"So what?" His body tenses and the grip around my neck tightens even more.

"You. Are. Not. Available." I yank away from his grasp and move around him.

"Could have fooled me considering *you* are the one who sent me away. Besides, I have *never* made it seem like I am available."

"Elizabeth..." He grabs my arm. I stop and look down at his hand around my wrist.

"Let go."

"I can't."

"Lilies..." I grit out through my teeth as tears fill my eyes. He drops my arm instantly.

"Elizabeth..." His voice is gutted with emotion. He never said the safe word was only for sexual purposes, and right now, this is all too much for me. I have to get Luke to figure out if he's right. The only way I can do that is if Graham leaves me alone.

"*You* made me come here, remember?" I walk towards the door as he stands there and stares at me with every emotion flashing in his eyes. I drop my head; I have to tell him what I know. As much as I want him to kiss me, tell me he was stupid, and we move on from this stupid fight, I can't. I have to focus on what's more important—his safety.

"It's his brother. He's doing this to you."

27

Graham

That's impossible. Landon died three years ago in a car accident; I remember seeing it in the papers. I look at Liza and frown. There is no way he's doing this.

"Landon? He died three years ago." She shakes her head.

"He didn't die." She opens the door and I quickly reach the steps, walking in after her.

"What do you mean he didn't die?" Her parents' conversation stops and they all look at us with questions in their eyes. She sighs and spills the whole story.

"Luke said that Landon was positive that someone was trying to kill him. He said that the week leading up to his car accident, someone had been following him and sending him threatening messages. He said he told his father and he brushed it off, saying he'd look into it, but he wasn't sure he ever did. Three days later, their father was killed. He started investigating his father's death, and when he started to figure out that Joe had something to do with it, he realized that he was being followed. His accident was later that week."

"He thinks I had something to do with it?"

"No, but he knows that Joe had his father killed. He wants revenge for his father's death and his own attempted killing. You wiped out the rest of the cartel, so he figured you took your father's place."

"What the fuck?" Axel asks.

"And Luke?" I ask.

"He didn't want to tell you his brother was still alive without talking to him and seeing if the theory was true." She sits next to her dad on the couch and he rubs her hair. Bethany sits on the other side of her while Brant fixes himself a bourbon.

"Which is probably why he left how he did...he's going to figure out if it's true or not." I grab my phone. After all these years, he never changed his phone number. I didn't either, yet we still hadn't spoken in years.

He answers the call.

"Luke," I say.

"I take it she told you?"

"Let me help you. Don't go after your brother alone, he'll feel betrayed."

"I just need to know if it's true. He could have killed her trying to get to you. I care about her and grew closer to her when she was interning—"

"You can't have her, Lu." Using his childhood nickname still felt normal. I missed my friend, but he'd get his ass handed to him if he thought he was taking her away from me.

"I know that. What I was going to say was, that I don't want any harm to come to her. And if it's my brother causing this shit, I'm the only one that can talk sense into him."

"Let me help."

"Meet me tomorrow. I'll text you the details."

I hang up and a sense of some relief washes over me. Even

though I know he wants Liza, I also know that he's helping me end this shit to keep her safe. I want to hate him for his feelings, but I look at her and can understand. Liza is cuddled into her dad's side, her eyes drowsy.

"Lizzie, why don't you get some rest?" Axel suggests. She looks at me and then back at her father before nodding. She stands and heads for the stairs, stopping briefly to glance at me.

"Graham, sweetheart, it's late. You should stay and get some rest as well," Bethany offers.

"I don't want Elizabeth to feel—"

"It's fine. Stay," she interjects. I stand, following behind Liza. Bethany kisses me on my cheek and smirks at me, whispering, "It'll all be fine." I give her a small smile and hope to God she's right.

Liza and I walk up the stairs in silence, both of us thinking what neither of us will say. Both of us wondering how this night will go. Will we sleep in the same room? Same bed? We haven't spoken about our issues. The last thing she said to me was to fuck off, basically. She used her fucking *safe word*. I'm the one who pushed her past her boundaries.

She walks into her room and I stop in the door frame, watching her move to sit on her bed. She looks at me and bites her lip. As always, my dick twitches and I have to remind myself that right now, she isn't happy with me.

"You can come in."

"Are you sure?" She nods and I shut the door behind me. I sit next to her and she turns to face me.

"Why'd you come here?"

"To fix my mistake..." She puts her head down and runs her hands up and down her thighs. "I should have never made you leave," I continue. She shrugs her shoulders.

"We have other things to focus on right now," she mutters. I take her hands in mine, looking into her eyes.

"I can't focus on that until *this* is fixed."

"There's nothing to fix. You said I had to leave, so I did."

"I was scared. I didn't think I could keep you safe."

"I don't want to talk about it, Graham. Not tonight, I'm tired. Can we just talk about it when this shit is over?"

"If that's what you want. I'm going to get a hotel tonight, give you some space." She frowns.

"You don't need to do that. There's plenty of room here. Besides, I'm sure you'll insult my mother if you leave now. Take the room next door." She points to the conjoined bathroom. "It's right through there." I kiss her cheek and head for the room I'll be sleeping in. I stop and turn to her one last time.

"Elizabeth?"

"Hm?" she responds, throwing her night clothes on.

"Enjoy this night alone, because it's the last fucking one you're having without me." She sucks in a breath and I turn for the other room, shutting the door behind me.

28

Liza

The whole night Graham's words replayed in my head. Twenty- four hours ago he was adamant that we couldn't be together. He refused to listen to me, acknowledge I was right, and let us solve the problem together. Now here we are apart, or at least in my mind we're apart, and we're still trying to solve the problem together. Why the fuck can't we just figure our shit out for once?

Luke texted me and told me that they were meeting tomorrow to question his brother. I knew Graham probably planned on doing that without me, but that's not how this is going to go. I'm going with them whether he wants me to or not.

I roll over and look at the clock. *3:00 a.m.* I can feel my body being pulled to him. I'm so pissed with him, but my body still wants him. I told him he'd have to grovel to fix this and he started demanding me back the moment he laid eyes on me. I don't know what's wrong with me. I should be able to resist him; *he sent me away*. I'd be completely stupid to put him out of his misery so soon.

Call me stupid, then.

When I first saw him standing at the door, I felt rage and happiness at the same time. I knew he'd come after me. I didn't expect it to be the next day, but I knew he'd come. I left because I was hurt—hurt that he constantly thinks it's not my job to protect him, too. I didn't know how to make him see that we were better together than apart. I knew that me leaving would make him feel how I felt once I left: powerless.

I finally sit up and yank my covers back. I walk into the bathroom and splash water on my face. Moments later, he opens the conjoined bathroom door and stands in the doorway.

"Can't sleep either?" he asks. I shake my head and dry my face.

"We can talk, if you'd like," I offer. *Why did I say that?*

"You used your safe word..." His voice is almost a whisper and I tuck my lip into my mouth.

"I know..."

"I think I'm pushing you too hard..." he says cautiously.

I fill up my water bottle and take a sip, heading back for my bed. "Lay with me?" He looks surprised at my offer. "I think it's the only way I'll get any sleep tonight," I explain. He tries to hide his smile and climbs into bed behind me, pulling my body to his.

I inhale his scent and close my eyes. "You're not pushing hard enough...for us...you're not believing in us." My eyes water and I bury my face into my pillow. He wraps around me tighter and snuggles into my neck.

"Angel...I'm sorry."

"I'm tired of you being sorry. I'm tired of us being here. Pushing each other away. Not fighting for each other."

"I'll always fight for you. I may be stupid sometimes and

I'm sorry, but I'm learning and I'm trying." I nod my head at his words. My body settles into his and I wipe my eyes, finally closing them.

"Marry me." My eyes widen and I turn to face him.

"Excuse me?"

"You heard me, Elizabeth. Marry me."

"Is that how you grovel?" He chuckles and kisses my forehead. "You're serious?" I ask.

"As a heart attack," he says, his eyes half closed, rubbing my back. He's hard as a rock and my body reacts the moment I feel it.

"Ask me when you're not half asleep with a hard on and I'll think about it." I feel his smile on my forehead, and within seconds, I hear a soft snore escape his mouth. I smile and suddenly I forget that I'm so utterly pissed with him.

Four hours later the sun peers through my curtains, pushing me to open my eyes. Graham comes out of the bathroom with a towel wrapped around his waist and his hair wet.

"Good morning," he says. *Does he realize he told me to fucking marry him last night? Am I supposed to forget that?* I clear my throat and stand up, stretching my arms above my head.

"Good morning. I'm going to have a shower." I try to walk around him to the bathroom when he puts his arm out in front of the door to the shower.

"Stop doing this to me," he says.

I raise my eyebrows and tilt my head in question. "Doing what, exactly?" I ask.

"Making minutes go by without the certainty of knowing we're ok. Tell me we're ok."

"I want us to be," I whisper. He pulls me into his arms and

looks me in my eyes.

"I want that, too." I wrap my arms around his neck and he leans his forehead against mine.

"You told me to marry you last night…" He chuckles and tucks a piece of my hair behind my ear.

"I know…but it wasn't right of me. I'm sorry." My heart breaks a little. *What did he mean it wasn't right?* As if he could hear my thoughts, he continues, "You deserve a proper proposal. And when I propose to you, it's going to be when I have your full attention, when you aren't thinking about a cartel chasing after me, and when I don't have a *hard on.*" I smirk and lean into his touch. "How do your ribs feel?" he asks.

"Doesn't hurt much anymore…" I graze my hand over his cock and he groans.

"Elizabeth, no. I'll hurt you."

"Then hurt me." I kiss his neck and yank the towel from his waist. If he thinks he isn't fucking me before our lives turn into a shitshow again, he's mistaken. He runs his tongue across his bottom lip. I slowly start to drop to my knees in front of him, taking his cock in my mouth. He tilts his head back and groans.

"Fuck, don't do this to me right now." He pushes his hand in my hair and tugs, pushing himself deeper into my mouth as I take all of him. He withdraws himself from my mouth and stares down at me. "I come nowhere other than inside of you. Up, now." He grabs my arm and helps me to my feet as he lifts me and puts me on the bathroom countertop. "Wrap your legs around me."

He pushes himself inside of me slowly, withdrawing and pushing again. He's being too gentle. "Graham, please."

"I don't want to hurt you." I bite down on his shoulder and buck my hips toward him. He groans and pushes deeper and harder into me, giving me what I want.

"Fuck." He quickens his pace, lifting me and pushing me into the wall. He thrusts and thrusts in and out of me. I completely forget the fact that we're at my mother's house and let out a loud moan.

"Quiet, baby. We'll get caught," he says, smirking.

"I don't care. It's so good." He places me on my feet and turns me around as I brace myself for the intrusion to come. He pushes his cock inside of me and rubs my clit with his fingers.

"You're going to come now, understand?" I bite my lip as my body convulses. He pumps in and out of me harder and faster as he reaches his climax. He groans my name and I'm filled with his warmth. He slides out of me slowly, turning me to face him. He kisses my nose and tucks my hair behind my ear. "Ok?" he asks. I nod.

"I know you're meeting Luke today. I'm coming with you," I say. He kisses my forehead.

"Take your shower, Elizabeth." He walks into his room and starts getting dressed.

"Don't you dare leave without me."

"I won't."

I eye him and climb into the shower.

29

Graham

Downstairs, Bethany has a breakfast spread laid out on the table.

"Good morning, honey," she says, kissing my cheek. "Help yourself to some coffee, breakfast is almost ready. Is Elizabeth up?'

"She's showering."

"How'd it go last night?"

"We'll be ok, she wasn't kidding about the *making me grovel* part. I have a lot of making up to do."

"Have you picked out a ring?"

"Not yet, I plan on it once this shit is all sorted out."

"I'm so happy for you both. The happiness you've brought her, we never thought—" Her eyes fill with tears.

"She makes me happy, too, Bethany. I'll spend the rest of my life showing her what happiness is. You have my word." I turn and fix my coffee, grabbing another mug and making Liza's, too.

"Good morning, Mama." Liza trots over and kisses her mom on her cheek. "Where's Brant and Dad?"

"They're outside. Your dad is on his morning run, trying to get his health back to where it was. Brant tags along with him, they should be back by—" The door opens and they walk in, right on cue. "There they are."

"Morning, Lizzie," Axel says, kissing her forehead. Brant kisses her cheek and goes over to Bethany, kissing hers next with Axel following behind. Liza walks over to me, eyeing the coffee mug that's next to me.

"That for me?" she asks.

"It is." She picks it up and takes a sip of it, smiling.

"Perfect."

"Indeed," I say referring to her and not the coffee. She smirks and nudges me.

"Still mad at you."

"You didn't seem mad twenty minutes ago when I fucked you against your bathroom wall," I whisper in her ear. She chokes on her coffee and I chuckle. We grab our seats at the table and I kiss her cheek. We all quickly eat our breakfast. My phone dings and a message from Luke comes through.

Luke: *Meet me at my place here in thirty minutes.*

Graham: *Same address?*

Luke: *Yup.*

Graham: *On my way.*

"Gotta go, angel." She wipes her mouth, kisses her parents, and follows my heels.

"Elizabeth." I was surprised to turn around and see her father was the one calling her that. She stops in her tracks and turns to face him.

"I'll be careful," she says, already knowing what he was going to say.

"Graham, you call if you need help. If anything goes wrong,

you protect her with your life. I don't like her going with you—but I know it's her doing and not yours," Axel says.

"I'll take care of her." We walk out of the door and I stuff her into my rental.

Twenty-five minutes later we pull up to Luke's apartment.

"How'd you know where to go?" she asks.

"Our places in New York were close to each other growing up. When our fathers went into business together, we moved out and got our own places here for when they traveled."

"You two must've been close."

"We were, but that was a long time ago. Come on, let's go." We head toward the entrance and I stop, turning her towards me.

"Listen to me, you stay directly beside me. If I get any feeling that this is a setup or that there is any danger, we leave. Understand?" I ask, taking her hand into mine.

"Yes. Let's get this over with."

I knock twice on Luke's door before he opens it. His face looks weird. He seems worried—or maybe scared.

"G...Elizabeth, come in. We need to talk..."

"What is it? Why do you look so weird?" Liza asks. My phone rings and it's El.

"I have to take this."

"It's your security, isn't it?" Luke asks.

"How do you know that?"

"Because I talked to Landon before you got here; it's him. He's convinced you knew about your father's plan to kill our father and then tried to kill him. He knows you're here, you need to leave." My phone continues to ring.

"How did you know it was El calling me?" He puts his head down and I grow impatient. I push him into his kitchen counter and wrap my hand around his neck. "I don't want to hurt you. But so help me..."

"He has..." He coughs as he gasps for air.

"Graham, let him go. Let him speak." I ignore her and keep my gaze on him.

"Has who?"

"Your mother, he has your mother." I drop my hands and freeze. My phone rings again and I put it to my ear.

"Graham! Get out of there, he knows you are there. I'm going after your mother. Get out, now!" El yells. *Click.*

"We need to get out of here. Now. He knows we're here and he's coming." I grab Elizabeth's hand and yank her toward the exit.

"He's here," Luke says, looking out of his window. "And there's a lot of them." I look out the window and see six or seven men rushing into the building. I turned to Liza and hand her a gun.

"You remember how to use this?" She nods. "You shoot anyone that you see. Do not shoot Landon, he's confused right now."

"How will I know what Landon looks like? I've never met him."

"He'll look like me, we're identical twins," Luke says.

Liza gasps, but quickly nods and regains her composure. "Go out the back. If you hurry, you'll miss them. I'll try to talk to him...and G?"

"Yeah?"

"Take care of her."

"I don't need you to tell me to take care of *my* girl," I grit out, pulling her out of the back door.

30

Liza

We rush down the backstairs, Graham's hold on my hand tightening once we get to the door.

"If there's anyone in the way of us getting out of here, shoot them. Do you understand me?" I anxiously wait to see what our fate holds behind that door. "All clear, let's go," Graham directs.

We run to the car, quickly merging ourselves. "You, ok?" he asks, looking at me.

"Let's just get out of here." He starts the car and his phone rings.

"It's Lu," Graham remarks.

"Lu?" Graham asks with his phone on speaker.

"Not Lu. Lando here." He gives an evil chuckle and Graham pulls out onto the street.

"Landon. What the fuck, man? What is wrong with you?"

"You. You and your fucking family is what's wrong. I'm tired of the Salandos getting away with everything they did to my family."

"I had nothing to do with whatever happened with our

fathers. I didn't even know he was into the shit he was into until he got taken." Silence falls on the other end.

"Bullshit." *Click.* Moments later his phone rings again.

"G, I tried," Luke says over the phone. "He won't listen. He told me that I always picked your side. He left and he's *pissed*. You need to disappear."

"Lu, I'm not afraid of your brother. If he wants war, he'll have it. I've gotta go, I have to find my fucking mother." He ends the call. *War?* What the hell does that mean? And why am I suddenly not afraid of it?

"She'll be fine," I reassure. He gives me a small smile and makes the drive to my parents' house in complete silence.

"You're staying here. I need to get to my mother. Call your brother and tell him not to let Selle out of his sight." He pulls me out of the car, but I yank away.

"I'm not leaving you. You need my help." He grabs my hand and pulls me up the stairs into the house.

"Axel!" he roars. My dad comes around the corner.

"What is going on?" His face is confused as he looks from Graham to me.

"She needs to stay here. They took my mother. I have to go after her."

"I am *not* staying here. I am coming with you," I argue.

"Elizabeth—" Dad starts.

"Dad, save it. I'm going. End of story." I fold my arms and glare at both of them. Graham shakes his head and turns to me.

"Go get your stuff. Hurry up."

"If you leave me, I swear to—"

"Go, Elizabeth." I dash upstairs and I hear Graham and my dad speaking. I grab my suitcase and shove what I need in quickly. Then I hear the door shut.

No. He didn't. He wouldn't.

I run downstairs and collide with my dad's arms.

"No! Let go of me! He needs me!"

"Lizzie, stop!"

"How could you? How could you let him leave me here!" I kick and scream until he finally releases me and I crumble to the floor.

"Lizzie, look at me." I sniff and he wipes my tears. "If he loses you, he won't make it."

"Dad, if *I* lose him, I won't make it." My mom and Brant walk through the door and she's at my feet in a second.

"What happened? Where is Graham?" she asks, rubbing my back and looking at my dad.

"He's gone. They took his mother, Beth." Her breath hitches and silently cries while comforting me.

"Sweetheart, come on. Let me make you some tea." Brant and my dad pull us up and walk us to the kitchen.

My mom busies herself making tea, wiping her tears as she goes. Madeline is her friend and I'm sure she's just as worried as I am. I walk over to her and give her a hug.

"I'm sure she's fine, Mom. They'll get her back, I'm sure of it." She nods and hands me my cup of tea.

"Come on, let's sit," she says, giving me a small smile.

Brant and my dad are in the other room whispering to each other. I can't make out their conversation as my mother tries to distract me, asking how I'm feeling and how our talk went last night.

"What are they talking about..." I whisper to myself.

"What's that?"

"Sorry, Mom, nothing. Can you excuse me? I'll be right

back." She nods. I run upstairs to my room and pull my phone out.

Graham's phone rings and rings. No answer. I call again and this time he answers immediately.

"Angel."

"You stupid, stupid man. I'm coming after you."

"No, you're going to wait until I come back to you." I actually laugh. He is clearly mistaken if he thinks I'm going to sit here and wait.

"Nothing about this is funny. You're not going to follow me, Elizabeth. I need to know you are safe."

"We are stronger together. You know that and I know that."

"Did you call your brother?" *Shit, I forgot.*

"I'll call right now. Where are you?"

"I'm almost at the plane."

"Wait for me, please."

"I can't. You have to promise me you will stay with your father." I don't answer. I'm not lying to him. "Elizabeth, promise me." I fight back every tear I have forming by the second. "Say it," he demands.

"I promise."

"I love you." I can't help it anymore; I cry. I cry hard.

"Come on, don't do this to me. Don't cry," he says.

"I'm sorry..."

"Tell me you love me," he demands.

"I love you."

"Good girl. I'll see you in twenty-four hours, not a second later." He hangs up and I grab my suitcase. He's clearly lost his fucking mind if he thinks I'm staying behind.

I quickly call my brother and fill him in.

"Do not let her out of your sight and don't tell her about

Madeline being taken. She'll try to come with me."

I'm not sure if that was the right call, but I can't worry about that right now.

"Ok, Lizzie, be safe. You know he's going to be pissed at you for going," Eli says.

"I know. Love you."

I grab my things and go to the bottom of the stairs to see my father waiting with his suitcase.

"Told you. I know my daughter," he says to Brant.

"I have to go after him..." I say.

"We know. Call us as soon as you get there," Brant says. My mom pulls me to her chest.

"Please be careful, sweetheart."

"I will, Mama." I turn to my dad and he opens the door.

"Ready?" he asks.

"Ready."

Graham Salando, you're getting my help whether you want it or not.

31

Graham

I call El as soon as the plane lands.

"Are you here?"

"No, I sent Ralph to get you. I am not losing this fucker."

"You're still following him?"

"Yes, he hasn't stopped yet. And the moment he does, I'm taking him."

"What?"

"He knows where they took your mother. He was there." I walk off the plane and see Ralph waiting for me.

"I'm on my way to you." I hang up and tell Ralph to track Ellis' phone.

"Get me there. Quickly." I slide in the back of the SUV and rub my hands up and down my thighs.

Elizabeth. I need Elizabeth. I pick up my phone and look at the picture I have of her on my screensaver. She's sleeping and her hair is slightly covering her eye. She's beautiful. I took it the first time she spent the night with me and it's been my screensaver ever since. This woman is the only thing that keeps me going and right now. She's the only thing that's keeping me focused. I need to find my mother; put an end to this shit so I can get back to Elizabeth and make her my wife.

My phone rings and pulls me out of my daze.

"I've got him. Meet me in the warehouse your father owned."

I look up at Ralph and he nods, acknowledging he heard Ellis' instructions.

"We're six minutes away. Make him fucking talk." I hang up the phone and quickly call Elizabeth.

Voicemail.

What? She always answers. I call again. *Voicemail. Bethany.* She must know where she is.

"Graham?" Bethany asks, answering the phone.

"Bethany, where is she? She's not answering her phone." She doesn't answer my question and I know instantly that my firecracker of a woman left.

"She's not alone. Her father is with her. I couldn't stop her. They took Brant's plane."

"Fuck. Alright." I hang up the phone as we pulled outside of the warehouse.

"Ralph, we're fine here. I need you to go to the tarmac and wait there. Elizabeth and Axel will be arriving soon. Do not bring them here. Take her to the lake house and don't let her out of your sight."

"Are you sure you both are alright here? I can keep watch and send another security unit for them," he suggests.

"I don't trust anyone else with her other than you and El. Send another team here."

"Got it boss. I'll call when I get her."

I walk into the warehouse, removing my suit jacket and laying it over the abandoned desk chair that my father used when he worked here.

"El!" I call out.

"In the den, Graham," he answers.

I walk in and I see a man tied up with blood dripping from his forehead and Ellis in his face. "Where did they take her?" he demands.

"You'll never find her," he laughs. I step forward and El looks at me. I roll my sleeves up and grab the knife from him.

I pick up the man's hand up, grabbing his ring finger. "You know, this is the finger they cut off my father." Fear strikes in his eyes. "Then they sent it to my mother." I let out a low, evil chuckle. "I'll ask you once: where's my mother?"

"I can't. He'll kill me if I tell you."

"*I'll* kill you if you don't tell me. You're collateral damage. It'll be easier if you come to terms with the fact that you are going to die either way. So, my mother. Where is she?" He shakes his head and I grab his ring finger tighter, pushing the knife against his skin. He screams. "Tell me," I demand.

"I can't!" In one swift motion the knife slices through his finger. It hits the ground and I shake my head, picking up his index finger. "We'll do this one next."

"No, stop. Stop, please."

"Where is she?!"

"She's at...your father's office." I drop the knife and look at Ellis.

"His office? Why?"

"He wants to end it where it all started." I jolt at the sound of my phone ringing.

"The team is on their way to you," Ralph informs.

"Tell them to head to my father's office, that's where she is. Do you have Elizabeth?"

"They are landing."

"Good luck, Ralph...with her. She won't like that you're not bringing her to me."

"I know, sir." He hangs up and Ellis looks at me.

"Let's go," I tell him. He looks at the man and back at me. "What do you want to do with this fucker?" he asks.

I shrug. "Leave him here. I'll send someone for him later."

We get in the car and within a second, Ellis is flooring it to my father's office.

32

Liza

I climb off the plane to see Ralph standing there with his hands in his pockets.

Fuck.

"How'd you know we were here? Where is he?" I ask.

"Ms. Crambell."

"Don't Ms. Crambell me, Ralph. Take me to him."

"I can't."

"You can and you will," my dad says, stepping off the plane. He's pretty much back to his normal self, only stronger. He worked out every day and reinstated his security business. He decided that he wasn't going to leave New York until he felt comfortable with everything happening. Ralph is tough, but he's not tough enough to deal with my father.

"Mr. Salando gave me strict instructions to take her back to the lake house." I walk up to the car, turning to Ralph before climbing in.

"Ralph, I like you, I do. But let me explain something to you. You, or no one else for that matter, will keep me from getting to him. You can either get me to him safely or you can spend the rest of your night explaining to Graham how the fuck you let me get away without you. And trust me, I *will* get away." He gives me a smirk and shakes his head.

"He's going to have my ass either way. Get in the car, Liza. I'll take you to him," Ralph relents.

My dad grins and climbs in after me.

"That's my girl," he says. I lean back and close my eyes, saying a prayer that he stay safe. If I lose him, I'll lose myself.

I can't lose him. I can't lose him. I can't lose him.

My dad puts his hand on my thigh and squeezes.

"Relax, Lizzie."

"Where are they?" I ask Ralph.

"On their way to his father's office. That's where they took Ms. Madeline."

"Oh, no." I pull my phone out and call Luke.

"Elizabeth? Are you ok?" he asks.

"Your brother took Madeline to Joe's office. Why?"

"Do not go in that building, Elizabeth. Get as far away from it as you possibly can."

"You know I can't do that; I have to help him."

"If you want to help him, you'll tell him to stay away from the building."

"Why?"

"I heard him on the phone talking about explosives with someone and it all makes sense. Joe's office is the first place he started being followed. He said he needed to destroy every memory of Joe, he said he needed to finish it where it started."

"Oh my God. He's going to bomb the building..."

"There's no hope for Madeline. Not unless they get there before Landon does." I hang up quickly and called Graham.

"Eliza—"

"He's going to bomb your father's office. You need to get there before he does. Get your mother out, Graham!" I hear him talking to Ellis.

"Do not come here, Elizabeth. I mean it. I love you." He hangs up and I look at Ralph.

"How far?"

"Five minutes." I look at my dad.

"You are not going into that building if he's there, Elizabeth." I freeze at the sound of him using my full name. "I am not risking your life for anyone else's," Dad says. I stare out of the window, willing Ralph to drive fucking faster.

33

Graham

"The door is locked," Ellis says. I pick up my key ring and toss it to Ellis. "It's the gold one." I watch our backs as he slowly opens the door. We're on high alert—there's no telling if Landon is here or not. He should have known we'd figure it out sooner or later. And if he's the same Landon I know, then he wants a show. I know he's here. I can feel it.

"I'm going to find your mother. Stay here. If he shows up, call me and get the fuck out of here."

"She's *my* mother, I'm not staying behind. Meet back here in ten minutes." I go left and he goes right. I know exactly where she is. I inch my way up the stairs and head for my father's office.

I push the door open and I see my mom tied to my father's desk chair. Her head hangs low and I can see a gash on the side of her face. I race to her, pulling my phone out of my pocket to call El.

"El, I've got her, she's knocked out. Bleeding pretty badly. My dad's office, hurry." I shove the phone in my pocket. "Mom, can you hear me?" I lift her face up and she flinches, groaning. "Mom, I'm here. We're getting you out of here." Ellis is there in a second, helping me untie her.

"Graham, I'm going to kill him when I see him. Look what he did to her," El growls. I shake my head at him.

"He's not himself, El. He thinks I tried to kill him. He's out for revenge over something I never had anything to do with. He's beside himself."

"Not a good enough excuse for me."

"Mom, can you walk?" Her eyes shoot open in a panic and she starts fighting against us.

"Maddy! Maddy, relax. It's me. It's me." She calms once she hears Ellis' voice as she searches his eyes. "Can you walk?" She nods and stands, but collapses the moment she steps forward.

"Fuck's sake. Let me carry her." Ellis pulls her into his arms and we dash for the exit.

Ellis pushes through the door with me on his heels.

"I wouldn't do that."

I halt my steps and Ellis stops. I turn around to see Landon with a gun pointed straight for me.

"Ellis, get her out of here."

"I'm not leaving you."

"Now, El. I'm fine."

"No, you aren't. I will blow this fucking place up with you and me in it," Landon says. Ellis runs and I start to move closer to the exit. "Stop fucking moving, G."

"I had nothing to do with what happened to you or your father. What reason would I have to do that? We were friends."

"Stop lying to me."

"Lando, I swear. I had no idea."

"Doesn't matter. Your father ruined my life and now I'm

going to ruin yours as payback."

"You and your uncle already killed him. Isn't that payback enough?"

"Not in the fucking slightest." I move closer inch by inch. I need to get out of this building. I can hear the commotion outside of the door. *Elizabeth.* I know she's trying to get in here.

"Looks like we've got company." Landon chuckles. I shake my head. "Leave her out of it, Landon. It's between me and you."

"I meant it when I said I was going to kill every member of your family. I can't wait to start with her."

"You'll have to kill me to get to her." The doors push open and I hear Ellis yelling after her.

"Graham!" she yells. Landon grins at me, turning his attention to Liza. My heart stops immediately.

"No!" I scream. He lifts his gun and I throw my body in front of her. He fires his gun and our bodies slam to the ground.

34

Liza

My eyes fly open and I feel crushed. I can't move, there's something on top of me. I look and I freeze—there's not *something* on top of me, there's *someone* on top of me.

"Graham? Graham? Answer me!" He doesn't move or answer me. Ellis barges into the building, exchanging gunfire with Landon while my father pulls Graham and I out of the building.

"Elizabeth, are you hurt?" Dad asks, panicked.

"Daddy, help him! He's not waking up! Help him!" Gunshot after gunshot goes off. I flinch at each one, flipping Graham over onto his back. There's blood, so much blood. *No.* The gunshots suddenly stop.

"Graham, come on, baby. Please, wake up." I shake him and my dad rips his shirt off, pushing it into Graham's abdomen.

"He's losing too much blood. We need to go, *now.*" Ellis comes out of the building, running towards us. Something's behind him, *someone's* behind him. *Landon.* Was he wearing that before, though? I can't see through my tears.

"Ellis, down!" My dad pulls his gun and fires it, hitting

Landon in his leg. He fires again, hitting him in his chest. He falls to the ground and I cry. Turning my attention back to Graham, Ellis is at my side in a second.

"We've got to get him to the hospital, now." I don't move. "Elizabeth, look at me." I look at Ellis through weeping eyes. "Unless you want him to die here, you have to let me take him." I let go and follow him to the SUV.

"Keep pressure on his wound. Keep talking to him." I push down on his abdomen. The moment we pull off, I hear a loud *boom*. The building is in flames and I silently thank Luke for the inside information.

"There's so much blood, Ellis." He looks up in the mirror and pushes down on the gas, jolting us forward. I look down at Graham, his breathing is more and more shallow.

"Baby, stay with me. Listen to my voice, you're going to be ok." I cry and cry, pushing down on his wound. "Ellis, please hurry. Please!"

"We're almost there, ok? We're almost there."

"You hear that? We're almost there. Open your eyes, Graham, please."

"We're here. Get ready, this will be quick. They're going to take him straight to surgery. It will be chaos and you will not have any answers. You need to let them work. Do you understand?"

"Yes, I understand." The door flies open and Ellis pulls him out. I run into the hospital. "Help us! Someone help!" A nurse runs behind me. "I need a gurney!"

In a flash, he's gone. They rush him in the back and then it hits me. I'm dizzy, I can't breathe, and my heart feels like it'll stop.

"Elizabeth!" My dad runs to my side. I drop to my knees

and he cradles me.

"He can't die," I wail. He kisses my forehead, hushing me with comfort.

"He won't. He needs you to stay strong, Lizzie. You have to stay strong." I bury myself in my father's chest and will the time to go by.

An hour later we are joined in the waiting room by Selle, Elias, Hogan, my mother, and Brant.

I'm still wrapped against my father's chest when the doctor comes out.

"Madeline Salando's family?" We all turn towards him, standing. "She's fine, just needed a few stitches on her forehead. We're getting her discharge paperwork and she will be all set to go."

"What about my brother, Graham?" Selle asks.

"I'm not sure about that, but I will find out for you if you give me a few moments." I sink back into my seat, my tears rolling again. *I need to get out of here.* I stand and my mother looks at me in confusion.

"Where are you going, sweetheart?"

"I need some air, I'm fine."

"You need to be checked out, Lizzie," Eli insists. I shake my head.

"I'm fine." I walk out of the doors of the hospital, the cool air hitting me in my face. I sit on the bench next to the door and pull my knees to my chest.

"Is he ok?" The voice startles me. I look up to see Luke a few feet away with his hand shoved in his pocket.

"He's in surgery. Landon?"

"He's gone."

"I'm sorry." Even though I'm not, I still say it. I can't be upset with him because of what his brother did. It wasn't his fault. Even though he's the reason we're in this situation, he lost someone, too.

"You shouldn't be. He tried to kill you."

"He was still your brother." He shrugs. Something's different about him. "I've got to run. I hope Graham makes it."

Graham? He doesn't call him Graham. Then it hits me.

"Landon?" He smirks at me and turns towards his car. "He'll find you; he won't stop until he does," I say.

"Make sure you tell him I could have killed you, but I didn't. This is my truce. I know he didn't have anything to do with what his father was into. I found all of the information on his father's computer. *If* he makes it out alive, he'll never hear from me again."

"*When* he makes it out."

He raises his eyebrow. "Right."

"Wait. So, who did my father shoot?"

"Luke...he shot Luke." My breath hitches and tears fill my eyes.

My father killed Luke.

"See you around, angel of mine." I cringe at him calling me that name; that's only reserved for Graham to call me. I stand and start towards him when I hear Ellis' voice. Landon speeds down the road away from the hospital and Ellis shakes his head at me.

"Let him go. The doctor wants to speak with you."

"It's only been two hours; they can't be finished yet."

"Elizabeth, calm down."

"You finally called me by my name." I give a small smile.

I walk into the hospital with Ellis on my heels. What is he

going to do about Landon? There's no way he's going to let him just drive away. He's the reason Graham is here, the reason why I could have been dead today, the reason Madeline was abducted and hurt.

"Don't you worry about that boy; he's not getting far," Ellis says, reading my mind.

"Don't hurt him. I don't think Graham would want that."

"Even after everything he's done to you today, you still manage to want peace for him..." Ellis shakes his head and directs me to the doctor.

"Ms. Crambell?" the doctor asks.

"Yes, that's me. Is Graham alright? When can I see him?"

"We managed to get all of the bullet fragments out. He'll have a hell of a scar, but he did well throughout the surgery. But I want to prepare you."

"Prepare me for what?" My mom is at my side and Selle is on the other side, holding my hand.

"Mr. Salando is in a coma." My heart flutters. I open my mouth to respond, but nothing comes out. *A coma?*

"When will he wake up?" Selle asks.

"That depends on Mr. Salando. He's young, he's strong, and I believe in him. He seems to have the support he needs to pull through this. But I want to be clear: this will not be a walk in the park. His body has been through a significant amount of stress and trauma. It needs to heal. It could take days, weeks, sometimes even months...the bottom line is, he needs you to be strong."

Selle nods her head and looks at me, wrapping her arms around me. "He'll be ok. It's Graham—our Graham. He's got this."

"You can see him as soon as we get him settled into his

room," the doctor offers.

"Thank you," I whisper.

A coma. He's in a coma. Graham is in a fucking coma.

35

Graham

Come back to me, baby. I'm here. We're all here.

Elizabeth. I can't reach her. It's so dark in here. Where the fuck am I? How did I get here?

Landon. He shot me, no, he shot her. Did I make it to her in time? Why can't I move? Her voice, I can hear it again.

No, I'm not leaving him!

Leaving me? Where am I?

Baby, wake up. Open your eyes. Please open your eyes.

She's crying. I hate when she cries.

I'm trying, but I can't. They're too heavy. I can't breathe again. What is happening to me?

Darkness, again.

36

Liza

Three weeks. It's been three weeks since I've heard his voice. Three weeks since I've seen his eyes. The longest three weeks of my life.

The doctors say that he's doing better; that he's getting stronger every day and all his tests look normal. So why hasn't he woken up? No one has the answers for me.

"Sweetheart, you have to eat. He'd lose his mind if he knew you weren't," my mom says.

"I ate earlier, Mama."

"Chips are not a meal, Elizabeth. I'll stay with him. Go down to the cafeteria with your brothers and Selle. Get some food. You'll need your strength when he wakes up."

"I'm not leaving him. Stop. *Please*." She sighs and looks at my father.

"You talk to her. I won't watch her make herself sick."

"Lizzie..." he starts.

"Daddy, don't. I'm not leaving."

"How about I go get you some food and bring it to you. Will you eat it then?"

"I'm not hungry."

"Please, for me?"

"Fine."

He kisses my forehead and leaves the room, my mother giving him an appreciative smile at the door. The door is forever revolving; Ellis and Madeline, Selle and my brothers. Everyone, every day, constantly. It's overwhelming. I'm trying to be strong, I'm trying to be nice, but I want everyone *out*. I just want to talk to him without being interrupted because they want to *check in*.

The nurse comes in. "How's my favorite man today?" she asks.

I enjoy her company and I like the fact that she talks to Graham. I like that she pays attention to me, too. She opens the curtains, checking his IV site and pump.

"You know, Graham, you're hogging the best view in this hospital." She looks at me and raises her eyebrow. "Have we eaten today, Elizabeth?"

"Not you, too, Gina."

"When this man of yours wakes up and tells you that he can hear how stubborn you've been, something tells me he won't be too happy that you haven't been eating." I smile at her.

"My father's bringing me food. I promise to eat it."

"Mhm. I'll get the things for his bath." She leaves the room and I'm finally alone with him. I grab his hand and kiss it.

"Hi, baby. It's just me and you now. I'd really like it if you opened your eyes." I put my head down and start to cry. "Because our families are driving me crazy. And because you have to ask me to marry you again." Gina comes in and drops the bucket off with the bath supplies and slowly backs out, shutting the door. I can hear her tell someone to give me a second.

I wipe my tears and put my head down, resting it on the side of the bed when I hear the voice I have been waiting three weeks for.

"Marry me," he grumbles.

"Graham?"

"Marry me," he says, clearer.

"You're awake!" I kiss his hands and stand quickly. He slowly reaches up and strokes my face. I lean into his hand and tears fall again.

"No more tears, angel." He wipes the tears from my face.

"I missed you so much."

"I'm here...how long was I out?"

"Three weeks."

He nearly jumps out of the bed. I ease him back down softly, smacking his shoulder.

"Fuck! That hurts," he groans and starts coughing. I pour him some water and bring it to his lips.

"Then stay down, you crazy fucking man! I'm getting the nurse."

"No, no. Just you. I want time with you."

"Baby, you're in pain. Let me get her." He grabs my hand and pulls me toward him.

"Just you," he croaks out. I slowly climb next to him. Even after three weeks in a coma he still smells like him...

He tries to sit up again and groans in pain. "Damn it, Graham. Stay down!"

"Fuck, fuck, fuck, fuck," he whimpers. I slowly rise from his side and grab his call light. "You need pain meds," I insist.

Gina walks in right on cue. "Well, well, well. Mr. Handsome himself decided to join us today?" I smile at her and her eyes well up with unshed tears. "This lady here of yours refused to leave your side. She talked about you a lot. I'm glad to finally see you putting her out of her misery."

"Gina, is it?" Graham asks. She nods and I frown. He grins at me. "She warned you that I could hear everything," he says. I back away from the bed and let Gina do her assessment over Graham. "How about we get you a bath?" she offers.

"A shower, not a bath," Graham says.

"You are not walking." I argue. Gina chuckles and hands me the bath supplies.

"We'll compromise, you two. We'll help him walk to the shower; there's a chair there. Then you can wash him like you've been doing for the last three weeks...Deal?"

"Fine." We both get on either side of Graham. The door swings open as my mother and Madeline barge in.

"Sweetheart." Madeline runs towards us and pulls his face into her hands, kissing his cheeks. "You're ok."

"Mother. I'm fine, how are you feeling?" She waves her hands in dismissal.

"Graham, I'm so glad you're awake," my mother chimes in. I feel myself getting frustrated again. I take a deep breath and Gina and Graham glance at me. Gina clears her throat.

"I know we're all happy he's awake, but he has requested his first shower. Can we give him some privacy?" Our mothers smile in unison.

"Of course, we'll go tell everyone you're awake." They retreat from the room and I give Gina an appreciative smile.

"Thank you," I say earnestly. She nods.

"It can be a lot, I get it. I'll be the bulldog, I don't mind. Now, let's get this handsome man of yours in this chair."

Graham leans over and kisses my cheek. "You need to stand

up for yourself, angel. You want time for just us, tell them to get the fuck out."

"She's your mother, I can't be rude. These three weeks have been hell for her, too. I can't tell her off because she sees that her son is finally awake."

"Yes, you can," he argues. We sit him in the shower and Gina grabs the soap, handing it to me.

"If you need me, use his call light." I nod and she leaves us alone.

37

Graham

I pull her towards me and she stands between my legs. I lean into her and kiss her stomach. The thought of her being pregnant comes to mind. If I had died, she'd have nothing to remember me by. I'm not ready to share her, but creating someone who's a part of us both makes my heart burst.

"You know I have to turn the water on at some point, otherwise sitting in this shower is extremely weird," she says, untying the back of my hospital gown and pulling it towards her. I wince in a little pain.

"You ok?" I reach for her shirt.

"You need to take yours off, too, you know, or you'll get—"

"Wet?" she asks, finishing my sentence with a grin.

"Take your clothes off, Elizabeth. You wash me and I'll wash you." She shakes her head. "Absolutely not. I'm not going to be responsible for you being stuck in here any longer than you already have been." I put my hand down the front of her pants and tug them.

"Take them off. Now."

"Good to know you didn't lose your need to be in control

while you were out." She quickly strips her clothes and steps in with me, the water coming from either side of the shower.

"Not a chance," I reply. She grabs some soap and starts washing me. She lifts my arms and slowly washes my stomach, her face filled with hesitation. I rub her back.

"I'm ok. Keep going." She quickly washes the rest of me. I try to stand up and she grabs onto my arms to help me. "I've got it, I promise." I bend down to kiss her neck and she stiffens. She groans and pushes her hands in my hair. I wrap my arms around her and use her as a crutch.

I inhale her scent and groan. "Your turn."

"Graham," she warns. I glare at her.

"Don't do that to me, angel. I want to wash you."

"How about you get better and get out of here, then you can wash me as much as you want when we're *home*?" I kiss her shoulder and bite down.

"Stop defying me." She turns and cuts the water off, grabbing a towel and slowly drying me off. Before I know it, she's on her knees in the shower with my cock in her hand.

"I live to defy you. Maybe you should sit down for this."

"I think you're right." I sit as quick as I can. I'm sure sexual activity isn't the smartest thing for me to be doing right now, but I am sure as hell not turning down a blow job from Elizabeth. She licks the tip of my cock and I groan a bit before she takes my cock entirely.

"*Fuuuck.*" She speeds up her pace and takes me deeper until I'm hitting the back of her throat. My body painfully tightens and I realize that three weeks with no sexual contact has turned me into a minute man. I push my hands into her hair and spurt my cum into her mouth. She takes it all, swallowing it down.

"Damn you," I curse.

She licks the bottom of her lip and dries herself off, pulling her clothing back on. I catch my breath and she helps me into a clean gown.

"I guess I need to get ready to share you now," she says sadly.

"Pretty girl, if you want them gone, I'll tell them to go." She shakes her head and helps me back into bed.

"No, it's ok. They've all been waiting anxiously just like I have. You scared us."

I rub her cheek. "I know, I could hear you."

"You could?"

"Yes and I don't like that you've been skipping meals."

"I didn't want you to wake up and me not be there." She pulls the blankets over my legs, pushing the pillow under my head. "Comfortable?"

"Perfect."

"Let me get the herd," she says, jokingly. "Be prepared," she warns. She leaves and returns moments later with her family and mine. Selle throws herself into my arms and I wince.

"Shit. I'm sorry, G."

"It's alright, Selly. You ok?" She nods and wipes her tears. "Hey, stop that. I'm fine," I reassure her. The doctor walks in and cuts off the conversation.

"You are more than fine, Mr. Salando. Your tests look fantastic and I'd say, if you're feeling up to it, you can go home tomorrow. Of course, you'll have to walk on your own first, but if you can do that, then I see no reason why you cannot heal the rest of this time in the comfort of your own bed." Liza rubs my shoulders.

"Are you sure he's ok to walk?" she asks. I nudge her. "Fine, fine," she gripes.

"Oh, honey, let me get out of here and make sure everything is perfect for you at home," my mother offers. Liza fidgets next to me at my mother's comment and I know it's bothering her. She wants to be the one taking care of me, but she isn't going to say that.

"Mother, it's fine. I'm sure Elizabeth can manage."

"Oh nonsense, she's exhausted and needs to be catered to herself. I'll have a chef come to make you both meals and bring in a cleaning crew. That poor girl needs rest." I look at her and she nods.

"Fine. Where's El?" I look around and don't see him. The room is silent. "Is anyone going to answer me?"

"He went after Landon," Eli says.

"Axel didn't shoot him?" I ask.

"No, Dad shot Luke. Apparently, El thought he shot Landon. He said when he left the building, Landon was lying face down. He didn't check if he was wearing a vest. Turns out, Luke came and Landon told him he was still going to bomb the building. Luke came running out of the building, El and Dad thought it was Landon, and then shot him."

"Luke's dead?" I whisper. Elias nods and hangs his head.

"I'm sorry, I know he was still your friend, G," Selle says, sitting on the bed. I swallow and look up at Elizabeth who's biting her lip. She's hiding something.

"Can you all give us a minute?" Within seconds the room is cleared.

"What aren't you telling me?" I ask. She sits in the chair next to my bed and runs her hands down her thighs. "Elizabeth..."

"Do *not* call me that." She hates it when I call her anything other than angel or pretty girl, but she needs to know that I'm not fucking around. She sighs and leans back into the chair. "Landon came to the hospital when you were in surgery. He could've killed me if he wanted to, but he didn't. He told me that it was his truce, that he knows now that you weren't apart of your father's business."

"He was at this hospital?"

"Yes. The night of the shooting." I grind my teeth together.

"Where's my phone? I've got to get the fuck out of this hospital bed."

"No, the doctor said tomorrow." I glare at her and she folds her arms, standing her ground.

"Ellis is my family. He's searching for someone that tried to kill not only me, but you and the woman he loves. He'll kill him the moment he sees him."

"He won't kill him. I asked him not to," she says. I chuckle.

"Ahh, pretty girl, Ellis has no boundaries when it comes to my mother. Give. Me. My. Phone." She huffs and hands it to me. I dial his number.

"El."

"Good to hear your voice, Graham. I'll be there soon; I'm wrapping something up here."

"Don't kill him..." I say.

"Don't ask me to let him go. He tried to kill you, your mother, and Elizabeth," he argues.

"Then teach him a lesson, but don't kill him," I negotiate. There's silence on the other end for a few minutes. Then I hear him release a long, drawn out breath.

"Alright. I'll be there in the morning," he concedes.

"Thanks, El."

"No thank you...for waking up. She was a wreck; I couldn't stand seeing her that way. She loves you, I'm happy for you." I look at Liza, ending the call.

I pat the bed next to me. "Come here." She slowly climbs in and cuddles into me.

"I'm glad you didn't die," she says, running her finger up and down my arm. I chuckle.

"I'm glad I didn't, either. Now, about you marrying me..."

38

Liza

It's been three months since Graham's accident and every-thing is starting to return back to *normal*, whatever that means. After he was discharged from the hospital, he went to see Landon and told him to stay as far away from us as he possibly could. Landon was reluctant to listen, but we haven't had any issues since then. Luke apparently was very prepared if he ever died. When Landon faked his death, Luke made a very descriptive will including how he wanted his business ran and who he wanted to run it in case something happened to him. Turns out, he had a back-up president for his clinic. Even then, I never returned to his office to work. They hired a new CEO and continued on with his work. Graham took his death a little harder than he expected, but seemed like he was finally trying to move on and find his new normal. His last doctor's appointment is today and I've never seen him so nervous.

I reach for his hand in the waiting room and give him a smile. "It'll be fine. I'll tell him you were the perfect patient...even though you weren't." He smirks at me and kisses my hand.

I wasn't lying; he was determined to do things on his own,

resisting help constantly. But I never expected anything less. He hated that I waited on him hand and foot and hated even more that he couldn't be with me sexually yet. There were so many times I had to take every ounce of strength I had to fight him off.

"Mr. Salando," the nurse says. We follow the nurse into the back. I watch tentatively as she takes his vital signs and fills him with questions. Moments later we're left alone again. Graham pats his lap and I shake my head.

"No way. We're in a doctor's office." He raises his eyebrow and tilts his head at me.

"Do I need to start counting down for you to listen to me?"

"Counting down? What am I, five?"

"I said to come here, Elizabeth."

"Not. A. Chance."

"Five...Four...Three..."

"What happens when you get to zero?"

"You wanna find out? Three months too long, baby."

"You haven't been cleared yet..." I tease. He stands up and starts to stalk toward me when there's a knock at the door. I grin as the doctor walks in.

"Salando. Sorry to keep you waiting."

"No apology necessary, Doc. We were just having a little game of cat and mouse." He grins. I blush at his honesty and sit in the chair, crossing my legs to try hiding the heat fuming from them. Graham sits next to me and faces the doctor.

"So, can I get back to my life now or what?"

"You can, everything looks good. All of your scans are clear and your incision has healed completely. Your stress test showed significant improvement and it would seem that you're in better shape than you were *before* your accident. How that's possible when I specifically told you no physical activity, I'm not sure. But, I'm also not going to ask."

I raise my eyebrow at Graham and shake my head. About a month into his recovery, he started exercising again by running and lifting weights. Despite his mother and I scowling at him about it.

Graham rests his fingers over his mouth to hide his smirk. He shrugs his shoulders. "I'm not quite sure how that's possible, either."

"Right. Either way, you are in top notch condition. I see no reason for us to have any further appointments." Both men stand to shake hands.

"Elizabeth, always a pleasure to see you. You two have a good weekend." I smile at him and nod. Graham places his hand on my lower back, ushering me through the door and whispering close to my ear, "Oh, we'll have a *great* weekend. You just wait."

"Keys," he says, when we are near the G-wagon. "The only reason I've ever let you drive this, baby, is because I had no other choice."

"Whatever, you love my driving. It's superbly better than yours." He opens my door and rounds the SUV to his side. He turns to me and pulls my face into his hands.

"You ok?" he asks. I lean into his hands and he kisses my forehead, then my cheeks on either side, then my nose as I giggle. "I want to take you somewhere this weekend," he says.

"Ok," I say willingly. A weekend away is just what we need to get back to our normal lives.

"You're not going to ask me a million questions?" He leans back and raises his eyebrows.

"Nope. I don't care where we go. I just know that a mini

vacation with you, wherever it is, is just what I need." I push my knees into the seat and lean myself forward until I'm an inch in front of his face. "But now I'm curious."

He pushes his hands through my hair and pulls my face to his, pressing his lips to mine. The heat between my legs returns with a vengeance. I deepen the kiss, crawling over the console and onto his lap. I push my hands into his hair as he brushes his lips over my neck. My mind reminds me of the last time we did this, how I thought he was crazy for telling me to crawl in his lap while he was driving. The only difference this time is we're in a parking garage and I'm the idiot who initiated something I know we won't be able to finish.

"Fuck," I sigh, pulling back. He frowns.

"What? I'm fine. You heard him say I'm clear."

"Not that, I just realized that you are *not* fucking me in a parking garage, in the middle of the day." He gives me an evil grin and pushes his seat as far back as it'll go.

"You're right, *I'm* not fucking you in a parking garage, because *you're* going to fuck *me* in a parking garage." I open my mouth to protest, quickly shutting up and scanning the parking garage. "Angel, no one will see you. These windows are dark enough," he coaxes. He pulls me down to his mouth again and I forget where we are, just taking him in. The man I could've lost, the man I love, the man I want, always. He pushes his hands up my dress and suddenly I'm happy I decided to wear it today. He quickly frees himself and moves my underwear to the side. Within seconds, I lower myself onto him, slowly. "Ah, pretty girl, don't tease right now. I'm seconds away from fucking you until you beg me to stop." He pushes himself up towards me, forcing me to grab the door handle. He fills me as I move up and down on him, finding my rhythm.

Graham leans his head back on the seat and groans, giving me the confidence I need to move at a quicker, harder pace. I place my hands on his chest and throw my head back. Feeling my body tighten against him, I moan his name and he pulls me to him, pumping in and out of me.

"You wait for me. You come when I say."

"I can't, I can't…"

"You can and you will. I'm almost there." He pounds harder and deeper inside of me. I fight every urge in my body telling me to come. I dig my nails in his arms and bite down on his shoulder when he starts to tighten.

"Now. You come, now." I fall apart at his demand and he wraps me in his arms as his cum pulsates in me. "Fuck, I have to get you home. I have three months' worth of fucking to do." I groan as he slides out of me and pulls my underwear back into place. He kisses my forehead and then my lips softly.

I climb back into my seat, quickly fixing myself in the mirror. I clearly look like I've just been fucked, my face flushed and my hair sweaty. The windows of the car are coated with fog and I giggle at what we just did.

"All set?" he asks, starting the car. I nod and buckle my seat belt as he drives us home.

39

Graham

When we got home we barely made it through the door before I started undressing Liza. Three months since I'd had her. That little quickie in the parking garage may as well have been ages ago because I need more. I push her against the door and shove my tongue in her mouth. I crave her, she is fucking insatiable. I need her every second of every day. Not being able to have her was torture, and now that I am cleared, nothing is stopping me.

"Graham, honey, how was your—oops." The sound of my mom's voice pierces through me. Liza jumps and reaches to adjust her dress, but I quickly pick her up and throw her over my shoulder, briskly walking past my mom and heading for the stairs.

"Mother, please, go home." She chuckles and grabs her things. Liza buries her face in her hands in embarrassment. I kick the door to our room close and throw her on the bed, pulling my shirt off and kicking my jeans off in record time.

"Your mom just saw…"

"Do I look like I care what my mom just saw? Lay down."

She bites her lip and leans back.

"Bu—"

"Elizabeth…" I say in a warning tone. She grins and motions that she's zipping her lips. "Good girl." I pull her dress over her head and hover over top of her.

"Missed you," she whispers, reaching for my face. I pin her hands above her head and smirk. "Oh, pretty girl, you have no idea." I make quick work of her bra and underwear, throwing them onto the floor.

I take my time licking and sucking every inch of her body. Slowly lowering myself to her pussy, I flick my tongue in and out of her.

"Please, you, just you," she moans. I replace my mouth with my fingers, pushing them in and out. "Graham…"

I know she's close; just a little more before she comes apart. Her body tenses and I remove my fingers. She gasps as I push myself into her, making her close her eyes.

"Eyes on me, angel mine." She quickly opens them and I push my dick deeper inside of her, her back arching. "Fuck, I missed this view," I groan as my body pushes in and out of her. She claws at my back and I know I'll be wearing her marks for at least a week. I wrap my hands around her neck and fuck her as hard as I can.

"Ahh, I'm going to—I can't."

"Come. I'm right behind you," I say through gritted teeth. She explodes over my cock and I come with a force I didn't know my body had. I can't stop fucking her, even with my body tightening. My speed goes quicker and I fuck her with an urgency I've never had. I pull her off the bed and she wraps herself around me.

I walk us into the shower, turning it on and slamming her

back into the wall as the water pours over us.

"Hold onto me." She wraps her arms tight around me while I wrap one arm around her waist, holding her in place. I push in and out of her slowly at first. She sinks her teeth in my shoulder and I push myself harder into her. "So good, you feel so fucking good," I groan as my pace quickens again. "Mine. Say it."

"Yours. Always yours."

* * *

"I really can't know where we're going?" Liza asks, putting the last bit of her clothes into the bag. I shake my head, grabbing our toothbrushes. "It's just for the weekend?" she clarifies.

I grab the bags and head down the stairs. "Just the weekend," I confirm. She huffs behind me and I chuckle.

"Come here," I say, putting the bags on the kitchen counter. She walks into my arms, wrapping hers around my waist. "You're sure you're ok?" I ask.

She's been a trooper these last couple of months, waiting on me and dealing with me, not listening to a damn thing her or my mother said. I knew that everything that happened was traumatizing to her. She wore it well, but I know my girl. I knew that she would make sure everyone else was ok before focusing on herself.

"Mhm," she answers. I cup her face and tilt it up toward me, looking her in her eyes.

"Angel...I know you." Her eyes fill with unshed tears. "Hey... no tears. Just talk to me, and if not me, then someone. You went through a lot and you haven't said a word about any of it."

"You haven't either..." She's right, I haven't. To her, at least. But I see my therapist often and was dealing with it. I ignore her comment and kiss her cheek. When I pull back I see her tears stream down her face. I wipe them and frown.

"What is it? Tell me, please. I can't fix it if I don't know."

"I...I keep thinking about you being shot...about what would have happened if you never woke up."

"I'm here Elizabeth...I'm not going anywhere."

"I could've lost you. What am I supposed to do if I lose you...I don't know who I am without you." She crumbles and I pick her up, sitting her on the counter.

"You'll never have to figure that out. It's all over and I've got you. Ok?" She nods and I arch my eyebrow. "Words, angel."

"Yes. Ok." She leans in and kisses me, giving me a smile.

"Now, let's go. The plane leaves in an hour." Her eyes widen.

"The plane?!" I chuckle as we head out the door.

She'll never forget this weekend.

40

Liza

When we arrive at the landing strip Ellis is there waiting for us.

"Hi, El!" He smirks and nods.

"Ms. Crambell." I roll my eyes at the formality.

"I really, *really* can't wait until you stop calling me that." He chuckles, turns to the SUV, and grabs our bags.

"Get on the plane, Elizabeth," Graham says, smirking. I cross my arms and raise my eyebrow.

"Not until you tell me where we're going." He chuckles and pushes his hands into his pockets.

"You sure you wanna play this game with me again?" I walk up to him and stand on my tippy toes so that I'm face to face with him.

"Oh, I am absolutely sur—" He hauls me over his shoulder and I shriek in surprise. He carries me onto the plane and deposits me in a seat, sitting next to me.

"Baby, when will you learn? I will always win," he says, pushing a strand of hair behind my ear. I hold back my smirk and roll my eyes. "Ah, the eye roll. This will be a fun trip." He sits back and Ellis climbs onto the plane.

"El is coming?" Graham nods as the captain comes out of the cockpit.

"We're all set to take off for Rome, sir. It'll be about an eleven-hour flight." He returns to the pit and it hits me. Rome? *Did he fucking say Rome?* I look at Graham and he's watching me, smirking.

"Rome, as in Rome, Italy? Oh my God! Oh my God!"

"I take that as you're happy?"

"Yes! Yes, I'm happy, I've never been!" He kisses my cheek.

"It'll be amazing, I promise. Now, buckle up."

I do as I'm told and lean back, smiling from ear to ear. I quickly text my parents, letting them know our flight is taking off and that I will call them when we land.

The plane takes off smoothly and Graham entwines our fingers together. I lean my head on his shoulder, realizing just how tired I am from him fucking me for hours. He looks down at me and kisses my forehead.

"Sleep, Elizabeth." And I do.

I wake sometime later to Graham kissing my cheek.

"Wake up, angel. I want you to eat something." I yawn, looking out the window and back at Graham. "What would you like?" he asks.

"Whatever you're having is fine," I say, unbuckling my seat belt and stretching. He looks up at the stewardess and nods at her. "I've gotta pee," I say.

I walk into the restroom, splash water on my face, and fix my hair. Remembering the bedroom, I leave the restroom and wander in. I smile at the thought of what happened the last time I was in this room.

"Reminiscing?" Graham asks behind me in a low voice. I

clear my throat and turn to him.

"Maybe." He smiles at me and continues.

"If I recall, the last time you were here, I fucked you right there...and over there...oh, and my favorite." He turns me around, my back to him, turning my face to the wall. "Right against this wall...here." I bite my lip and lean against him. He pushes my hair to the side and plants a kiss on my neck, sending a rush of energy through my body. "Maybe I should do it again...hmm? What do you think?"

"Yes, please," I say, breathless. I wonder if this feeling will ever leave. The feeling that I always want him, the feeling of my body igniting from his words. Being with Graham is exhilarating and it seems that the feeling would never end.

He turns me to the door and kisses my cheek.

"As tempting as that is, I need to feed you. We have a lot to do and so little time to do it when we land." I frown, poking my lip out in disappointment.

When we return to our seats, our trays of food are waiting for us. I take in the scent of the perfectly cooked steak and twice- baked potato.

"Would you like wine with your meal, Ms. Crambell?" the stewardess asks. I nod and give her a smile. She pours me a glass, topping off Graham's.

"Does Ellis drink?" I whisper to Graham, watching El sip his diet Coke and rip through his food.

"Never seen him drink a day in my life, angel." He shrugs. I nod and return to the dish in front of me. Shoving a piece of steak in my mouth, I let out a groan, realizing just how hungry I must have been.

"Good?" Graham asks, raising his eyebrow. I close my eyes and groan again.

"Mhm, perfect. How much longer is the flight?"

"About four to five hours. You slept for a long time. Must've been tired..." he says with a sly grin, sliding a fork full of the steak into his mouth. I elbow him and he laughs.

41

Graham

The moment Liza saw the plane start to descend she was glued to the window. I never believed that I'd bring anyone other than my family here. I found myself wanting to show Liza every part of me, show her every place that meant something to me.

Rome has always been special to my family; it was where my mother and father met and we took family vacations here often growing up. We hadn't been back in a few years, but I thought it was the perfect place for Liza and me to get back on track after the fiasco we went through.

"This is beautiful, Graham," she says as we pull into the driveway of my family home. I watch her take in the scenery around the house, pushing my hands into my pockets and leaning against the car rental we got.

"It is, isn't it?" I ask, looking at her and not the house or the view. She turns around and smirks at me.

"I'm talking about the house."

"I'm talking about the view." She wraps her hands around my waist and beams at me.

"I love you, you know." It's the truest words I've ever said.

"I do, and I love you, too. Let's go inside." She pulls me towards the double door, eager to go inside.

This was the house we owned for as long as I could remember. It was what Selle and I called a *mini-mansion*. A seven bedroom house sits next to the ocean, with a pool and hot tub in the backyard. It is a typical Rome house, with small balconies on the two biggest rooms.

The door opens before Liza could open it herself and our family chef and housekeeper, Marco and Abigail, step out.

"Grahamie! It's been so long since your last visit, my God! Look at you." Abigail smiles at me, pulling me into her arms for a hug.

"Ms. Abby, it's good to see you." I kiss her cheek and Marco smirks at me.

"You can't visit more often, Grahamie boy?" He shakes his head and gives my shoulders a quick squeeze.

Liza stands beside me with her hands entwined together. I grab her hand and pull her in front of me.

"This is Elizabeth. Elizabeth, this is Abigail and Marco. They've known me since I was–"

"Since he was six! Six! Now look at him!" Abby says, squeezing my cheeks. She turns to Liza and pulls her in for a hug, kissing each side of her cheek. "Come, come in. Let's get you settled in."

"Well, I guess, I'll just meet her in the house, eh?" Marco barks out to his wife. Abby and Marco have been married for twenty-seven years and love each other more today than before they said I do. They were one of the firsts to show me that love, *true love*, truly exists.

"So, you finally can make it up here and right before your

birthday!" Marco says, patting my back. I cringe at him for bringing up my birthday. I've managed to ignore my birthdays the last couple of years. My family always tried to plan parties, but I'd always find a way to stay for an hour and sneak out. Liza has asked me numerous times when my birthday was and I have constantly given her wrong dates. I know it's only a certain amount of time before she takes matters into her own hands and asks Selle.

"I'm happy to be back. Do me a favor, though, don't mention the birthday around Elizabeth."

"You're fucking kidding me. She doesn't know?"

"I keep telling her the wrong dates...you know I hate birthdays."

"How are you going to wiggle your way out of celebrating it when your—"

"There you two are. What are you doing? Hurry and get in here," Abby yells. Liza is behind her, sitting on the kitchen stool laughing. "I tell ya, those two are trouble together. You just wait and see," Abby says.

I kiss Liza's cheek and slide on the stool next to her as Abby hands us an Aperol Spritz. Liza raises her eyebrows and I pick my drink up.

"Try it, you'll love it." She tips the glass back and closes her eyes, taking in the citrus taste. She licks the bottom of her lip and smiles.

"That's amazing." Abby nods, smirking as she leans over the counter.

"So, Elizabeth, you got my Grahamie to settle down? Tell me how the hell you managed that?"

"I'm still trying to figure that out myself. Not quite sure how I got so lucky, Ms. Abigail," she says playfully, leaning against me.

"Ah, angel, don't flatter me." She gets up from her chair and smirks.

"Bathroom?" Liza asks. Abby nods and directs her to the bathroom, quickly coming back.

"Angel? You call her *angel*?" Abby asks, smiling. I take another swig of my drink. Marco and Abby know me inside and out. I may not have been back here for a few years, but we talk as much as we can. They know everything, even unspoken things.

"The dreams...they—"

"Stopped?" Marco cuts in. I nod in confusion.

"How did you know?" I ask.

"Abby stopped mine. That's how I knew she was heaven, sent just for me." He wraps his arm around his wife, kissing her cheek.

Marco used to be a part of the Special Forces and had an assignment that should've ended his life, but didn't. He was lost, confused, and wanted to be dead. He takes any moment he can to tell people that Abby was the only one who made him want to be alive, who made him *feel* alive.

I lean over, looking down the hall and ensuring Liza is out of earshot.

"I'm proposing..."

"Grahamie! When?"

"Soon, Abby. I have a plan. I just hope nothing fucks it up."

"Language," she scolds. I apologize under my breath.

"What could possibly go wrong? You've finished the things your father had. You've turned his business into a legit one. You kept her safe from that fucking psychopath of a stalker. Everything is falling into place for you," Marco says.

"Marco! You watch your language, too!" Abby says, beside herself. Like I said, Abby and Marco may live here, but I talk to them; keep them updated on *everything*. They haven't missed a beat. Marco runs a lot of things here for me on the business side, so when things started getting messy at home, it was important for him to know. Not only that, but he's important to me. He's been through a lot of shit in his life, I knew he'd help me see straight.

"That's what I'm afraid of. When has my life ever been the way I wanted it to be? Something always comes and fucks— sorry," I glance at Abby, "screws it up."

Abby tugs me into a hug and rubs my back. "You are getting the happiness you finally deserve. Don't let your past or your fear keep you from living."

42

Liza

This house is amazing. The bathroom, the rooms, the homey feeling, the smell of lavender and cinnamon all over the house. I smile to myself, wondering if Graham had a hand in that. I snoop throughout the house, looking at pictures that hang on the walls, some of Graham and his family throughout the years. I stop at a photo of an older gentleman who looks a lot like Graham's father.

"You're supposed to be using the restroom." Graham slides his arms around my waist and kisses the side of my head. I smile and lean into him.

"Who is that?" I ask, continuing to look at the photo.

"My grandfather."

"He looks like your dad, and you, actually." He chuckles and turns me to face him. I tilt my face up to him and press my lips to his. "Where's your room?"

"Why, you need something in there?" I run my hand across his cock and gently squeeze. He groans and wraps his hand around the back of my neck, pulling me closer to him.

"Where. Is. Your. Room?" I ask, emphasizing every word.

In true Graham fashion, without notice, he hauls me over his shoulder. I laugh, settling into his grip. I learned a long time ago not to fight him when he goes into his alpha mode—and he is in full-on alpha mode right now. He chugs me up the flight of stairs; you'd think I was light as a feather with how quickly he launched up them. He kicks through a door, quickly slamming it shut and pushes me against it.

"You make me fucking crazy, Elizabeth." I smirk, pulling his mouth to mine. Kissing Graham is one of my favorite things to do, especially when it is sloppy, raw, and rough. That's when it's full of emotion, full of things he can't say yet but wants to, full of promises and future. I moan and he lifts me, wrapping my legs around him. "I need to be inside of you." I hear him tussling with his belt and zipper.

"Mmm." He yanks my dress up, slides my panties to the side, and shoves himself inside of me. I throw my head back at the fullness of him, sinking my teeth into my bottom lip.

"It'll be fast, we have somewhere to be." I groan as he pushes harder and harder into me. I buck my hips against him, forcing him deeper. "Fuck, angel." He pushes me against the wall, my legs still wrapped around him. His strokes speed up and my body responds immediately.

Sweet Jesus.

"Baby..." I moan. He puts his hand around my neck and I sweep my tongue across my bottom lip. I feel myself tightening around him and I know I'm right there. "I'm going to come." He licks my neck and kisses it.

"Music to my fucking ears. Let me have it," he says. As if that were what I needed, I explode on command and Graham follows me. When will I grow tired of this, of this feeling, of this man? *Never.* I know the answer immediately. This is the man I'm holding onto for the rest of my fucking life. I knew that the moment I laid eyes on him.

Graham sets me on my feet. I struggle a bit to gain my balance and he steadies me, kissing my temple. "Ok?" He raises an eyebrow, smirking at me.

"Just fine." I turn for the bathroom and he grabs my arm, pulling me back to him.

"Absolutely not, I want my cum dripping out of you for the rest of the day." I gasp and open my mouth, but he silences me, pressing his fingers against my mouth. "Give me your panties," he commands. I quickly obey, sliding them down my legs and pushing them into his hand. He brings them up to his nose with a deep inhale and groans. If I weren't already wet, I sure as hell am now as I watch him take in my scent. He shoves them into his pocket and slides his fingers inside of my pussy, pushing me back against the wall.

"Graham…"

"I think we have time to make you come *one* more time." I'm breathless as he pushes his fingers in and out of me. I groan and he wraps his fingers around my throat, squeezing. "Come on, my dirty fucking girl. Tell me how close you are."

Fuck, when he talks to me like that my brain turns into mush. I can't find words, I can't think, I can't fucking *breathe*. He finds my G-spot and pulses it with a come hither motion.

"So close. So, so close," I pant. He growls, he fucking *growls*, and my walls tighten. I'm done for, there's no hope for me. I crumble and shake beneath his touch and he chuckles. But then he pulls his fingers out before I can get my release. "Fuck you," I moan breathless.

He yanks me by my hair, pulling my face to his. "One." I roll my eyes and he smirks. "Two." I get excited as he counts higher. He hasn't spanked me since before his accident, and my God, am I craving it. The heat, the pleasure, the fucking sensation. I smirk at him and bite my lip, knowing that'll be another. He opens his mouth and I push my lips against his.

"Let me guess, three?" I whisper. He pushes his fingers inside of me, this time adding a third and I come hard. He quickly turns me around, my palms slamming to the wall and his hand coming down my ass. *Once. Twice.* I inhale waiting for the last one.

"You. Are. Mine. Mine to spank, mine to make come when *I* want, wherever *I* want...but you already know that, don't you, Elizabeth?" I shake my head. That's not my name. "You'll get the third and two more at my convenience."

"Don't call me that." He laughs again and faces me toward him. I look at myself in the mirror positioned behind him; I look like I've just been purely fucked. Like I just came twice in under six minutes. I look like a dirty fucking slut. My ass is stinging in pleasure and I feel my head spinning. I want more. I need more.

He looks at me and rubs the side of my face as I sweep my tongue across my lip. "Don't look at me like that," he says. He knows, he always knows.

"Like what?" I ask, breathless.

"Like you want my cock in your mouth." I do. That's exactly what I want.

"But—" He kisses me gently.

"We have somewhere to be. But trust me, later, oh angel, later when I get you back here, I want you on your knees waiting for me so I can fuck that pretty little face." Puddle. I'm a fucking puddle as I nod and follow behind him out the door like a puppy.

He entwines our fingers as we climb in the back of the SUV, giving my knuckles a soft kiss and laying my hand over his knee. "Where are we going?" I ask.

"You'll see. I know you're tired from traveling, but give me a few more hours and I promise we can sleep for the rest of the day. We'll drive to a drop off spot and walk the rest of the way." I raise my eyebrow.

"Will that be *before* or *after* you fuck my face?" His neck snaps to me and he does that fucking growl again.

"Filthy fucking mouth you have, angel." He pulls me onto his lap and buries his face into my neck. He pushes two fingers into my mouth. "Suck," he orders. I suck them hard, lapping them with my saliva. He rolls his eyes shut. "Fuck, you'll kill me one day," he groans. Yanking his fingers out of my mouth, he pushes them into my pussy and I gasp.

"Quiet, unless you want Ellis to hear me take everything you've got." I nod, but I make no promises. I know I can't be quiet, but fuck's sake I'll try. He shoves his fingers in and out of me as I ride them slow and deep. "Look at you, riding my fingers, not caring if he just looks up and sees you. Slutty fucking girl."

He's right; all El has to do is look in the mirror and he'll see me. I wish it made me care, instead it made me wetter, turning me on more. I reach for Graham's cock. If I'm going to be seen riding something, I much prefer it be his cock. He throws his head back.

"That's what you want? You want me to fuck you right here while he's only feet away?" he asks. I nod and continue riding his fingers. He groans and frees himself from his pants, pulling his fingers out of me and replacing it with his cock. "Sit all the way down, take all of it." I sink down and take every inch of his cock. My head falls back and I let out a moan, I can't help it. He pushes his hand over my mouth, muffling my moans. Fuck, at this point, they're screams.

Pushing deeper with every thrust I feel euphoric. Graham pumps in and out, over and over again, and I feel my body tightening. It's happening and fuck, I can't control it. I don't want him to stop, but my body can't hold out any longer. "I think someone's about to come," he whispers, pulling himself out of me. I whimper at the loss of him.

"Not yet," he says, pushing himself back into me. He brings me to the edge again, over and over.

I hate him. I love him. I hate him. Fuck, I love him.

"Please," I breath. "I need to come." He buries himself in me, this time pushing me so far down that he feels embedded in me.

"I make you come when *I* want. Say it." *Ugh. I hate him again.* I try to move my hips, but he stills my movements. "Say it and I'll give you what you want."

"You make me co—" He slams into me and I swear I see fucking stars. He puts his hand over my mouth, knowing I can't keep quiet. I'm about to explode, and if he rips that from me again, I might actually kill him. My pussy convulses around his cock and my body turns into jelly as he pumps in and out of me, chasing his own release. He spurts into me and I smile into his hand.

He slides out of me and slips me next to him. He kisses my cheek and stuffs himself back into his pants. I giggle when I look up to see Ellis shaking his head.

"Sorry, El," I whisper, not quite enough because he chuckles in response. Graham looks out the window, his hand resting on his chin as he smirks. *Proud fucker.* He doesn't even care...I can't help but wonder if he's ever done that before.

"Have you…" I say, quickly removing the question from my mind. He turns to me.

"Have I what?"

"Nothing. It's stupid."

"Say it."

I huff and pick at my dress.

"Have you done that before?"

"Are you asking me if I've fucked a girl in the backseat of my car while my driver was merely feet away?" He grins at me and I shift in my seat. "No, not until you."

I look at him and know he's telling the truth. I wish I was weirded out about the fact that Ellis practically witnessed us fuck, but he didn't see anything besides what probably looked like me sitting on Graham's lap for a make out session. He didn't hear anything because Graham was practically suffocating me with his hand.

"Good."

He turns back to the window, taking in the scenery of the water as we pass it. I reach for my phone and quickly snap a photo of him.

43

Graham

This place still brings me so much peace. I look around at all the memories I still hold here, knowing that I'll be making many more with the woman I love this weekend. The truth is, I know she won't want to leave Sunday. She'll fall in love with this place as I did the first time I came here as a kid. Not just the place, but the people, too. Everyone works hard for what they have and no one treats anyone any different.

Ellis parks at the marina. Liza can't stop smiling as we reach it and I quickly check my phone for the time. Our families should be getting here tomorrow. I asked for one day with Elizabeth, just me and her. They all dreadfully agreed; none of them have spilled the fact that my birthday is Saturday. I'm grateful, but I also know that when Liza finds out she'll be pissy about her not getting me a gift. I watch her climb out of the car and circle around to me, smiling.

This woman is the best gift of all.

"This is beautiful," she says, stretching her hand out to me. She pulls me down the dock and it's a view I can't wait to look at for the rest of my life. I take a picture with my phone. She's insane if she thinks I didn't see her take that photo of me in the car; she's not the only one with a new screensaver. I snap the picture of her looking back at me smiling, tugging on my hand. It's beautiful, encasing her perfectly. The water is in the background, her hair is tumbled over her shoulders with loose curls, and her beautiful brown eyes are glowing.

This ring is burning a hole in my fucking pocket. Every moment feels like the right moment since we've gotten to Rome. I know she's tired, hell, I'm tired,but I want to keep her to myself before our families come and rip our time apart.

"What's going on in your head?" She tugs my arms around her waist and leans against the railing. *Is this the time? Do I want to do this now?* I have it all planned out, but I could easily turn that into an engagement party. I'm sure our mothers would have a field day with it. I already know this woman is it for me, I just have to make it official. She raises an eyebrow when I don't answer and I smile.

"Such an impatient girl." She grins and tilts on her tippy toes to give me a kiss.

"*Your* impatient girl." I groan and pull her closer to me.

"Damn right." I deepen the kiss when her phone rings. She giggles and reaches for it. I let her go and she answers it, smiling.

"Hi, Selly." *Oh no.* "We're at the marina, it's beautiful here. I never want to leave." I'm itching to know what my sister is saying. The family coming was a surprise and I was sure to tell her that, but she doesn't know not to mention my birthday. This isn't the moment I want to piss Elizabeth off. She walks off after a few *mhms* to my sister, holding her finger up to me. I try my hardest not to follow her.

I pull my phone out. *Should I text Selle and tell her to keep her mouth shut?* I type the message out, hovering over the send button when an arm slides around me.

"Feed me. I'm hungry," Elizabeth groans. Well, I guess I'm safe. I entwine her in my arms and kiss her cheek.

"Yes, ma'am."

I take her to a restaurant that overlooks the water. As usual, she huffs and puffs, saying she's not dressed appropriately for where we're going. I will never understand how she still, after all this time, doesn't see herself how I see her. She could wear a fucking trash bag and still put anyone next to her to shame.

"This is beautiful," she says, gazing over the water.

"You've said that already." She rolls her eyes at me and smirks. "One," I count.

"If I roll them again, will you add another?" she asks, leaning across the table.

"You're playing a very dangerous game, Crambell."

"Just how dangerous we talking, Salando?" she sasses as she finishes her bowl of pasta.

This woman will be the fucking death of me.

"We're leaving," I growl. She giggles as I pay the check quicker than I've ever done anything. I grab her hand and stuff her into the back of the car.

"Home, El, and quickly." He grins and pulls out onto the road.

44

Liza

After we arrived back, Graham made good on his promise and showed me just how dangerous of a game I was playing.

He smooths my hair out of my face and pulls me to him. "I have one more surprise for you tonight." I turn to him and snuggle his side.

"I'd ask, but you're not going to tell me anyway," I say. He kisses my nose and I close my eyes, drinking in his scent.

"Take a nap, angel. I'll wake you in a couple of hours." He goes to get up and I reach for him.

"Sleep with me. You're tired, too." He sighs and lays back down. "Thank you, you never sleep."

"Just this one time. Because it's been a long day and you're right, I am tired." He lets out a yawn and closes his eyes. I smile as I trail my hand up and down his abdomen.

Before I knew it my eyes were closed and I drifted off to sleep to the small sound of Graham's breathing.

* * *

Graham's alarm blares in the distance and I groan. "Cut it off."

"Time to get dressed," he says, removing me from his body.

"Can't we just stay here? You said we could sleep all day." I pout.

"I promise it'll be worth it." I smile and nod.

"Fine. But only because you've been making *very* good on your promises so far." I slide out of the bed and dip into the bathroom.

"Have I now?" he asks, following me and starting the shower. I pull my shirt over my head, nodding my head.

He smirks as he tests the water and pulls his clothes off. I stop and stare at him, tugging my lip in between my teeth.

Christ.

"Get in the shower, Elizabeth." I narrow my eyes at him, removing the rest of my clothes as he gets in.

"Don't. Call. Me. That," I say pushing my finger in his chest. He smirks and grabs my finger, pulling me into the shower with him.

"That's the name you were born with, I'm sorry to break it to you."

"Yeah, but I always feel like I'm going to get in trouble." He wraps his arms around me and dips us under the water, nibbling on my ear.

"Maybe you are," he teases.

My thighs clench together and I feel myself mindlessly pushing my ass back against his already hard erection. He groans and kisses my neck.

"We don't have time for this, angel."

"Don't make me beg..." I turn around and cup his erection in my hand as he hisses.

"Fuck...turn around." The tip of my mouth goes up in a small smile as I turn around. "Brace yourself, it'll be fast and fucking hard. We've got somewhere to be."

Fast and hard was quickly becoming my favorite. I put my hands on the wall and he kicks my feet apart, slamming inside of me not a second later.

"Graham!" He thrusts in and out of me, digging his fingers into my hips. I push back, matching his force and he groans.

"Shut the fuck up and take it, baby." I let out a strained groan. He leans next to my ear and whispers, "Your body was made for me and only me." He spanks my ass and sinks further into me, speeding up his pace.

"Harder. Fuck me harder." He wraps my hair around his hand and pulls my face to him as he gives me a bruising kiss, digging his fingers deeper into my hips. He pushes in and out of me with so much force I feel like my entire world is spinning.

"Come for me, baby. I know you're right there, I can feel your filthy pussy tightening around me." I scream out as he pushes me over the edge. He thrusts in and out of me, faster and faster until his body starts shaking from his own climax.

He bites down on my shoulder and groans, "Mine." I smile as he slides out of me. I turn towards him, wrapping my arms around his neck. "Always."

45

Graham

"Is everything all set, El?" I ask, walking into the kitchen. He finishes his water and nods.

"The helicopter is ready and the winery is all set to go, as well." He looks around me and smirks. "Does she have any idea it's your birthday Saturday?"

"No."

He chuckles. "I'll be at the car waiting for you two."

"What time does everyone get in tomorrow, Graham?" Abby asks as she pulls out ingredients for a dish.

"I think around 10:00 a.m., I'm not quite sure. It wouldn't surprise me if they showed up tonight, instead." She bites her lip and looks down. I narrow my eyes at her.

"Ms. Abby...what do you know?"

"They're coming tonight...your mom called me about an hour ago from the plane and said their plans changed and the pilot needed to leave today. It was supposed to be a surprise for you, for your birthday."

"Please don't tell me they're planning a surprise party? Liza doesn't even know they're coming. Fuck's sake."

"Language!" she scolds. "You have some time. It's only 6:00 p.m., they won't be here until at least 11:00 p.m." I shake my head and Liza walks in, wrapping her arms around me.

"You ok? You look pissed."

"I'm fine, angel. All ready to go? You look beautiful."

"Back at you, handsome. I'm ready when you are." She kisses Abby on the cheek and heads towards the car. Abby smiles at me and kisses me on my cheek. "Good luck."

Liza looks perfect tonight; she's wearing a low cut, black dress that hugs her body in a way that should be fucking illegal. She looks at me from inside of the car and smirks.

"Whatcha staring at, Salando?" I climb in beside her.

"Come here."

"Nope, not a chance. You are not messing up this lip combo. It took me forever to nail it." She slides next to me and turns her cheek to me. "You'll have to settle for kissing me on this pretty little cheek."

"If you think I'm keeping my lips off yours for the entire night, Crambell, you are sadly mistaken." I kiss her cheek and rest my hand on her leg. She sighs and turns to me.

"Not telling you, so don't ask," I say before she can even start with me. She huffs and I chuckle. "We'll be there soon, I promise." She leans back and closes her eyes. Moments later I hear soft, deep breaths come from her. I tuck her into my side and kiss the top of her head.

"You nervous?" El asks, glancing at me and back at Liza.

"Not the slightest. Is that odd? Shouldn't I be nervous?"

He smirks and pulls up to the helicopter pad. I tap Liza's shoulder and she groans. "We're here." She blinks her eyes open and smiles at me.

"Hi, baby," she says, touching my chin.

"Hey, pretty girl." I kiss her nose and El opens the door for us. "Alright, let's go."

"Where are we?" she asks, climbing out.

"We're going to go sightseeing around the city and then to my winery."

"*Your* winery?" I chuckle and rest my hand on her back, directing her around the car. She stops and turns to me. "Graham...what the fuck is happening? Why is there a helicopter here?"

"That would be our ride, angel mine." She looks at me in disbelief.

"Why do I ever expect a normal date from you?"

"I have no idea. Get in." She shakes her head and smiles, climbing into the helicopter. She stops and looks at me.

"These shoes were not made for this," she says, gesturing to her black, red bottoms. I grab her arm and bend down, gently removing her pumps.

"Better?" I ask. She smirks and quickly climbs into her seat. I climb in after her and buckle her in tightly.

"I can do that myself, you know." I raise my eyebrow at her and she shrugs.

I quickly secure myself in the pilot seat and she almost breaks her neck trying to turn to me. "Absolutely not. Where is our pilot?"

"Oh, baby, I am the pilot. Hold on tight." I pull us up into the air and she laughs.

"Just get me there safely, please, and I hope food is involved. I'm starving."

The sun is starting to set. The sky looks beautiful and Liza is in complete awe. She points to every building and smiles at every angle of the sunset she sees. I mindlessly reach for her hand and she squeezes it.

"This is amazing. You're amazing," she says. I bring her hand up to my lips and place a gentle kiss on it.

"The night is just beginning, angel." She shakes her head and smiles, looking back out the window. She points and clasps her hands together.

"Is that the vineyard? Over there?"

"Yes, it is." She goes to unbuckle her seat belt as we get closer to the landing pad. I reach out and stop her. "Angel... wait, we're landing." She sits back impatiently, staring out the window. The moment we land she unbuckles herself.

"Elizabeth, wai—"

"Wait for you to come around, yes I know," she sasses. I scowl at her and quickly round the helicopter, her shoes in my hands. I kneel and gently grab her ankle, slipping her shoes back on one at a time. I push my arm out for her and she takes it as we walk to the vineyard.

"So, when were you going to tell me you owned a vineyard?"

"I own a lot of things, baby."

"Mr. Salando, welcome," the waitress greets us. "So glad you could join us today. We have your dining room set. Please let me show you to your seats." Liza tugs on my arm and I look down at her, raising my eyebrow.

"I'd like to try some wine while we're here," she says. I nod at her as we follow the waitress. I place my hand on Liza's lower back as usual, caressing it with my thumb as we walk.

"We have the chef preparing everything as you requested. Would you or your wife like a wine menu before your hors d'oeuvres arrive?"

"A wine menu would be great, please," I respond. The waitress leaves and Liza turns to me. "Your wife, huh?"

"You didn't correct her," I remind her.

"You didn't, either," she retorts as I pull her chair out.

"Sit, Elizabeth." She nudges me, but sits down.

"I thought this was just a vineyard. This place is huge."

"It's a vineyard and a restaurant," I explain.

"Can we go to the waterfall after dinner?"

"Anything you want, angel." I knew she would want to tour the grounds so I made sure everything was exactly perfect for her. She smiles as our waitress comes back with a wine menu.

"Here you are. I've got some sparkling water here for you both in the meantime and your starters shall be out soon." She looks over her shoulder as the doors open and two people with trays of food glide in. "Here they are now. Crab cakes, calamari, stuffed mushrooms, and roasted brussel sprouts," she introduces. "If you need anything in the meantime while we're preparing your meal, just let me know. Do you know what wine you'd like, ma'am?" Knowing Liza, she is probably secretly flinching at being called *ma'am*. She doesn't like formal conversation.

"Just the house sampler will do," I interject, handing the menus to her.

"Very well," the waitress says, departing swiftly.

I stare at Liza as she sinks her teeth into a crab cake. Her eyes roll and she lets out a moan.

"Good?" I ask.

"That's the best thing I've ever had in my mouth." I arch my eyebrow at her.

"The best thing you've ever had in your mouth is my cock, angel; don't you forget it." She chokes on the crab cake and I smile, shrugging my shoulders.

"Try the stuffed mushrooms next." She shakes her head.

"I don't think I'll like mushrooms." I pick one up and hold it to her mouth.

"Open." She obeys and I gently place the mushroom in her mouth. "Chew and swallow." I watch her do both and she groans again. "Good girl." I smirk.

"Ok, fuck, that's good. Give me another." I feed her another as our dinner arrives.

"Seriously? This is too much food for two people. This steak is the size of my head."

"Oh, come on, it's definitely not as big as your head, baby." She throws a calamari at me and I catch it in my mouth. "Nice try," I say, smugness lacing my tone. She huffs and shoves another in her mouth.

"Eat up so I can show you around."

She eats her steak and samples all of the wines. Her face scowls with every wine that's too sweet or extra dry. I watch her in amazement, because without even realizing it, she chooses the wine that I knew would be her favorite. It's a sweet Moscato with hints of strawberry, apple, and a hint of lime.

"I'm disgustingly full," she says, standing up and walking over to me. I slide my chair back and pat my leg as she quickly sits, wrapping her arms around me.

"Did you enjoy the food?" She nods and leans back into me. "I haven't been here in quite some time. I did some remote updates, but hadn't seen it in person," I say.

"Who runs this place while you're not here?"

"Abby and Marco do a pretty good job at popping in when I need them to." She leans back and searches my face with a small smile.

"You take really good care of them, don't you?"

"I do." I push a strand of her hair behind her ear.

"They're lucky to have you."

"I'm lucky to have them, too. Come here." She leans down to me, her face just inches from mine. I push my hand through her hair and pull her lips to mine.

Intensifying the kiss, she straddles me as her dress rides up. I push my hands up her dress and squeeze her ass.

"Anyone could walk in," she gasps as I move her panties to the side and push my fingers inside of her.

"You want me to stop?" I ask pushing in and out of her with more force. She closes her eyes and begins to ride my hand. I kiss her neck, adding another digit. "Answer me," I growl.

She whimpers. "No, no. I don't want you to stop." She moves faster, trying to find her release.

"Of course you don't. Because my little dirty slut wants to get off, so be a good girl and ride my fingers." She moans and I push further into her. I can hear voices outside and she freezes. "Looks like we're going to have company if you don't hurry and get yourself there." She groans and I push my fingers in and out of her faster than before. She moans louder and I yank her face to me, planting a bruising kiss on her lips.

I feel her pussy clench around my fingers before she soaks them with her release. I pull them out of her, sticking each in my mouth and licking the sweetness of her off.

"Ready for a tour?" I ask as she smirks at me.

"Mhm." She climbs off and I smack her ass. She laughs as I take her hand and guide her out of the door.

When I took over this place it needed a lot of work. It was a distraction when my father first cheated on my mom and our *perfect family* dynamic started shifting. My mom acted oblivious while my dad didn't even seem to be hiding his monthly sluts. I buried myself in renovating this place, escaping the realities of my home life. I originally planned on turning this into a country club, but it seemed wasted being that the vineyards were already here. So, I improvised, keeping the vineyard and adding a five-star restaurant with venue for events.

"Graham, this is beautiful." We walk by the venue area towards tall weeping willow trees with strings of twinkling lights draped throughout them. Behind it is the waterfall and an open area with a fire pit.

She looks up at the tree and the twinkle in her eyes reflecting the lights tells me this moment could never get any better. I stand behind her while her back is to me and reach into my pocket, grabbing the ring that I hope the woman in front of me will be wearing for the rest of her life.

I watch her staring up at the sky and the lights strung in the tree in awe. I begin what I had rehearsed in my mind since the day I bought the ring.

"You know, from the first day I fucking met you, I knew you were it for me. I knew that even though I didn't deserve you, that I had to be selfish and keep you anyway. I promised myself that no matter what, I'd do whatever I had to do to keep you happy. I remember sitting in my room that first night you stayed over trying to talk myself out of wanting you." She turns around and smiles at me. I close my hand over the black, velvet box and sink to one knee. She looks in confusion and then gasps.

"Graham..."

"I tried so hard not to want you. I tried so hard to push you away, so that you could be with someone that deserved you. But fuck, that thought made me murderous." Her eyes fill with tears and I open the box. "Elizabeth Crambell, I know I'm not what you deserve, but I want to spend my life showing you that I can be. Marry me?" Tears start to spill over her face as she closes the distance between us.

"It's always you, Graham. There's no one else."

"Is that yes?"

"Yes, of course it's a yes." I slide the ring on her finger, bringing it to my mouth and kissing it. I pull her into my arms and spin her around. She giggles and cries at the same time.

I wipe her tears and kiss her nose. "You know I hate when you cry, pretty girl."

"We're getting married?"

"We're getting married."

46

Liza

As the helicopter lands I'm still shaking. I can't believe what just happened. I'd think it was a dream if it weren't for the huge fucking emerald cut diamond sitting on my finger, staring back at me.

I'm engaged. To Graham fucking Salando. The man who *couldn't be tamed.* The man who was *Seattle's bachelor.* He chose me, or rather, he'd say that I chose him. But regardless of how much he thinks he doesn't deserve me, he does. He deserves someone who will love him for him. Who will be there to pick up the pieces when he feels like he'll break. He deserves someone who is all in for him and who he is, not for what he has. He deserves me.

He reaches for my hand and kisses it and then my ring as I smile brightly at him. I unbuckle my seat belt and climb into his lap.

"I love you," I say, breathlessly. He gathers me in his arms and squeezes me so tight that I gasp in response.

"I love you more."

"Not possible."

"Don't care," he says with finality. I climb off and we exit the helicopter meeting Ellis.

"Congratulations, you two," Ellis remarks. I smile at Ellis as he pulls Graham in for a hug and me after.

"Thank you, Ellis." I climb into the back of the car and lay my head back. Graham pulls me into his side.

"You're tired, I'm sorry. I should have thought about it."

"I'm fine, today was perfect. You got a clean health bill, you brought me to the most beautiful place, and you made me your fiancé. I never want this day to be over."

"I do. Unless you plan on marrying me tonight," he says as I giggle. "Just saying." I swat his arm as we head back home.

* * *

Thirty minutes later, we're pulling back up to his home, except it's different. It's decorated with candles lined down the driveway and flowers surrounding the door frame. I look at him in confusion and he smiles down at me.

"Got enough energy for one more surprise?" I put my thinking face on.

"Hmm, I guess one more won't hurt." He pulls me out of the car and I stumble. "Oops, too much wine," I say, giggling. He shakes his head and steadies me, wrapping his arm tightly around my waist.

"You sure know how to set the mood, don't you?" I ask as I stare at all the decorations.

"I had some help," he says, pulling me in for a kiss.

"What would you have done if I said no?" I ask jokingly.

"Well for starters, the surprise would have been very embarrassing." I frown and he pulls me down the driveway to the door.

"Is this not the surprise?" He shakes his head.

"No, pretty girl, this is." He opens the door and I walk in.

"SURPRISE!!!"I jump and run back into Graham's chest. He encircles me in his arms and laughs. I look to see all of our family standing in the hallway with smiles on their faces. I can't help it, I cry and run straight to my parents.

"Hi, Mama! What are you doing here?"

"Oh, sweetheart, Graham invited us to surprise you." She hugs me tightly and my dad squeezes me next.

"How's my girl?" he asks. I kiss his cheek and he smiles. We say hello to the rest of our family and I smile at Graham across the room. He nods his head towards the kitchen and I follow him.

I run right into his arms and kiss him. "I don't deserve you. You bought them here and I know that was hard for you to do."

"Why's that?" he asks.

"Because you don't like sharing me," I say, smiling as he laughs.

"They don't know yet, I figured we could tell them together." I nod and he turns for the family room. I catch his wrist and yank him back to me.

"I want a little more you time before we're bombarded in there." He lifts me and sits me on the counter, stepping between my legs. He puts his arms on either side of my thighs and leans in.

"Whatever you want, angel." I rest my forehead against his and breathe in his scent.

"I can't wait to marry you. Thank you for choosing me," I

whisper, holding back the tears forming in my eyes.

"Baby, it was always you." He kisses my forehead and salty tears slide down my face. "Hey, don't cry. You know I hate it." He wipes the tears from under my eyes and places a soft kiss on my lips.

"I'm just happy."

"Me, too. Now let's go tell these crazy people we call our family." He pulls me down and entwines our fingers as we walk into the family room.

Here goes nothing.

47

Graham

Everyone is laughing and talking amongst each other. I stop and sit in the recliner, pulling Liza into my lap. These are the moments when I feel at peace, like my life isn't so fucked up after all. It's these times where I feel like I must've done something right to have the love of my life, surrounded by a family who loves her just as much as I do.

I clear my throat and Selle looks at me with a smirk. Liza shifts nervously and I grip her hip to steady her.

"Don't be nervous, they'll be happy for us," I mumble at her. She takes a deep breath.

"But my dad, what if he's upset?" she whispers. "Did you ask him? Oh, God, what about Brant? What if he feels left out—"

"Elizabeth." She turns to me and frowns.

"Don't call—"

"Calm down. We're getting married, they'll all be happy." I smooth out her hair and kiss her forehead.

"Ok...I'm sorry. I'm ready when you are. I'm tired of hiding my hands." She smirks.

Selle sits on the arm of the recliner. "You two are really packing on the PDA tonight, huh?" I elbow her and she giggles. "I'm sorry we came early, G. The pilot said there would be weather tomorrow and didn't want to chance it."

"When were you supposed to come?" Liza asks, looking at her. I glare at her, hoping she doesn't mention my birthday being tomorrow.

"Tomorrow. It's Gra—" I push her off the recliner and she falls on the floor. "Fucker." She laughs.

"Giselle...language," my mom says. I chuckle and look at Liza as she nods.

"We have something to tell everyone," I say. Liza smiles nervously and pulls her arm from around me to sit up.

"We're getting married!" we say. The house breaks out in happy screams. Selle yanks Liza out of my lap and pulls her in for a hug.

"YES! Finally, you're going to be my sister!! Let me see that rock!" Selle yells. She stares down at the custom ring I had made for Liza and she smiles. Emily helped me pick it out. She'll be here tonight as well, I assume. The pilot left for another pick up, but I haven't told Liza that yet. They haven't seen each other since graduation, and as much as they talk, I know she misses her. Emily's been traveling abroad since graduation and they hadn't been in the same time zone since she's left.

"My God, that's beautiful. Good job, G." She hugs me tighter than normal. "I'm so glad you're getting the happiness you deserve," she whispers to me. I hug her back and kiss her cheek.

"About time you asked her. I thought I'd croak over before you grew the balls to ask her," Axel says, pulling me in for a hug. "Congratulations, you two." He turns to Liza and hugs her tightly.

"My girl is going to get married." His eyes get watery and hers does, too.

"Daddy..." She smiles. "Don't cry, then I'll cry. I got Mom not to cry. Save it for the wedding."

"I'm proud of you, both of you. Graham, you sure took your time asking," her mom says, smiling at me. Liza cocks her head to the side and grins at me.

"What does she mean?"

"I asked them, all of them. Your mom, dad, and Brant. I knew how much that would mean to you."

"When?"

I grind my teeth together and she puts her hand on my arm, running her thumb over my skin. "Before your accident?" she asks. I nod in response and she kisses my cheek.

The women all get into wedding talk and I silently stare at Liza, soaking her in. *My wife.* She's going to be my wife. I look at Elias and Hogan to find them smirking at me. Elias leans forward, placing his arms on his knees.

"I hope you know what you're getting yourself into. She can be a handful, and for fuck's sake don't let her get hungry. Oh, and don't leave an empty roll of toilet paper on the hanger—" Hogan cuts Elias off. "Definitely don't drink her last bottle of anything or she'll be out for blood." We all laugh and they pull me into a hug.

"Congratulations, man. Make our sister the happiest in the world."

"I plan to, and Elias, you do the same. I'm not oblivious to the fact that you'll probably end up being my *double brother-in-law.*" Liza chuckles and goes into the kitchen.

The front door slings open and I hear Emily and Travis before I see them.

"YOU'RE ENGAGEDDDDD!!!!" Emily yells, throwing her suitcase down and running to Liza.

"Em! Em! Oh my God! What are you doing—" Emily points to me and then pulls Liza into a hug.

"That man of yours! Let me see that ring, we worked hard on that shit!" I chuckle as Travis rounds the corner.

"G man! Congrats!"

"Trav! Glad you could make it! I know it was short notice."

"Man, all I'm doing is following her around the world like some type of whipped pussy cat. Let's get fucked up, your birthday is tomorrow!" I punch him in his stomach.

"Keep the birthday shit quiet. I didn't tell her." He groans and flips me off. "But follow me, the kitchen is fully stocked."

48

Liza

I look at the clock and see its 11:50 p.m. I have been up for over twenty-four hours and I am fucking exhausted. I can't believe Graham flew all our friends and family out this weekend for our engagement. He really thought of everything.

Drinks are flowing and everyone is dancing. Graham is swaying with my mom and I smile at them. I am determined to change his mind about birthdays. Selle called me earlier. She told me that he hated birthdays, that he never celebrated them, but that she wanted to celebrate him when we got back. This place is too perfect and means too much to him not to celebrate him here, surrounded by people that love him.

"Selle...about that party. Let's do it here. Tomorrow."

"Absolutely not, he'll kill me."

"Everyone is already here, it's perfect. I want to. I'll take the blame, he won't be mad at me," I say, winking at her. She does a gagging motion and whispers to her mom.

"I think that's a perfect idea, we'll tell him it's an engagement party. Speaking of which, your mother and I have already started planning. Does next Saturday work for you to go over things?" Madeline asks.

"Mom, one thing at a time," Selle says, smiling. She pulls out her phone and starts scrolling. "I can get caterers, décor, and everything ready. Invites will be tricky because it's literally the day of." She looks around and giggles. "Actually, this is everyone he'd want around him."

"Thank you. I know this is a lot, I just want to show him that birthdays don't have to be painful." Madeline gives me a warm smile and cups my face. "Ahh, Elizabeth, you are perfect for him." She kisses my cheek and stands next to Ellis. I smile when she stands in front of him and he quickly glances down at her, giving her a peck on the cheek before going back to his usual stone stare.

It warms my heart seeing them both so happy. He was beside himself when he couldn't find her. When he thought he lost her he was brutal, no remorse for anyone who stood in his way.

"Mama, I need to steal my fiancé away. I'd like a dance of my own." She smiles and kisses Graham's cheek as I slide into his arms.

The music changes and it's another slow song, but I don't hear it. I'm too focused on the man in front of me. I wrap my arms around his neck and he pulls me close to him. "Are you happy?" he asks as we sway slowly, left and right.

"I am. Are you? I know they said they weren't supposed to come until tomorrow."

"Baby, I don't see anyone but you. I don't care that they're here, but I know you do." He kisses my forehead and I quickly glance at Selle. I mouth the word *time* to her. She glances at her phone and smirks.

I stand on my tippy toes and rub my nose against his.

"Happy Birthday, baby."

He arches his eyebrow; he knows how much that turns me on. I smirk at him and he shakes his head. He spins me and pulls me back to him. "Who told you?"

"*You didn't.* That's the most important part of this conversation."

"I hate birthdays."

"I missed your birthday last year; I'm not missing another. This one will be your favorite, I promise." He chuckles and dips me, planting a kiss on my lips.

"Happy Birthday, G," Selle says, handing him a shot. I take one from her, as well. Elias, Hogan, Emily, and Travis are all surrounding him with a shot in their hands.

"Another year older!" Travis says, raising his glass. We all raise our glasses and down the shots. My body instantly feels warm as we shoot another.

"Fuck, I do not think getting drunk while I'm exhausted is a good idea," I groan. Emily hands me a third and Graham cocks his head to the side, watching me quickly swallow it.

"Careful, angel. We know you're a lightweight when it comes to shots," he whispers in my ear.

"Alright, honey, we're all tired. We're going to turn in and we'll see everyone tomorrow for brunch. Happy Birthday, sweetheart," Madeline says, hugging him.

"Thank you, Mom."

"You kids stay up as long as you want, but I expect to see each one of you at family brunch tomorrow at 10:30 a.m. You are all staying here, so you have no excuse to be absent." She looks at us and waits for a response. She raises her eyebrow at us. "Understand?"

We all nod and she smiles. They all leave and my parents

give us all quick hugs. "See you all in the morning."

Eli, Selle, and Hogan are all dancing together and I smile at them. Honestly, it's like she belongs to both of them. I chuckle at the drunken thought and Graham nudges me. "What's so funny?" he asks.

I scrunch my face up at him. "Trust me, you wouldn't like it." I glance back over to them when I hear Selle laugh and he follows my gaze. He groans and shakes his head. "I just think that maybe she's the common denominator in *both* of their happiness..." I say.

"You're clearly drunk. That is not what's happening." Selle laughs again and Graham looks over at them with an arched eyebrow, then back at me. "Christ, is she fucking them both?"

"Probably not on a regular basis, but I'm sure it's probably something they've tried."

I laugh and pull him towards the kitchen. "Not our business." I push him against the counter and start kissing him. He groans in response, trying to take possession of the kiss. He pulls me closer, but I push him away. I reach for his belt buckle and sink to my knees in front of him.

"Elizabeth...what the *fuck* are you doing?"

"Giving you your first birthday present. Let me." He looks at our friends in the next room and then down at me as I smirk.

"Dirty goddamn girl." I push his briefs down just enough to free his already hard cock. I lick my lips and pull him into my mouth. "Fuck..." He pushes his hand into my hair, thrusting himself deeper into my throat. I lap my saliva around his cock, squeezing his balls in my hand while I work the tip of his cock with my tongue. I look up at him and he throws his head back as he continues to fuck my mouth.

I love giving him what he wants. I love making him forget

all his responsibilities and problems. Even if it is just for a few minutes. I suck harder and faster, helping him find his release. His balls tighten in my hand and I ready my mouth for the blow it's about to receive.

"Angel, I'm going to come. You're going to swallow every fucking drop." I keep sucking, moving up and down as he steadies my head, shooting his load deep into my mouth. I swallow it as it hits my mouth, humming in response. "Fucking perfect," he whispers, wiping my mouth and pulling me to my feet. He yanks my mouth to his and lifts me on top of the counter.

He runs his hand up my leg and brushes his fingers over my bare pussy. "Mmm, your needy fucking pussy shows exactly how much of a slut you are for my dick. You're dripping, Elizabeth." I open my mouth to protest, but he shoves his fingers into my pussy, shutting me up. "It's your fucking name, *Elizabeth*," he whispers, pushing his fingers in and out of me. He drops to his knees and covers my clit with his mouth.

"No, not for you," I moan, chasing the rhythm he's began. He adds another finger and laps his tongue inside of my pussy as my head falls back. He leans up to kiss my neck and gently bites my shoulder.

"What is it? Tell me. What's your name, then?" He pushes his fingers further into me and I moan a little louder this time.

Fuck.

49

Graham

I reach up and put my hand over her mouth as she moans louder. I go down and suck her clit harder, fingering her faster.

"What. Is. It?" I growl into her pussy. She practically screams as she nears her orgasm. "You want to come? You answer my question first." I pull my fingers out and she whimpers.

"Angel..." she says, breathless. "I'm your angel." I plunge my fingers back into her, curling my fingers up to her G-spot. Her pussy tightens around my fingers and descend again, increasing the speed of my tongue. My fingers continue their assault, fighting my tongue for first place.

"Mmm and soon you'll be my wife. Now come all over my fucking face." She soaks my face and digs her nails into my shoulder as she steadies herself. Her body shakes and I'm trying my best not to fuck her on the countertop right now. The loud whimpers I'm trying to muffle with my hand are loud enough to wake this whole fucking town, making self-control really fucking tough.

She comes down from her climax, trying to catch her breath.

I stick my fingers in her mouth. She sucks obediently, as always, and I groan at the sight. "Good fucking girl." I give her a quick kiss and pull her dress down.

"Fuck, that was hot." We both whip our heads around to the door to see Emily and Travis standing there. I can't tell if they're aroused or shocked, but based on the tent growing in Travis' fucking pants, I'd guess the first. Emily is out of breath and her legs are clenched so tightly together I think she's going to collapse at any moment.

I lift a red-faced Liza over my shoulder, smirking at her. "See everyone in the morning," I groan as I walk past them both.

"Sorry," Liza squeaks out to them as we walk towards the stairs.

I kick our door close and throw her on the bed. "I want you to be extremely aware, that the only reason I am not fucking you senseless right now, is because my need to make love to you tonight is stronger. Come here." She crawls up on her knees and over to the edge of the bed. I pull her to stand and unzip her dress, sliding it down her body. I start kissing her ankles and work my way up her body. "Now, this house is full of family, so be a good girl and stay quiet. Can you do that?" She nods and I stop kissing right above her navel, staring up at her with my eyebrow arched. "Words."

"Yes, I'll be quiet." I continue my quest up her body, lifting her as I walk us back towards the bed. I gently lay her down and push her legs open, planting myself in between them. *Fuck, how is it that she's always so wet?* She arches her back as I flick her clit with my tongue. She moans, grabbing a pillow and putting it over her face. I chuckle as I fuck her with my tongue, slow and steady.

"This is torture, please," she begs. I hope she knows it's just as torturous for me, too, but I'm not fucking her until she begs me to. I ignore her and continue my assault on her pussy, lapping in between her folds until I start to feel her body tighten.

"Graham..."

"What, angel? Tell me what you want," I say, sucking on her clit. She moans louder at that and pushes my head further into her.

"Please, no more. Just you. I just want you."

"Not yet."

"Please, I need you." I pull her legs up and yank her deeper into my mouth. Her legs begin shaking as I add two fingers into her pussy. "Shit...Graham. I can't be quiet."

"Yes, you can," I say, adding third finger, stretching her pussy more. She starts to clamp down on my fingers and I quickly stand up and push my dick into her. She lets out a scream and wraps her legs around me, securing me inside of her. "You come on my cock with me buried inside of you for the rest of this weekend, no exceptions. Understand?"

"Yes, yes!" she moans even louder. "You're so deep, I feel you everywhere." I bite her ear and move in and out of her, brutally slow. "Faster," she begs.

"Savor it, baby. I'll fuck you like my slut later." She moans again and digs her nails into my back. My head falls back as I thrust in and out of her, harder and harder. Pushing her legs back so I can get a deeper angle, she loses it. Her pussy squeezes my dick so tight I struggle to move. "Your pussy is strangling my cock, pretty girl. I think someone may be coming." She screams my name and I silence her with a devouring kiss. "Shh, you'll wake our parents."

"I don't care...I need you." She grabs onto my ass and pushes me deeper into her as she comes. "Mmm, so good," she breathes. I quicken my pace and chase my own release. I cup her face and kiss her as I begin to fill her with my cum.

We stay that way for a few minutes, our breathing interchanging. I roll off her and pull her into my side, running my hands up and down her back. She looks up at me and I kiss her forehead.

"We're getting married..." she whispers.

"Soon, I hope." She smirks at me and nuzzles into my arms, her eyes closing. "Don't make me wait, Elizabeth. I want you to be my wife."

"I won't, I promise," she whispers before she drifts off to sleep.

I say a silent prayer that nothing in my fucked-up life stops her from keeping that promise. Or *anyone,* for that matter.

50

Liza

It's only 7:00 a.m. when my eyes open. I roll over, fully expecting Graham to already be awake with his laptop over his legs. Instead, I feel his breath on my neck and his arm draped protectively over my middle.

He's sleeping. He hasn't slept since the accident. He tosses and turns at night, always up before the sun. I watch him as he sleeps; at how peaceful he looks. I brush a piece of his hair out of his face and he groans a little, tugging me closer into him. I kiss his chin and nuzzle back to him, letting sleep find me again.

"Angel…" He kisses my lips. I moan at the touch of them and he kisses me again. "Give me those eyes." I smirk at him—I love it when he says that to me. My eyes flutter open and he smiles at me. I brush my fingers across his lips.

"You slept past seven, ya know."

He nods and kisses my hand.

"I guess I'm finally feeling normal again." He pushes his hair back off his face. "I'm sure that's because I get to marry the woman of my dreams."

Don't make me wait, Elizabeth.

I frown, remembering the desperation in his voice last night. *Did I dream it?*

"What's going on in that head of yours, pretty girl?"

"Last night, you said not to make you wait." He nods, sitting on the edge of the bed, turning to face me. I try to read his face, waiting for him to say something, anything, regarding the concern I thought I heard last night. "Why?"

"Because I'm afraid that you'll change your mind," he whispers. I gasp at his honesty.

"Graham..." I crawl over to him and straddle his lap. Cupping his face in my hands he looks away. I tilt his face back to me and his eyes close. "Look at me, please." I'm begging at this point. He takes a deep breath and I say the only thing I can think of. "Give me those eyes."

Graham takes a deep breath again, but this time, he opens his eyes. "Elizabeth, I'm fucking *scared.*" I search his face in confusion, pushing his hair back a bit more.

"Of what?"

"Something or someone taking you away from me." I shake my head and silence him with a kiss.

"I'm not going *anywhere.*" He pulls me off him and he stands up, pushing his hands through his hair.

"Elizabeth, I got shot, for fuck's sake. The only thing I keep thinking about, is what if I had died? Who would've taken care of you? You would've had nothing. I know you. You would have lost yourself, you would've given up. You would've blamed yourself. If I had died, nothing would've been left behind to remind you of me. Not a ring, not a last name, not a child. *Nothing.*"

"Stop talking to me like I'm weak. Stop talking to me like I am incapable of being strong on my own! I left once because I needed *you* too much, because you made me feel like I couldn't do it alone. Don't make me regret coming back!" I stand, pushing into his chest as I breeze past him. I don't get very far before I feel him yanking me back to him by my hair. It's painful and the roots of my scalp sting.

"Do *not* threaten me. You wanna leave? *Fucking try it.*"

"Fuck you, Graham. You basically just told me that you want me to marry you as soon as possible, because you think I'd crawl in a hole and forget existence if you die. That I'd off myself...because I'm, oh yeah, *weak*. Fuck you, " I say, spitting the words in his face.

"That's not why I want you to marry me and that is not what the fuck I said." I chuckle in disbelief. He wraps his hand around my neck and slams me against the wall. I arch my eyebrow, challenging him. "I want you to marry me because if it were the other way around, who would've taken care of *me?* *I* would've had nothing. I would have lost *myself. I* would've given up. And I sure as fuck would've blamed *myself.* It's not *you* that I'm worried about being weak if something happens, it's fucking me. Goddamnit, it's me."

I push against his hand, making his grip tighten. "What about the ring, last name, and child part?" He looks down at the ring on my hand. He drops his hand from my neck, picks up my hand, and brings it to his mouth as he plants a kiss on my ring.

"Ring? Check. Last name? I hope so, but I'll settle for hyphenation. Child? Whenever the fuck you want."

I let out a sigh and step toward him. He immediately pulls me into his arms and I wrap mine tightly around his waist. Tears well up in my eyes and I bury my face into his shirt.

We're fighting and we shouldn't be. We just got engaged, for fuck's sake. He tilts my chin up, making me look at him.

"Why the fuck are we fighting?" I ask. He wipes the tear from my cheek, resting his forehead on mine.

"I don't want to fight with you. But don't ever, and I mean ever, threaten to leave me again, Elizabeth. Even if you did, I'd find you. But you already know that."

"I'm sorry," I whisper. "I'm so sorry." I start crying. I don't know why, but I do. He rubs my hair, lifting me and taking me into the bathroom. He starts the shower and begins undressing me.

"Arms up." I lift and he pulls the oversized t-shirt over my head. He bends down, sliding my underwear down my leg as I step out of them. I reach for his shirt and pull it over his head. Then I push his briefs down, freeing his cock. He pushes me into the shower under the hot water, streaming down my back. I stare at him as he steps in behind me. His cock is semi-erect and I can't control my next movements. I drop to my knees in front of him and pull him to me.

"Liza..." he groans. I shove him into my mouth, pushing him as deep as he can go until I gag. I repeat the same movement repeatedly as his head falls back. "Fuck."

I increase my speed and he entangles his hands in my wet hair, forcing himself deeper as he hits the back of my throat. I love it when he's like this with me. His hand slams against the wall and the other one steadies my head. I push my fingers inside of me, chasing my own climax. Seeing him almost there makes me want to come.

"Look at you, on your knees. My cock in your mouth and your fingers in your pussy. My little slut." He yanks away from me, pulls me up, spins me around, and pushes inside of me without warning.

He licks my ear and gives it a tug. "I told you, you come nowhere but on my cock." He slams inside of me. It's sloppy, and rough, and full of need. He reaches around and toys with my clit while his cock slams in and out of me. My body begins to shake. "Good girl," he praises. I feel his body tense and we start to come together. It's loud, but we don't care. He groans my name as he finishes inside of me, our cum sliding down my leg. He takes his fingers and runs it up my leg, pushing it back into my pussy. "Wouldn't want you to miss a drop." He sticks his fingers in front of my mouth and I wait for his order. "Open." I open my mouth, keeping my eyes on him, and suck our juices off his finger. "That's my girl."

He kisses my forehead and begins washing me before I do the same to him. "I'm not leaving you, Graham, and nothing or anyone is going to change my mind." He nods and turns the water off, grabbing a towel and wrapping it around me. I find his eyes and I narrow in on him. "I mean it. You want to get married tomorrow? I'll do it. You don't want to wait? Well, I don't either."

"Our mothers would kill us both," he says, pushing my wet hair out of my face. I smirk at the truth. "We'll give them three months, that's it." My eyes widen as I think about how telling them this will make them lose their fucking minds.

This will be fun.

51

Graham

"THREE MONTHS?!" Bethany screams as my mother interjects, saying the same. I chuckle and Selle does the same.

"How the hell do you expect us to pull off a wedding in three months?!" Bethany continues.

"Graham, honey, we want this to be perfect for you two. But three months? Are you pregnant?" I hold up my hand, stopping my mom from continuing—even though I wish like fuck that were the case. All of my tampering has been in vain.

"Mother, it's either three months or tomorrow. We're giving you three months out of respect for you two. If we had it our way, we'd get married right now. And no, she's not pregnant."

"We don't want to wait, Mama. So much has happened in our lives these last few months, I could have lost him." Liza shakes her head at the thought. "I'm not putting off marrying him. I don't want to and you can't force me." I reach over and grab her hand, planting a kiss on it. She looks up and smiles at me. Brant clears his throat and we all look at him.

"Bethany, I'm sure this has you in a frenzy, but if anyone

can pull off a spectacular wedding in a few months, it's the women sitting at this table." He places his hand over hers and she gives him a reassuring smile. Axel looks at Liza and winks as she smiles.

My mom is deep in thought when she starts smiling. "I know just the person who can pull this off. I'm going to make a few calls. Elizabeth, don't you worry; your mother and I will take care of everything." She gets up and pulls her phone out. She's excited as she waves Bethany to follow her, them both cackling down the hall. I know this because she has a strict *no phones at the table* rule and you definitely don't get up in the middle of a meal.

"G, what do you want to do for your birthday?" Selle asks, changing the topic.

"I vote to get drunk," Travis says, shoving a piece of watermelon in his mouth. Emily elbows him and he looks at her. "What?" She glances at Axel and Brant at the end of the table. "Oh."

"That's alright, Emily, we weren't always old. We used to do the same things you kids do. The parties, the drinking, the sex." Liza chokes on her champagne. I pat her back and the table laughs. "How do you think you got here, Elizabeth?" Axel chuckles. She turns her face up in disgust and I chuckle.

"Alright, well we're going golfing. We'll see you all later. Be careful and be safe," Brant says, standing with Axel following him.

"I think it's so weird how they're so close when Mom and Dad literally fucked like yesterday," Elias says, throwing back his mimosa. Liza tenses under my arm and glares at him.

"Could you fucking not, Elias?" She glances at Emily and Travis. Even if they didn't know, they would never judge or say anything.

"You may like to pretend like it didn't happen, but it did. I don't give a shit that it happened, but them being so close afterwards is just weird. He began living with them right after it happened, Lizzie."

"Right after Dad *almost died*. Fuck, Elias." She stands up and walks away into the kitchen with Emily following after her. I turn and glare at him. He pushes his hands through his hair.

"What the *fuck* is your problem?" I ask. He shakes his head. I know she's pissed at her brother—she's never called him by his full name before.

"It's just...weird."

"It's their business."

"I'll go talk to her," Hogan says, rising. But Elias grabs him and shakes his head.

"It's my fault, I'll talk to her." Selle shakes her head at him and looks away, tucking her hair behind her ear. I glare at him as he walks into the kitchen.

"He won't admit it, but it still bothers him. His mom drilled monogamy and fidelity in our heads since we were twelve. Always told us if we weren't happy, leave. When she failed to do that herself, Eli acted unphased, but I knew," Hogan says, looking towards the kitchen.

"Then why doesn't he grow the fuck up and talk about it? I will admit how close they are is a bit...unconventional, but what the fuck ever. If anything, we should all be glad that they can be around each other." I hear Liza raising her voice and I stand, heading for the kitchen with Hogan, Travis, and Selle on my heels.

"She made me feel like shit when I *kissed* another girl in

fucking high school, but she can cheat on her fucking husband and it's fine! Stop fucking sticking up for her, Lizzie!"

"I'm not sticking up for her! I talked to her and Dad about it. I got fucking clarity, something you should've thought about doing." She gets in his face and continues, "Your relationship isn't going to last if you let what our parents did haunt you. They've moved on, they made a mistake! We should be happy they can stand each other. Do you know how fucking hard our lives would be if they went back to hating each other?! Do you know how hard these last few months would've been if we didn't have both of our fucking parents here!" Tears well up in her eyes and she pushes him. "Grow up!"

"Elizabeth…" I start, but Elias holds his hand up to me. "She's right. I'm sorry, Lizzie. I'm…I'm trying. I'm going to get some air." He gives Selle an apologetic look and walks out the backdoor. She looks at me and runs after him.

"Selle," Hogan says. She stops in her tracks, concern written all over her face. "Give him a few minutes to calm down." She shakes her head. "I can't. He's been weird since we got here and now I know why. He needs to know I'm here for him." She shuts the door and goes after him.

"You didn't have to be so hard on him, Lizzie. He knows he needs to talk to them. He's trying," Hogan says, shaking his head. She looks up and wipes her face. "If he doesn't let it go, it'll ruin him. It'll ruin *them*," she says looking at the door he and Selle walked out of. "If he doesn't either talk to them or let it go, it's going to cost him *her*." I rub her back and kiss the side of her head. "Come on, angel. Let's take a drive."

52

Liza

I look out the window the entire way to the shopping center. Emily is talking about some dress she wants to find, but I'm barely listening. First, I get into a pointless fight with Graham, now with Eli. I don't fight with my brother—ever. We've always talked to each other, always told each other everything. Why wouldn't he tell me this was still bothering him? I guess I can't put all the blame on him. I didn't tell him I talked to them about it, either. I pull my phone out, scrolling to his name.

Liza: *I'm sorry.*

My phone vibrates not a minute later with a text back from him.

Eli: *No, I'm sorry. I'm an ass.*

Liza: *Just talk to them. You'll understand after and it'll give you closure. I promise.*

Eli: *So, you do think I'm an ass?*

Liza: *Oh, definitely.*

Eli: *I don't like fighting with you, Lizzie.*

Liza: *I know, I'm sorry I pushed you.*

Eli*: Eh, barely felt it. Love you, see you later.*

I smile and pocket my phone back into my clutch. Graham raises an eyebrow at me. He leans into my ear and whispers, "That better be your fucking brother who has you smiling that way." I look up at him and smirk, bringing my lips an inch away from his face. "And if it's not?" I ask, tilting my head to the side. He yanks me to him and kisses. "Don't test me, angel."

Travis clears his throat and I pull away from Graham's grip, turning to face him and Emily.

"Sorry," I say, blushing. Emily smiles and giggles, leaning into Travis' embrace as he shakes his head.

Ralph opens the door for us once we get to the shopping center. Graham gave Ellis the day off today since we all leave tomorrow. We walk towards the first store and Graham reaches his hand back for me to grab. I grab it absentmindedly while talking to Emily about what she wants to buy.

"I need a new bathing suit for starters. Oh, and a black dress. Someone burned my other one," she says, looking at Travis. He shrugs his shoulders, looking down at her. "It was too fucking short," he growls. *These fucking men and their obsessions with our dresses.*

We walk into the first store and Emily and I head for the bathing suit section. "Sooo..." she says, awkwardly picking through the selection. I raise my eyebrows. I know she saw Graham and me yesterday, I was waiting for her to say something about it. "Is he always like that?" she asks. I shrug. "Pretty much, yeah. Is Travis not like that?"

"Oh no, he is, but he's not nearly that intense. He knows what he likes and he loves telling me exactly what to do."

"And do you like that?"

"Yeah, I love it. But he holds back; I can tell. Like I can feel how rough he wants to be with me, but he always stops himself." She shrugs and I frown a bit.

"Tell him. Tell him how you want it and what you want. Tell him you trust him. He'll do it. Trust me." I wink at her. She looks down at an alert she sees on her phone. Her face is blank as she glances up at me. "Oh, shit."

"What is it?"

"The entire world now knows you're engaged..." I snatch the phone out of her hand, quickly reading the article.

It seems like Seattle's most eligible bachelor is no longer available. According to ex-fiancée, Madison Pinsley, her and Salando were rekindling things when she found him and Elizabeth Crambell rather close at a party. Pinsley claims she ended things that night and soon after heard the news of the engagement through an extremely reliable source. She states that she feels blind-sided and naïve. There has been no comment from Salando or the alleged fiancée, Elizabeth Crambell.

What the *fuck*.

"I will fucking ruin her." I grit through my teeth. "That slutty, lying ass bitch!" Emily's eyes widen and I turn around looking at Graham. He has his phone in his hand and his cheek is tense. *He's reading it.*

"Wanna go fight a bitch? I'm down." She's always down, that's the problem. Emily was always getting into trouble from her temper during freshman and sophomore year. She finally got it under control, but every now and again it comes out. As for me, I stay nice for a reason. I was taught at a very young age how to protect myself. I still take the classes every Wednesday night, especially since Graham was shot.

My phone rings, it's Giselle.

"Hey," I answer. She starts screaming on the other end and I almost have to rip the phone from my ear.

"THAT *BITCH*! SHE'S LYING! HE'D NEVER REKINDLE THINGS WITH HER, PLEASE DON'T TELL ME YOU BELIEVE HER! I CAN PROM—" I cut her off.

"I know she's lying. I'm not leaving him. You can relax, Selle." She takes a deep breath and then another. "Thank God...Mom's on the phone with our media team now. What do you want to do about it?" I look outside to Graham and then to Emily who gives me a small smile.

"Nothing, don't say anything. It's his birthday. She did this on purpose. I will not let her ruin this day for him. I'll personally deal with her when we return home tomorrow."

I can hear Madeline in the background agreeing with my decision. "Ok, we're getting everything ready for tonight, bring him back around 6:30 p.m., ok?" I let out a sigh. "It'll be ok, Liza. I'll see you later."

53

Graham

Rekindling things. Blind-sided. Naïve.

The words float through my head from the article. She thinks she's going to take one of the happiest moments of my life and make it about her? With her lies and manipulative fucking ways, she's crazy if she thinks anyone will believe her.

"Graham..." Liza touches my arm and I look down at her. My hand is wrapped so tight around the phone I can't make myself reach for her.

"It's not true," I blurt out. She has to know I'd never leave her. She has to know that I haven't seen Madison since the charity event that night.

"Baby, I know," she says, pushing the phone away from me. She takes it and pushes it into my pocket, pulling my arms around her. I sigh in relief and wrap her tightly against me. She nuzzles into me and I kiss the top of her head.

"I'm going to kill her..." I mutter.

"Not if I do it first," she says as I chuckle. She looks up at me and smirks. "I told your mom not to comment and that we'd deal with it once we got back home. It's your birthday and *she* of all people will *not* fuck this one up."

"She had one thing right in the article." Liza leans back and looks at me with a slight frown. "She definitely is naïve if she thinks she's getting away with this." She smiles at me and pulls me toward the next store. I raise an eyebrow at her when I see it's a lingerie shop. "Be good, angel. Remember the last time I brought you to a shop like this?" She bites her lip at the memory and I groan.

"You good, man?" Travis asks. I nod my head and watch Liza pick up pieces of lingerie, stuffing them into the basket. She looks at me and winks as I smirk. "Who do you think told her?" he continues.

"Fuck if I know, but I'll find out when time permits. Right now, I'm going to enjoy my stupid fucking birthday with my fiancé and our sex-watching friends." He laughs at that and I grab his shoulders, squeezing. "Seriously, how much did you see?" He holds his hands up and shakes his head. "Just you devouring what clearly must taste like the world's best pussy to you." I shrug my shoulders. As long as he didn't see her pussy, I don't give a shit. "How do you trust yourself to let go?" he asks.

I look at him in question and he looks at the floor. Travis and I have always been alike sexually. We've had threesomes and fucked in front of each other freshman through junior year. He's walked in on me fucking someone and I've done the same, so I know he likes it on the rougher side. "It was hard at first. I was always rough, but I never completely let go until she begged me to. She begged me to trust her to tell me when it became too much. Once I did that, it was easy to be myself. Hell, I'm probably rougher now," I say. He grunts and shakes his head.

"How the fuck is that even possible...I remember that girl I walked in on that time sophomore year." I shake my head and he chuckles. "I want to get there, man. She practically begs me to choke the fucking life of out her, but I can't."

"You can...you think you can't because she's different. She's different because you love her and you don't want to hurt her. But just like she trusts you not to hurt her, you have to trust her to tell you when to stop. You both need to be comfortable with your safe word. Just try it. The fucking house is big enough, no one will hear you."

"Yeah, unless I do it in the kitchen."

"Fuck, let it go Trav." I laugh and he walks behind Emily, looking in her basket.

"Wanna see what I got?" Liza asks, holding her basket up. She turns for the fitting room and I follow like the fucking lost puppy I am; drooling over her constantly, following whatever command she gives me. She thinks I'm the one always in charge, but she has no fucking idea.

I sit in the chair in the small, private dressing room and wait for her to change. My phone vibrates and I pull it out, knowing it's probably our media team again.

Unknown: *You proposed to that bitch?*

I dial Madison's number. It rings once before her annoying, little voice is on the other end. "Hey, bab—"

"You're goddamn right, I proposed to her. Call her a bitch again and see what happens. Stop texting my fucking phone and stop feeding lies to the press. You want to play victim? Play it. But make no mistake, Madison, you know I can end you." The dirt I have on her and her family could tarnish their name for good. She doesn't want to test me. When it comes to Liza, limits don't fucking exist.

"But, I—" I hang up, not wanting to hear whatever excuse was about to come out of her mouth. I take a deep breath and Liza steps from behind the curtain. She tilts her head to the side and raises her eyebrow. I look over her entire body. She's wearing a red, all lace one piece with a corset in the back.

"Fuck," I say, adjusting my immediately hard cock. She straddles me and I run my hands up her back.

"Why'd you call her?" she asks quietly. I pull my phone out and show her the message. She cocks her eyebrow and tenses up. "I handled it, don't worry about her." I kiss her nose and she sighs. "I like this one," I say.

"Yeah?" she asks. I run my hands up her back, loosening the corset. "Graham...don't," she starts.

"Ahh, you're under the impression that you make the rules again, aren't you?"

"Our friends are waiting on us," she protests. I shake my head. "She's trying on things, too. I guarantee we have all the time we need." I tug the tiny piece of fabric that covers her pussy to the side and push my finger in. She lets out a small moan as I push another in.

"Ride my fingers, angel," I whisper in her ear. She tucks her bottom lip into her mouth as she focuses on riding my fingers. I entwine my fingers in her hair, yanking her head back and exposing her neck to me. I run my tongue up her neck, placing a soft bite on her neck.

Moving my fingers faster, she moans a little louder. I cover her mouth with my hand. "Seems like we're having to keep you quiet a lot this week."

"Yeah, because you're an animal," she says, muffled by my hand covering her mouth. I pull my fingers out of her and stand us up, pushing her back against the mirror. "You want animal? I can show you an animal, baby." I quickly unzip my pants and shove myself inside of her. The groan she lets out goes straight to my cock and I pump in and out of her faster. She bites down on my shoulder and the mirror starts to shake. I turn her to the wall adjacent to it and thrust in and out her, deeper and faster.

"Liza? You all set?" Emily asks outside the dressing room. I add a finger and circle it around her G-spot as she yelps.

"Yes! I'm coming!" I chuckle at the double innuendo of her coming all over my cock as we speak. "Fuck yeah, you are, and I'm right behind you, pretty girl." I pump my load inside of her and she slumps against the wall, catching her breath. I kiss the side of her head and she smirks at me.

"Animal..." she says, walking behind the curtain to change.

54

Liza

"You're such a slut," Emily whispers in my ear as we take our seats at the bar and restaurant.

"Oh, shut up. I know you were doing the same thing I was in that dressing room." She shrugs her shoulders and bites her lip, fanning herself.

"Flashbacks," she says, laughing. I hit her arm and take my seat next to her, the boys on the other side of the table.

Graham and Travis are talking about the New York office and Emily hits my leg. "Bitch...what is it?" I ask.

"Are you going to end up moving to New York?"

"I don't know. I mean, he's opening his new office there. We haven't talked much about it." I take a sip of my drink and she taps her finger on the table.

"I mean, I guess I might as well just tell you..."

"Tell me what?" I ask.

"We're moving to New York." My eyes widen in surprise and Travis tilts his head at our conversation.

"What? Really?" She shoves a bite of her food into her mouth and nods.

"When?" I ask.

"Two weeks. We're looking at an apartment when we get back."

"But I thought you were traveling for a year."

"Honestly, I loved it at first, but I just want to settle somewhere. There's a great company that I have an interview with on Tuesday. I always love New York when we visit your parents and Travis already has a few offers. So, I figured why not?"

"As long as you're happy." I smile at her and Travis slides her hand in his. They seem so happy and that makes me happy for her. All throughout our childhood, and even more when Tim started stalking me, it was her constantly taking care of me and worrying about me. It's her turn to have someone take care of her.

"So, three months before the wedding?" Travis asks me.

"You know your friend here is not keen on being told to wait," I joke, gesturing at Graham.

"When it comes to you, angel, the word *wait* does not belong in my vocabulary. Or yours, for that matter," Graham says.

"Animal," I whisper to him as he snickers. The waiter brings our check and I quickly snatch it, handing my card over before Graham can hound him for it.

"It's your birthday, you don't pay on your birthday." He shakes his head and stands, helping me up as well. Ralph is waiting for us and the sun is starting to set.

"Oh, shit. I forgot something," I say. Graham raises an eyebrow at me. "I'll be quick, I promise."

"I'll come with you," he says. I put my hand on his chest and shake my head. "No, you will not. Emily is coming with me." She loops her arm through mine and we head to the jewelry store.

"Birthday present?" she asks with a knowing smirk. I nod at her. "Yes. I ordered it and it's ready to be picked up."

"At some point you also need to buy a wedding band," she says, tugging my arm. "Yeah, I know, I just want it to be special and to fit him," I say.

"I can't believe you're getting married."

"I know, it's fucking crazy, right?" We laugh as we walked to the jeweler. I pick up the birthday present I hope helps change Graham's mind about birthdays.

Graham holds my hand the entire drive back with me snuggled against him. Emily is sleeping soundly while Travis mindlessly runs his fingers through her hair. I'm not ready to leave this place tomorrow, Graham has been so happy here. Despite Madison and her ruthless antics, he's been so at peace here.

I look up at him and he's scrolling through his phone. His face is settled and he's calm. He peers down at me, kissing the tip of my nose as he starts running his hand up and down my back.

"What is it, beautiful?"

"I just don't think I'm ready to leave yet. We just got here and we already leave tomorrow."

"We can stay as long as you want, Liza." He tucks a piece of my hair behind my ear and traces my lips with his finger.

"No, no, I know you have to get back and finish the merge for the New York office."

"I can do that from here. We'll stay another few days," he says matter of fact. I smile and nod, laying my head back on his chest.

Ralph opens the car door for us and we all tunnel out of the car. Emily has a smile plastered on her face in excitement.

Travis opens the door with the rest of us trailing behind. "Where the fuck are the lights in this place, G?" Travis asks. Graham flips the switch on next to the door.

"SURPRISE!!!!" everyone says, jumping out of their hiding spots as flashes go off from every angle. Madeline and Giselle thought it would be nice to have this night photographed. Graham shakes his head and smiles at all our family and friends surrounding him. He hugs our moms and Giselle. I stand by the staircase watching everyone wish him a Happy Birthday with a smile on my face. He searches the crowd for me, his eyes finding mine almost immediately.

He walks over to me and pulls me to him, planting a searing kiss on my lips. "This was your doing, wasn't it?" he guesses. I wrap my arms around his neck. "You deserve to be celebrated." He kisses me again and a flash goes off. He smirks as another follows and turns me toward the camera. He tucks me into his side and we smile for the photographer. Then he cups my face and goes in for another kiss. The photographer snaps another photo before leaving us alone.

"I don't deserve you." he says, I smirk at him. "Too bad, you're stuck."

"The best kind of stuck. I love you, angel."

"I love you."

55

Graham

A surprise party was the last thing I suspected. Usually someone gives it away, typically Selle, so now I understand why I hadn't seen much of her today. She would've ruined the surprise the moment she saw me. I'm overwhelmed by our families laughing and bonding with each other. Overwhelmed with the constant feeling that I don't deserve any of this. Overwhelmed with the thought that I'll wake up and it'll be ripped away from me.

"Come with me?" Liza asks, approaching me. I raise my eyebrow and take her hand as she holds it out to me. I put my drink on the end table and follow her to the back balcony. Our mothers watch her leave with smirks on their faces. Knowing we have their support is comforting, which is interesting because I never cared if I had support for anyone for anything.

"Happy birthday," she says, pulling a small box and handing it to me. She fidgets a bit and I smirk, taking it out of her hands. She's nervous and it's cute.

"You didn't need to get me anything, you know that."

"Open it." I shake my head at her and open the box revealing a gold men's gold bracelet with a flat platform reading *I love you more* engraved on it. "Not possible, angel." I look up at her and she's biting her lip. I take it out and slip in on my left wrist, turning it over for her to clasp it for me.

"You like it?" I cup her face and kiss her forehead as she leans into me. "I'm never taking it off. It's perfect, like you. Thank you." She wraps her arms around my waist and we stay that way for a few minutes. Turning to look out over the grounds, she takes a deep breath and leans into me, her back to my front.

"This place...it just feels like peace," she says. I tighten my hold on her. She looks up at me and watches me as I look at the lights wrapped around all the trees in the yard, the pool glistening in the night.

"Peace is wherever you are for me." I kiss her forehead and she smiles. This was by far the best birthday I could've asked for.

After my family left, the week seemed to go by even faster. My time with Liza here in Rome went by quickly—too quickly. We promised Marco and Abby that we'd be back after the wedding and they promised to be there. Liza was quiet for most of the flight and that worried me a bit. I knew she had been worried about the press; our families had been hassled the moment they got back from Rome. Paparazzi bombarding them all with questions was a stressor for her. Knowing that Madison caused all of this makes my blood boil. I'm still deciding what I'm going to do about that.

When our flight lands, Ellis is there waiting for us, as usual. There's no paparazzi and I make a mental note to thank my mom for ensuring that no one knew when we were returning from Rome. I need to talk to Liza about how she wants to address the press. We climb into the car and I look at her as she gives me a small smile.

"We need to—"

"Talk to the press, I know," she says, reaching for my hand. "I've been thinking about it. This isn't a bad thing; this isn't a bad moment in our lives. We got engaged, we love each other. Madison is the one trying to turn a happy time into a bad one. I just want to tell the truth. That's it." I bring her hand up to my lips and kiss it.

"Then that's what we'll do," I say.

"I want to do it today. I'm not hiding our engagement and I'm not hiding from her." I nod and send a quick text to my mom to tell the media team our plans.

"Whatever you want, angel. Is that the only thing that's on your mind?"

"That obvious, huh?"

"I've told you; you wear every emotion on that pretty face of yours."

"I'm just thinking about wedding stuff. Selle texted me about my bridal appointment for a dress, Mom texted me about if we were going to have a wedding party, and your mom texted me asking about floral designs. I'm just a bit overwhelmed."

"I'll tell them to back off." I pick up my phone, but she grabs it from my hand. "No, don't. They're asking valid questions."

"Ok, so let's discuss it together." She smiles at me and nods. We discuss our wedding plans and it's like I see a weight fall off her shoulders instantly. We decide that the wedding will be intimate with just our family and friends. We wanted the ceremony to be outside, but since it'll be December, we'll find a venue that has tall, open windows to give an outside feel.

"I feel so much better." I raise my eyebrow and she giggles, crawling onto my lap. "I can't wait to marry you, Graham." I bring her face to mine and kiss her.

"I can't wait either, angel."

56

Liza

There are people surrounding our building with cameras and vehicles everywhere. Graham looks at me and focuses his eyes on me. "You ready?"

"As I'll ever be." He kisses my ring finger and somehow that gives me all the strength I need. I push my shoulders back and slide out of the car, putting my hand in his as we walk towards our front door.

"Mr. Salando! Mr. Salando! Can you confirm or deny the allegations Ms. Pinsley are suggesting?" He looks at me and I nod at him. He turns to the man with the microphone and shakes his head.

"Ms. Pinsley is lying. The only truthful thing she said in that interview is yes, Elizabeth and I are engaged. However, there was never any talk of reconciliation between Madison and me. We ended things years ago when she in fact, faked a pregnancy in hopes of me marrying her. While it may be hard for her to accept that we are over, I'm afraid that's not my problem." He reaches for me and pulls me into his side, kissing my forehead. "Elizabeth and I will be getting married this December. That should be your story, not Madison Pinsley and her manipulative ways."

We turn to head for the door when the reporter continues, but directs questions at me this time. "Ms. Crambell! First, congratulations. I wanted to ask you if there was anything you wanted to say about the accusations?" I turn to Graham who has his hand on my back. I keep my chin up. "As my fiancé said, Madison is a manipulator. She wants to play victim, which is fine, I could care less. The only thing I care about is finally getting to marry this man. If you'll excuse us, we had an extremely long flight." The reporter nods and smiles at us, moving out of our way.

When we get into the house Graham pushes me against the door, yanking my shirt over my head. His movements are fast and frantic, I can't keep up. I reach for his shirt, pulling it over his head. He lifts me up and I wrap my legs around him as he continues to devour my mouth, forcing his tongue in and out. He drops me on the couch and flips me over onto my stomach. I hear his zipper, and before I can catch my breath, he pushes into me. A moan rips out of me and he speeds up, fucking me harder and deeper. The sounds of our skins hitting fill the living room. He yanks me to him by my hair. "Mine. And now everyone knows it."

"Yours."

And I come with a vengeance.

The next few weeks go by in a blur from cake, food, all the way down to wine tastings. Graham has been present for everything, never complaining even when I have him try the same cake three times to make sure he likes it. He has to leave for New York today and he'll be gone for a few days. He told me to come with him, but I have a meeting with our wedding planner.

I watch him put the last tie into his suitcase before he zips it up. He looks at me and sighs. "Come with me."

"I can't, I have too much wedding stuff to do."

"Do it in New York. I don't like being away from you. What if something happens and I can't get to you?"

"Nothing will happen, I promise. Ralph, Selle, your mom, and my mom will all be here, too." He gives me an unimpressed expression and puts his suitcase by the door.

"I still don't like it. Madison has been radio silent since our interview and I keep getting these weird texts. I just feel like you need to be with me." Ever since we gave our interview, Graham has been getting text messages. The first was just about how I'm after his money and he was making a mistake. We figured that it was probably from Madison, but then he started getting texts from someone claiming to be his mother. Graham said it had to be a sick joke, because his father said she was dead.

"Graham, it's three days, I'll be fine. I can stay with Eli and Hogan if it makes you feel better." He raises his eyebrow, challenging me. "Don't even with me, I have to get this stuff done before my bridal appointment next week. Don't defy me on this. If I feel like something is off or something is wrong, I'll call you. I promise." He kisses my forehead. "You better. I love you, I'll call you when I land," he says. I nod and give him a quick kiss. "I love you more."

"Not possible."

"Don't care."

I watch the car leave and my phone buzzes. It's Emily texting our group chat.

Em: *I'll be over in fifteen minutes, we have shit to do.*

I quickly text back.

Liza: *I'll be here.*

I put the phone on the table when it sounds off again.

Selle: *Bring something cute to wear for dinner, Em! No way we're ordering take out tonight. Fuck that.*

Em: *Count me in. See you bitches soon.*

I don't bother telling them that I'm not in the mood to go out, instead I quickly hop in the shower and find something comfy to put on. I pour myself a glass of wine and start flipping through the floral designs Graham's mom sent me.

They're extravagant and beautiful, some more than others, but all still seemingly beautiful.

A knock on the door comes. "It's open!" I yell. A moment later, Selle and Emily come barreling through the door. They both have an overnight bag in their hand and I cock my head to the side. "I take it you're spending the night?"

"Yup. Sure as fuck am. Travis went with Graham to New York, so I'm shacking up with you tonight. Honestly, don't be surprised if I'm here for the next three days."

"I thought you were going with him to look at places there?"

"Well, Graham asked Trav for some help with the merger. I told him we could look at places next week, since he doesn't start work for another three weeks, anyway." She pours Selle and her a glass of wine and they both pop down on the floor, pulling wedding magazines out of their bags.

"Ok, now lets finish planning this fucking wedding."

57

Graham

"She still hasn't said anything to anyone yet?" Travis asks. We're at my office at the New York site. I shake my head at his question about Madison. "No. I'm assuming she got the hint."

"Yeah, I don't know about that man..." I turn around to face him and he's looking at the door with disgust.

"Oh, Graham, your office is coming along nice, baby." My blood is ice and I narrow my eyes as I turn and face her. "Madison, why the fuck are you here? And how the hell did you even get in?"

"Oh, easy. I told the guy downstairs I was your wife. Wasn't hard to believe." I glare at her and Travis' eyes widen at her admission. "After all, I was supposed to be, or did you forget that?"

"Get her the fuck out of my office," I tell Travis. He moves immediately, not questioning me.

"If he touches me, I'll make sure someone touches *her*." Travis freezes, glancing at me. I hold my hand up. "Travis, give me a second." He walks towards the door and shoots me a warning glare.

"Madison, how many times do I have to tell you? Do not threaten me."

"I'm not threatening you; I'm threatening your slut." I'm on her before I realize what I'm doing. I push her against the glass window and tighten my hand around her throat, cutting off her air supply. "Do *not* call her that. I don't know what exactly has gotten into you or that crazy fucking head of yours, but hear me clearly when I say this: you don't stand a fucking chance. *We. Are. Over.*"

Her lips start to turn a light blue and it's taking everything in me not to snap her fucking neck into two. "Here's what you're going to do. You're going to tell the press that you're happy for us, you're not going to lay a hand on *my fiancée*, then you're going to leave us the fuck alone. And if you don't, I promise I will end you and your miserable goddamn existence." I let go of her neck and she clutches it, gasping for air.

"You don't scare me. And you won't hurt me," she sputters.

"Wanna bet?" I ask, leaning against my desk. I cross my arms and watch her attempt to steady her breathing.

"You'll regret it," she taunts.

I shrug. "We'll see. Now get the fuck out of my office." I turn and look out the window as I hear the door slam shut. I let out a sigh, picking up my phone to call downstairs.

"Yes, Mr. Salando?"

"Who's working the front gate downstairs?"

"That would be, let me check..." I hear typing on the computer and I tap my finger impatiently. Whoever it is has officially gotten on my shit list for letting her in my fucking office. "Ok, here it is. It's Mr. Greg."

Fuck, I liked him. Oh well.

"Fire him."

"But, sir—"

"He let an unauthorized person up here, fire him. If you're incapable of doing your job, then I can fire you as well."

"No that's not necessary, sir, I'll do it right away." I hang up and dial Liza. She answers on the second ring and I let out sigh of relief when I hear her voice.

"Hi, baby." She giggles and I shake my head, looking at the time. I hear more laughter in the background. "Selle and Em are here. How's New York?" she asks.

"It's been...eventful, to say the least. If we end up moving here, I'll have to bribe Angie to move here, too. The staff here is fucking horrible. I want to fire them all."

"Be nice," she says. Suddenly I hear Selle yelling, "Yeah, G. Be niiiiiice."

"Are you guys drunk?" I ask. It's 6:00 p.m. there, so it wouldn't surprise me if they were. I knew they were going out for dinner tonight, now I'm wondering if they ever even made it there.

"It's 9:00 p.m. there, why are you still at work?" she asks.

"I'm letting the staff go home now, but they knew today would be a long day. They're being compensated accordingly."

"Don't work yourself too hard. Oh, you got a package today... " she whispers. "Hold on...let me go to our room." Once it's quiet I hear the door shut and she clears her throat.

"Did you open it?" I ask.

"No. That's a felony." I chuckle at her and run my hands over the bracelet she gave me.

"Open it."

"No. It's not mine."

"Open it, Elizabeth." She almost growls. Moments later I

can hear her ripping through it. "Wait, FaceTime me. I want to see what it is." Except I know what it is. I sent her a new dress for dinner tonight and there was not a chance in hell I wasn't going to see her put it on. Not even seconds later, her beautiful face is on my screen.

"Let me prop you up." She shuffles the phone until I have a perfect view of her opening the box. "Umm, Graham."

"What, angel?"

"What the fuck is this?" She picks the phone up and flips the camera. I frown at what's inside of the box. It's photos of Madison leaving my building wearing what she had on today—except she looks freshly fucked. How is that even possible? That was, what, ten minutes ago?

"Isn't this your building?"

"Elizabeth—"

"Did you see her today?" She looks through the pictures and I can already see the thoughts spiraling in her head. I hear my sister and Emily in the background yelling for her. "I'll be right there!"

She picks up the phone and glares at me. "I've gotta go."

"Do not hang this phone up. Let me explain."

"I don't care, Graham. It's fine."

"It's not fine and it's not what you think. She came here and I kicked her out, end of story."

"Ok."

"Angel."

"Graham, I said ok. I'll talk to you later." She hangs up the phone and I call back immediately. It gets sent straight to voicemail. I push my hands through my hair.

Fuck me.

58

Liza

At dinner I am distracted by the pictures, by Graham not mentioning it to me, but mainly by how badly I want to wrap my hands around Madison's neck.

The photos are on a slideshow in my head and I can't stop it from staying on repeat. After I hung up on Graham, another package arrived—I'm assuming it's the one Graham thought I was opening the first time. He sent me a beautiful, emerald green dress to wear for dinner tonight. But I'm so irritated with him that instead of wearing it, I decide to wear a tight, fitted, long, black dress that cuts low in the front.

"Earth to Elizabeth." Emily slams her hand down on the table. I roll my eyes, throwing back the shot she placed in front of me. "Obviously you're mad about something, so spill."

"It's nothing. I'm fine." Selle raises her eyebrow and leans in. "What'd he do?"

"Nothing, Selle, really. I'm just stressed with all the wedding stuff." I briefly look away to mask the lie I told. I know she knows it's a lie, but she doesn't pry. Instead, she just gives me a small smile and pulls her phone out.

"I can't wait for your bridal appointment, that's when it'll feel real! Do you have any idea of styles?" Emily asks I shake my head. "Not really. I mean, I know I want something that'll make Graham speechless, but I don't know what that dress looks like yet."

"We'll find it, I can't wait," Selle says, but she's distracted by the door...I turn and my eyes lock on the entrance. "What? Who is that?" Selle looks like she's seen a ghost; the color drains from her face and she doesn't speak.

"Giselle. What's wrong?"

"That's...impossible," she mumbles. I follow her gaze to an older woman, probably her mom's age. She is stunning. She has long, dark hair that tumbles down her back with a fierce look—and she's staring right at us. *Why does she look so familiar?*

"We need to leave, right now," Selle says. She stands and all but basically pulls me out of the door with her. The woman watches us leave with a small smirk on her face as we push through the door and head for the car.

Selle is quiet the entire way back to the house. Emily keeps giving me worried looks and I just shrug my shoulders in response. "Are you going to tell me why you freaked out or should I just call Eli?"

"It's nothing. I thought she was someone she wasn't, that's all."

I bite the inside of my lip and nod my head. Something is seriously wrong, but I won't force it out of her. All I know is that I'm running through every memory in my mind to figure out why I've seen her before. My phone rings and it's Graham. I ignore it, still not wanting to talk to him.

All I want to do right now is shower and go to sleep. I don't want to think about Madison, I don't want to think about the mystery woman that has Selle so quiet, and I don't want to think about the fact that I still have a few days before Graham comes home.

"I'm going to head home," Selle says, grabbing her things. I frown at her. "Look, I don't know who you saw, but I do know how it feels to have someone have that amount of power over you," I say. She sighs and turns to me, pulling me into a hug.

"It's not my place to say who she is, and if she is who I think she is, we're going to have a hell of a family meeting." She kisses my cheek and walks out of the door. My phone rings again and I sigh, answering it.

"Hi."

"Why aren't you answering your phone?" Graham demands.

"I did answer."

"I'll be there in two hours." He hangs up and I roll my eyes, moving to sit on the couch next to Emily. She has the phone up to her ear and pats the spot next to her. I lay my head in her lap and she runs her hands through my hair, pulling out the bobby pins I had for my hairstyle. "Ok, well I'll see you when you get back...I love you, too."

"Bitch, what the fuck is happening?" she asks, removing the last two pins from my hair. I turn over and look at her.

"Madison came to see Graham today at his office, paparazzi took photos and sent them to me of her leaving his building. She was smiling and she looked flushed, like she was out of breath."

"You think he cheated on you...be serious, Liza. It's Graham. He's obsessed with you; he'd never jeopardize that for anyone. Especially her...did you ask him about it?'

"He was on FaceTime with me when I saw the photos. He told me that she came to see him, he told her to leave, and that nothing else happened. It's just...he didn't tell me when it happened. I had to get photos of it first. He should've told me right away; she shouldn't even have access to the fucking building, Em."

"Men are stupid. Maybe he didn't think to put her on the New York list. Maybe he didn't expect her to be there. After all, she lives here." I shrug. Maybe she was right. I'm sure I'm being ridiculous, but I can't make myself care enough to call him and say sorry. My pride is really being stubborn today. I wonder how bold I'll be when he's in my face.

"He said he's coming home."

"I know, Travis called me. He said Graham is a wreck and has been on a rampage since you hung up on him. A bit dramatic, if you ask me." We both laugh and at the moment I'm beyond happy that she's here with me tonight. After about an hour, she decides that she'll head home since the boys will be back tonight. I give her a tight hug. "Thank you for comforting me."

"Always, you're my favorite, bitch." I smirk at her and watch her climb into the car. As she shuts the door I see a figure by the end of our driveway. I squint my eyes, thinking I'm seeing things. My eyes adjust to the darkness and the figure is gone.

Fuck, I must really be exhausted.

59

Graham

We land exactly two hours later after our call ended. I made arrangements to leave immediately. There was no way she was going to bed tonight thinking I was keeping things from her. Travis didn't complain when I told him we were leaving, he was practically jumping for joy.

"How is it possible that she got those photos that quick?"

"That's what I'm wondering, too. And I want to know who the hell dropped them off."

"Did you check your cameras?"

"I tried and it won't work. I don't know what the fuck happened, but something doesn't feel right. I keep trying to pull them up and it's glitching. I called Ralph, he said Emily made it home and Liza turned into bed like twenty minutes ago."

"Then maybe it's just something electrical." I laugh and shake my head. "Electrical?" He shrugs his shoulder. We land and both zip our way home.

When I get home the house is dark besides the lamp that is on in the security room. I sent Ellis home and drove myself.

He was not in agreement, but I told him Ralph was already at our house. I pull into the garage, taking a deep breath at how close I feel to her already.

Climbing out of the car, I stop in my tracks when a figure appears at the end of the driveway. I quickly pull the gun from my waistband; I never leave without it since everything that happened. The figure walks closer and closer. It's a woman, that's for sure.

Madison clearly doesn't give up. I shake my head and start walking closer towards her, gun still in hand and aimed. "Have you lost your mind? I told you to stay the fuck away from me, Madison." The figure steps into a beam of light from the house and I stop in tracks.

"Hello, son."

I almost fucking faint. Either I'm seeing a ghost or my biological mother is standing in my fucking driveway.

"How..."

"Can we...talk?"

"You're supposed to be dead...you killed yourself." I lower my gun briefly and she steps closer, shaking her head.

"No, your father paid me to stay away from you."

"Lies. I watched you leave, then you slit your wrists."

"Yes, you saw me leave after he paid me to. Please let's talk."

"Fuck you. I rather not. I've been just fine without you."

"Talk to me or I'll kill her," she says, nodding towards the house. I raise my eyebrow and stalk towards her. I wrap my hand around her neck and squeeze.

"You should know when it comes to her, I don't spare anything or anyone. Especially when she's being threatened."

"I'm your mother—" she chokes out.

"You're a surrogate. You had me, he paid you, and you left," I grit out. I release her and she tumbles back. "Get the fuck out of my driveway."

"There's things you need to know." I shake my head and make my way to the house. "Your father, your *family,* they're all lying to you. They've been lying to you for years."

"My father is dead!" I yell at her. She frowns, then a devious smile spreads across her face as the front door swings open.

"Graham?" Liza asks.

"Go back inside," I say, not taking my eyes off *my mother.* She walks closer to the door and I raise my gun at her again. She stops in her tracks and tilts her head at me. "You'd shoot your own mother?" she asks. Liza gasps and puts her hand over her mouth.

"I thought you were dead?" Liza asks in an almost whisper.

"Yeah, it seems everyone did. Tomorrow, Graham, we're talking," she says, walking back towards the road. "I'll be in touch," she adds. She climbs into a black car that pulls to the end of the driveway. I watch the car get smaller and smaller.

What the fuck.

"Graham..." Liza says.

I'm pacing, fuming, confused, and in dire need of hurting someone. *How is she alive?* And why the fuck did my father tell me she was dead? Not only dead, but that she killed herself. That was a lie, clearly. And what did she mean that everyone had been lying to me?

"Graham!" Liza says, taking me out of my inner thoughts. I turn to her and she has tears in her eyes.

I pull her into my arms. "I'm sorry. I'm sorry I didn't tell you Madison came to see me. It was nothing." Her tears wet my shirt and she shakes her head.

"We can talk about that later. Right now, I want to know why someone who's supposed to be dead was in our driveway at midnight. And how does she know where we live?"

"I don't know, but there's only one way to find out." I pull my phone out and hover over my mother's number. "Graham, it's midnight, you can't call her tonight. Do it tomorrow," Liza says.

"No, fuck that. She can answer my questions tonight." She answers on the second ring.

"Honey? Everything ok?"

"No, it's not. You want to explain to me why someone who's supposed to be dead, who looks an awful lot like my mother, just showed up at my house?" There's silence on the other end of the phone and I grind my teeth at the silent admission.

"I'm on my way. Stay put. Lock your doors. And, Graham, do *not* believe a word she says."

She hangs up a moment later and I stare at the phone, dumbfounded. She didn't even deny it. She didn't even plead her case. She didn't apologize. And here it is, the other shoe that I knew would drop on my perfect, little life.

60

Liza

"What'd she say?" I ask. "She's on her way..."

I look at the clock and sigh—it's clearly going to be a long night. I start a pot of coffee and change into a pair of Graham's sweatpants and t-shirt. He looks empty and deranged sitting on the couch, staring at the wall with a whiskey in his hand. I think about the restaurant; I'm pretty sure that's the same woman we saw there.

Had she been following us? It would explain how she found out where we lived. I pour myself a cup of coffee and sit in the recliner chair in front of him. I pick up my phone and send a text to Selle.

Liza: *Explain now.*

Selle: *I'll be there with Mom. We're not far away. Be there in ten.*

"They'll be here in ten minutes," I tell him. He chugs the last bit of his whiskey and stands. He's wearing my favorite charcoal suit as he sheds the coat and hangs it up. Rolling his sleeves up, he pours another whiskey before throwing that one back with ease as well. I bite my lip as I watch him pace again.

"Sit down," I say, feeling completely uncomfortable.

"I'll sit if you agree to talk to me."

"I am talking to you."

"You know what I mean, Elizabeth." I stare at the fire that's going and tuck my legs underneath me. I don't correct him when he calls me by my full name like I usually would. I don't want to fight with him, now just isn't the time. He just found out life changing news. And while I don't think his biological mother will be in our lives, I know there has to be a part of him that is curious. She gives off a dangerous vibe, but then again, so does Graham.

"There's nothing to talk about. Your ex came to see you. She was photographed leaving your building looking pretty flushed and freshly fucked. You didn't think to tell me. We're fine."

"Wait...tell me you don't think I actually fucked her." I turn away from him, looking at the floor. He yanks my chin up to look at him. "You think I fucking *cheated* on you?"

I don't answer him, instead I tuck my lip in my mouth and glance away.

"Answer me."

"No."

"No what, Elizabeth?"

"No, I don't think you cheated on me."

"Fucking liar."

He stalks away from me and heads upstairs to our room. A moment later I hear the door slam and the shower start. *What is wrong with me?* He'd never cheat on me. Whoever sent me those photos are getting exactly what they want, me jumping the gun and silently accusing Graham of doing things I know he'd never do to me.

I sit my cup of coffee down and sigh, looking up at the ceiling. Everything was going so well, I should have known it wouldn't last. We're supposed to have our engagement party on Saturday and now it's the furthest thing from my mind. We ironed out the last details this morning and everything was ready for the party, but what if there isn't one? I just accused my fiancé of cheating on me, someone who just asked me to spend the rest of my life with him. He probably thinks I don't trust him.

This night is shit.

The doorbell rings and I check the peephole, seeing Madeline and Selle outside.

"Why didn't you just use your key?" I ask, opening the door for them. Madeline kisses my cheek and Selle hugs me. "I'm sorry. It wasn't my place to say who she was..." Selle says. I nod, closing the door behind them.

Madeline's eyes are bloodshot red. Her normally perfect face is bare of makeup and her hair is in a messy bun. I've never seen her this way, but even now she's beautiful, flawless. "I made coffee," I say, handing her a cup. She gives me a small smile. "I'll go get him."

The shower is still going when I step into the steam filled bathroom. Graham is under the shower head with water pouring down his face, his head hanging down, taking deep breaths. Both hands are pressed against the wall and his shoulders are shaking a bit. *He's crying.* I weigh my options: I could comfort him, admit I was wrong and tell him I'm here for him, or I could give him his space and wait for him in the room.

I'm a coward and chose the latter, sitting on the bed and

waiting for him to come out. Five minutes later, he comes out of the shower with his towel wrapped around his waist. He pulls out a t-shirt and sweats, dropping the towel and ignoring my existence as he gets dressed.

"They're here." He nods, not even looking at me as I'm talking.

"Graham..."

"Don't. Not right now."

"I didn't mean to—"

"Elizabeth, I mean it. I'm so pissed at you right now. I can't be responsible for my actions if you keep talking."

"*You're* pissed?! You have nothing to be pissed about with this. Did I have *my* ex visit me while you were gone? Did you see photos of *me* leaving someone's building wearing a fucking trench coat and heels?" His eyebrows crease and he tilts his head.

"What?" he asks.

"What do you mean, *what*? How the fuck do you think it made me feel when I saw that? AND YOU DIDN'T TELL ME!" He ignores me and picks up the photos that are on the nightstand next to the bed. He shakes his head and smirks. "What is funny right now?" I demand.

"These are old photos. Because she was *not* wearing that when she came today." He throws the photos down on the bed and glares at me. I look down and bite my lip in embarrassment, but how could I have known?

"Which doesn't excuse the fact that you would think for a second I'd stick my dick in anyone besides you."

61

Graham

"I'm sorry..." she starts.

"Explain to me why you're marrying someone you don't trust." She lifts her teary eyes to me and swallows hard. "Answer me, Elizabeth. Why are you fucking marrying me if you don't trust me?"

"I do trust you."

"Lies, again." I turn for the door, but she grabs my wrist, stopping me. "I do, Graham. It's just...sometimes I just get in my own head. I'm constantly waiting for the ball to drop, for something to shatter what we have, or someone to shatter it. I just thought, maybe..."

"Maybe, what?"

"That maybe she made you see that she's the better choice. That she fits better." I grind my teeth at her words and take a deep breath.

When it rains it fucking pours.

"Elizabeth...I'm saying this once and only once. I've spent our entire relationship doing nothing but worshiping *you*, focusing only on *you*, what *you* need, what *you* want, what makes *you* happy, and being the kind of man *you* deserve. I've worked my ass off to eliminate any threats that come for us. I've worked my ass off to show you that I may not deserve you, but that I still wasn't. Letting. You. Go. But that still isn't enough, is it? You still don't believe in us. You said it was me, but it's *you*." I shake my head; I can't do this right now. I can't give her what she needs when right now it's *me* who needs her strength. I can't be strong enough for both of us right now. My mother just returned from the goddamn dead and I have no idea what I'm going to hear when I get downstairs.

"You know what, I'm not doing this right now. Maybe we need to think about our futures apart instead of together. I can't keep fighting you. You think so negatively about me, even when you say you don't. You have things you need to figure out and I have two women downstairs who need to explain to me why the fuck I've thought my mother was dead for my entire life." I pull out of her hold, glaring at the ring on her finger, and open the door. If looks could kill I'd be dead on the floor.

"We are *not* breaking up. So you can take everything you just said and fucking *choke* on it. You're mad and that's fine, but if you think for a second that I'm leaving you or you're leaving me, you really have no goddamn clue who you proposed to." She puts her hands on her hips and I try to hide the smirk that's threatening to show on my face. *That's my girl.* I admit, I didn't expect her to stand up to me. I expected her to stay quiet, think about it, and then come back fire burning.

She raises her eyebrow and waits for my response. I clear my throat and quickly wrap my hand around her throat, pushing her against the wall. "Tell me, who did I propose to then?" Her pulse quickens under my fingers and I tighten around her throat. "Did I propose to a runner?" She shakes her head. "Did I propose to a liar?" She shakes her head again. "Did I propose to someone who doubts me?" Another shake. Her eyes fill with tears and they spill over. "Want me to tell you who I think I proposed to?" She rolls her lips and I run my free hand down her cheek as she gasps for air. I loosen my hold on her throat briefly, just long enough for her to catch a breath.

Tightening again I tell her, "I think I proposed to someone who is used to running from *everyone*. Someone who is used to having to lie to keep her feelings safe. I proposed to someone who, unfortunately, is used to having to doubt not only the people in her life, but herself." I put my mouth to her ear and her breath hitches. "And I undoubtably proposed to the love of my fucking life." I let go of her throat and she drops to her knees in front of me, gasping for breath. "Don't ever question whether or not I'd cheat on you, Elizabeth. I won't be doubted in our relationship and sure as fuck won't be doubted in our marriage."

She looks up at me, her hands rubbing her neck. I crouch down in front of her and run my finger down her cheek, taking a deep breath. "I'm sorry," I say. She croaks again and I wipe the tear from her face before planting a kiss on her lips. It's quick, motionless, and feels foreign. I'm so pissed with this woman, but I'd never leave her in this state. I help her up and pull her to me in a tight hug. "Figure your shit out, angel...please."

We'll make up appropriately later. Right now, I need answers from the women I thought I could trust the most.

"Graham," Selle says, walking over to me. I hold my hand up to her and walk past her, fixing myself another drink. A drink I'm sure I don't need, but I do it anyway. Elizabeth comes downstairs and looks just as empty as I feel. It rips me apart, but I can't focus on it right now. I sit in the recliner and stare at my mother.

"Start talking." I throw the drink back and my mom audibly swallows.

"Graham," Liza growls. I glare at her. "She's your mother, " she says. I take a deep breath before turning my attention back to my mom.

"She was having an affair with your father," my mom starts. "We were trying for a baby, but for some reason kept failing. I had two miscarriages before we decided we'd just let it go. The problem with that was your father stopped touching me all together. He started coming home late and smelling like perfume that absolutely wasn't mine. When I questioned him about it, he told me, 'I'm doing this for you, so you can get what you want.' I didn't understand what he was talking about until he showed me the ultrasound of you." Selle sits next to her with her hand on my mother's leg. Liza is behind her, with her finger dangling on the side of her lip. She's watching me, waiting for my reaction.

"I planned on leaving him. I met with the lawyer and got everything in order to leave. But then he told me that you were for me and that it would never happen again. I was stupid, naïve, and believed him. After all, I wanted a baby, and after the miscarriages and the failed year's attempts, I assumed it'd never happen for me the normal way..." She takes a deep breath and looks at me, wiping her tears. "He ended things with her and she tried to kill herself. She tried to take you away from me before you were even here. Your father had her committed until she gave birth. Once she gave birth she visited him at his office, telling him that she never wanted you. She just wanted him and she'd kill you if he didn't take her back."

"Mom…" Selle says. My mom pats Selle's leg and gives her a small smile.

"Anyway, he asked her what he needed to do to keep her away. Neither of us were surprised that it was money. He gave her what she asked for, but she didn't stay away. Like I said, it wasn't about you. It was never you she cared about." She takes a long pause, crossing her legs. She takes a deep breath before she continues.

"She tried to kill you, twice. She snuck into our house when you were six-months-old and stabbed you. Ellis heard the alarm go off and shot her. The second time, she came for the both of us. Your dad was gone on business and you were about six-years-old at the time. I hadn't known she'd been visiting you at night, telling you who she was and that she wouldn't hurt you. But one night, she snapped. She tried to strangle me in front of you. The dreams you have, they aren't just dreams. They're memories."

I shake my head and my hand tightens around the whiskey glass. Liza notices and comes over to me. She sits on the arm of the chair and pulls my hand into her lap. I'm stuck in limbo—I can't believe what my mom is saying. I never knew how I got the scar on my back. Every time I asked my mom would always say, "You were a clumsy kid."

"What we didn't know was that you were becoming attached to her the more she visited you at night. So when she took you, you just went. She had you for three days. She left you in a room, only coming to check on you by giving you water and coloring papers. Your father and Ellis found you, and when they found her, she had slit her wrist and took a bunch of medications."

"How'd they find me?" I don't recognize my own voice as the words come out.

"She sent a picture to your father of her holding a knife to your neck with a location...I thought she was dead until last month when I started getting texts from her. Then she showed up at the house telling me that she would get her revenge on me taking Joe from her. She doesn't care about you; she's using you to get to me."

"Mom, why would you keep this from me?"

"You were healing. When I planned on telling you in Rome, you announced your engagement. I didn't want to worry you. I had already informed our security team and the police were aware with surveillance on the house. I wasn't expecting her to find you so quickly."

"That's what I don't understand...how did she find me?" I stand and run my fingers through my hair, thinking back to any moment I could've been vulnerable.

"Madison...her interview," Selle says. "She used the interview to trick you. She knew you'd wait to comment, she knew you'd set up a time to respond."

I think back to the day we arrived. I remember looking around for Madison, I remember looking around for anyone. There was a woman there dressed in all black wearing sunglasses, but I remember thinking she was with the press.

"I'm going to fucking kill her." I pull my phone out and send a text to Ralph and Ellis to come inside. I walk over to my mom as she's holding back tears. "It's not your fault. You were protecting me, I understand that. But do not lie to me again, Mother. My whole entire life I've been haunted by dreams; dreams about when we were taken and dreams about you being strangled. The dreams about Selle were different because I knew it happened, but those about you...from that night. My whole life I've tried to piece together any answers on why I kept having them."

"I'm sorry, honey. I'm so sorry, but you have to stay away from her. She's dangerous and she isn't going to stop until she gets to you; to our family."

"Guess what, Mom? I'm dangerous, too."

62

Liza

Graham is hugging his mom when Ellis and Ralph appear in the kitchen.

"Coffee?" I ask them. They both shake their heads, but I pour them both a cup anyway. "Take it, you know you both want to." They take the cup from my hands and I take a deep breath when Selle walks into the kitchen.

She looks back at Graham and her mom, pulling me into the hallway.

"Did you tell them we saw her?" she asks.

"I think *we* should. I'm not going to be the reason he's mad at me any further tonight."

"Wait, why is he mad at—never mind, not important. Just fix it before Saturday."

"How did you know who she was at the restaurant?."

"I stumbled upon a photo of her years ago in Dad's office and knew who she was. They look so alike, Liza. They have the same eyes and the same dark hair.I thought she was dead, as well; I'd never hide that from G. I thought I had to be mistaken when I saw her at the restaurant at first, but then I freaked out. I didn't want to tell you before I told him. I didn't want to put you in that position."

"I understand why you didn't say anything. It's ok." She wipes her eyes and nods. "But you need to tell him..."

"Tell me what?" We turn and see Graham leaning against the wall with his hands in his pockets. "What is it, Selly?"

"We saw her at the restaurant tonight, but that's not the first time..." she admits.

"Wait, what do you mean?" I ask.

"I saw her earlier today when I was picking up the flowers for the engagement party, I—I thought it was surely impossible that it was her. I was told the same story you were about her being dead. But then I saw her again at the restaurant and I knew. The way she was staring at us, I knew it was her. I guess she followed me, it's my fault...She knows where you live because of me. I'm —I'm sorry," she says, breaking out into tears. He engulfs her in his arms, closing his eyes and taking a deep breath.

"This is not your fault. She would've found me regardless. I don't care that she knows where I live, Selly, I care about your safety. You need to increase security. I don't know what this bitch will do to get to me or Mom." She nods her head and wipes her face.

"Call Eli, tell him you're staying here today, then go get some rest. It's late."

"Ok." She turns to me and I pull her into a hug. "Everything will be ok, Selle. Get some sleep," I say.

She turns to her brother and he gives her a small smile before nudging her towards her old room. "Love you."

"Love you, too, Selly. We're right down the hall and Mom is on the third floor with El." She nods. "I'm going to call Eli to come stay with me. I'll be ok," she says.

"Send Ralph to get him. I don't want anyone doing anything or going anywhere without security." She nods and walks to her room.

Moments later it's just Graham and me. I walk into the kitchen brushing past him as I cut the coffee off and pour the rest down the drain. I can feel him staring at me, how close he is to me. I gather my breath and turn around, coming face to face with him. He takes a deep breath and leans his forehead against mine. It's a normal thing he does when he needs to control himself, to control his anger. I didn't expect it, I expected him to ignore me for the rest of the night.

"Let's go to bed," he says. I nod, and as fast as he was standing in front me, he's gone a second later. My shoulder sags in defeat. I cut the lights off, leaving the lamp by the door on for my brother, and head upstairs.

Graham is already in bed, his back facing me when I climb in behind him. I lay on my back and stare towards the ceiling. This isn't us. I want to touch him, I want him to touch me. We have a *no going to sleep pissed off* rule, but I guess that doesn't matter tonight. We've never spent a night in bed together without sleeping entangled with each other.

The only way I can rest is if he's near. I have to be touching him. I have to have some piece of his skin on mine. I let out a sigh and turn on my side. I try to focus on the silence and turn off my inner thoughts.

"Stop thinking. I can hear your thoughts from over here. We're fine. Go to sleep."

"You haven't touched me...you always—" he turns over and faces me, cutting me off.

"I always what, Elizabeth...?" I flinch at him still using my full name.

"Please, don't call me that..." Except now I'm becoming irritated. He wants me to back down, to submit, to apologize? Well, I'm not doing it anymore. "You know what? Fuck you." I pull the covers off and start to move when a hand reaches around my middle and pulls me over.

"Stop," he growls. I try to move, but he tightens his hold on me.

"I want to take a bath, let me go."

"I'll take it with you," he huffs out, not giving me a chance to reject.

He watches me undress as he sits on the edge of the bathtub running the water. He doesn't add any of the lavender cinnamon salt and I frown.

"Aren't you going to put—"

"No, it'll burn your eyes," he says as he stands and undresses painfully slow.

"My eyes?"

"Yes, Elizabeth. You clearly need to be reminded of what's important.The only way you seem to remember that is when I've fucked the sense into you." My breathing hitches and my hand freezes on my panties. All I can think is what the fuck that has to do with my eyes. He stalks over to me, wraps his hand around my neck, and pushes me against the wall. My breath is constricted, but I know my eyes are matching the desire in his. "Don't be scared, you have your safe word. In here though, if you want me to stop, tap my arm twice. Get in the tub, Elizabeth." He releases his hold around my neck and yanks my panties down in one swift motion. "Now," he says when he's finished preparing the bath.

I climb into the oversized tub, which could almost pass as a hot tub. He climbs in after me and pulls me to him.

"Answer something for me, have you figured your shit out yet? Or do you need help? Because you're getting this punishment either way."

"You're acting like I mean nothing..." I say, my eyes swelling with tears. He runs his finger over my cheek and kisses me, bringing his mouth to my ear.He pushes my legs open to sink himself into me. I groan at his intrusion. He pushes further into me and I try to wrap my hands around him.

Instead, he gently bites my ear and whispers, "You're everything, now hold your breath." I don't have time to think about what he said before he pushes me under the water while thrusting himself harder and harder in and out of my pussy. I thrash around, unable to focus on anything other than the fact that he's drowning me, no, fucking me? I don't fucking know. He yanks me up and I cough, clutching onto him for dear fucking life.

"Graham!" I cough out. He smooths my hair out of my face and kisses me long enough to forget how deep his cock is seated inside of me.

"Breathe and focus. We're going to try it again okay?"

"Wait. What do I do?"

"Enjoy getting fucked by your fiancé underwater; enjoy giving me the power of having your life in my hands. Enjoy knowing that at the end of this, you're going to have the orgasm of your fucking life."

I swallow and my pussy tightens around his cock. He groans and smirks. "That turns you on, huh?" I nod because a part of me wants to see just how far I can go, how much I can handle.

"What's your safe word?"

"Lilies," I whisper.

"What do you do for your safe word when we play with water?"

"Tap on your arm twice."

"Good girl, now hold your breath. This time you're not coming up until you come all over my cock."

Seconds later, I'm back underwater. I tell myself to relax, that he won't hurt me, and he won't let me drown. I hear him in the distance over my heart beat. "Open those fucking eyes and watch me fuck you while you beg for air."

My eyes fly open and he looks feral, his thrust is so deep and slow at first, but when my back involuntarily arches, his speed picks up. My body is going through so many emotions. My chest is tight, but the ache in my pussy is more than worth chasing. So I focus on that, because I don't know how long I've been underwater, but I know my lungs burn. I truly feel like I'm seeing stars. Graham inserts two fingers into my pussy and praises me, "Be a good girl and come for me. Come on my cock, angel." I know I'm having an orgasm so fucking good that I'm in a state of euphoria. I don't register him pulling me up from the water, all I can feel right now is my body shaking and me coming so hard that it's still going.

Graham is pumping in and out of me with his hands tangled in my hair.

"I'm filling this pretty cunt up with my cum, and then you're going to come back to your senses and realize that if it's not you, I don't fucking want it."

I'm unable to form words because the orgasm is still fucking going. He thrusts in and out of me and when I feel the warmth of him inside me, I moan.

He kisses me and pushes my wet hair out of my face.

"Ok?" he asks.

I nod. "Yeah."

"You did good. So fucking good." He kisses my nose and I lean into him. His arms wrap around me and I cry. I cry hard. He pulls us out of the water, taking his time to dry my body. He brushes my hair and places small kisses on my shoulder before pulling one of his shirts over my head and depositing me into the bed.

He runs a hand over my face and sighs.

"You know how you felt under water? Like you couldn't breathe, like you were clawing your way out of darkness trying to reach the light?" I nod and he continues, "That's what loving you feels like; like I can't fucking breathe and like I'm chasing every piece of darkness away from you because you are my fucking light. Don't ever second guess that again, ok?"

"Ok..."

"Sleep, Elizabeth," he says in a raspy voice, but he turns his back on me once again. For the first time, I truly feel like I was used to be fucked. My heart shatters that we are right back to where we started tonight.

Maybe things aren't ok yet.

63

Graham

My alarm clock goes off at 6:00 a.m. like usual, but I'm exhausted. My body is spent and my head is all over the fucking place. I'm not mad at my mom for not telling me she wanted me to finally be happy. I understand why she didn't. My head is all over the place because Annika, my biological mother, thinks we're meeting today. If I see her I'll kill her. If she thinks for a second I'd chose her over my mother, she's fucking stupid.

I roll over, ready to kiss Liza good morning and tell her I'm sorry, but she's not there. Instead, there's a note on her pillow.

Spending the day with my dad. See you at the engagement party. Love you.

–Liza

The engagement party isn't until tomorrow. If she thinks she's not going to see me for an entire day, she's fucking crazy. I pick up my phone and send her a quick text.

Graham: *Why didn't you wake me?*

Not even a minute later she responds.

Liza: *You needed to sleep, you had a long night.*

Graham: *Come home, I'll work here today instead of the office.*

Liza: *No can do, Daddy/daughter day today. Go to work, you are already missing two days in New York because of me.*

I sigh at her reply. It didn't set me back much, I had everything in place. I only went because I wanted to see how the renovations were going; I could do everything else from my office here. Before I can respond, she texts again.

Liza: *Besides, I think we could use a day to clear our heads.*

That gets my attention.

I call her immediately… "Hello?"

"Did you fall and bump your head, angel?"

"What are you talking about?"

"We don't need a day to clear our minds, not when it comes to us. We argued, it happens in relationships. We're fine."

"Graham, you didn't want to touch me last night after our *bath*. You barely even looked at me before you turned your back again. You made me feel used. Clearly we're not fine." I sigh and secretly hate myself for how cold I was with her yesterday.

"I would never use you in that way. You thought I cheated on you…it hurt. I can deal with a lot of things, Elizabeth. I can deal with my mother coming back from the dead, I can deal with my parents lying to me my entire life, but what I can't deal with is the woman I'm marrying questioning my loyalty to her and our relationship."

"I'm sorry. You were just so…cold. When I saw your eyes, I didn't see love anymore, I saw anger."

"I was angry, Elizabeth, but not entirely with just you. I was angry with myself for not telling you right away. I was angry that I didn't think about the chances of her showing up. I was angry that I wasn't better prepared for what she could do. It wasn't just you, it was me, too."

"Are you meeting with Annika today?" She changes the subject and I'm grateful for it. I stretch out on the bed, crossing my legs and shrug.

"I'm not sure. I don't have anything to say to her. I know she'll just lie and now I know she just wants to hurt my mom."

I have to admit, hearing that I was a ploy to keep my dad with her hurt more than I expected it to. I mean, I knew my mom didn't want me, but I had no idea it was because my dad didn't want *her.* When my mom told me the story last night, the only thing that truly surprised me was that she tried to kill me multiple times. That tells me that she grew desperate, and when people are desperate, they do unconventional things. When I told Annika last night that my father was dead, she showed no reaction other than that evil tilt of smile she briefly gave.

I can hear Axel in the background. "Why are you two awake so early?" I ask.

"Dad always wakes up this early. I left around 5:00 a.m. He said he wanted to catch the sunrise, then we're going to breakfast, and to um..."

"To what?"

"To pick your ring out." I smile at the thought of her ring shopping for me. My phone buzzes again, bringing me out of my thoughts.

Unknown: *Meet me in thirty minutes, I know you're awake.*

"Well, have fun and be safe, I've gotta go. I'll see you tonight. Not tomorrow, you come home after you're done. Understand?"

"Ok, see you tonight." I hang up and text the unknown number back.

Graham: *Send me the location and don't waste my time.*

I know I shouldn't be doing this. I know this woman is dangerous and I know she has it out for my mom. But I'm intrigued; I have questions I need answered and I need to look her in her face and see just how dangerous she really is.

Thirty minutes later I'm pulling up to the downtown park. I sit on the bench and wait like she told me to. El and Ralph are both at tables in view of the bench and I have two snipers on the buildings above. If she tries anything with me, she'll be dead before she knows what hit her.

"I didn't think you'd show up. I know your *mother* told you to stay away from me."

I look up and freeze—I look just fucking like her. I always thought I looked like my dad, especially my grandfather, but when I look at her, I see my dark hair and my eyes. It's almost sickening. She gives me a smirk and tilts her head to the side, looking me up and down.

"Look at you. All grown up."

"What do you want, Annika?" She gives me a sad frown and then sits down. She crosses her legs and leans back, letting out a deep breath.

"You said your father was dead, that's not on my radar. Is that the truth or are you lying?"

"He's dead. I watched him blow up into a million pieces." She fidgets a bit. She does it quickly, but I catch it. I smile inside. *Bingo.* "That's what this is about? Don't tell me you're still pining over a man who didn't choose you?"

"Shut up. You know nothing."

"I know enough. I know that you were a surrogate that got too fucking attached. I know you were my dad's fuck toy that just had to have more. I also know that you tried your damnedest to kill me. Tsk, tsk. Seeing you yesterday, I thought maybe I got my wit from you," I say, turning towards her, "but clearly that's not the case." She grinds her teeth and I chuckle. "Now that," I point to the face she's making, "*that* I did get from you. Now, tell me what you want now that you know there's no chance of getting Daddy dearest back."

"Same thing I wanted back then."

"Money?"

"Your mother. Dead. Then I'll be happy and leave you alone for the rest of your miserable, little life."

"See, here's the thing, I can't let you do that. So, I'm going to make you a deal. I'll pay you a half of million to fall off the face of the fucking planet. Don't come near me or my family again. You took the money before; you'll take it again."

"I only took it because your father made me, I didn't want it. I wanted you and him." I grind my teeth, just like she did before and shake my head. My blood starts to boil. The lies I'm hearing through her teeth is pissing me off.

"You didn't want me."

"Yes, I did. Why do you think I willingly got pregnant?"

"Because you wanted to trap my father."

"I wanted you, Graham. I wanted to be your mom. But they took you away from me, made me think I was crazy, and then sent me away when I tried to come around and tell you who I was. That family, *your* family, they're monsters. They lie, they kill people, and they cover up the truth if it doesn't benefit them."

I watch her as she talks. Is she telling the truth? My mom said last night that she didn't want me, that she tried to kill me. My head is spinning. I'm going through everything my mom said last night. I'm struggling on who to believe.

"You tried to kill me...twice."

"It was an accident; it was just supposed to scare your mom enough for her to let me leave with you." I shake my head—that's not true. My mom would never lie to me to that extent. She'd never keep me away from my biological mom if she wasn't dangerous. I catch movement out of the corner of my eye and Annika sees it, too

Again, I would've missed it, but her body language gave it away. *She's fucking playing me.* I keep my composure; she thinks she's got me. I see a man pull a weapon out of his red coat and fasten a silencer on.

"My mom, she lied to me?" I ask, turning towards her. She nods and I grab her hand. "I always asked about you. I had dreams about you coming to visit me when I was small. They always told me it was my imagination."

"Let's take them down together. They don't deserve to keep breathing after what they've done to us. They robbed me of twenty-six years with you."

I yank her to me, pulling my own gun out and pressing it into her stomach. To passers it would appear that we're hugging, everyone oblivious to what's happening around them.

"I guess that's something else I inherited from you. Bluffing." She chuckles in my ear, the same evil chuckle I have, and it sends chills down my spine. "Tell your friend over there to leave or I'll shoot you in your fucking gut."

"You wouldn't." I cock the gun in response and push it where her heart is.

"Try me." Ellis and Ralph are already closing in on the guy on my left and I see another behind Annika. She raises her hand and they both stop, retreating. "Good Mother." I pat her back and put my gun away.

"Here's what's going to happen. You're going to take the money and I'm never going to see you again. If I do, I'll kill you. I don't take threats to my family well. I don't make threats like you, I make promises."

She gives me an evil smile and raises her eyebrow. "I should've killed you the moment I laid eyes on you."

"Yeah, you should've. Don't let me see your face again, *Mother*." She finches at me calling her that and I secretly get the closure I needed. My whole life I wondered what she was like. I wondered if she missed me or thought about me before she "killed herself." I got my answers today; she was going to have me taken out in the middle of a fucking park.

"I don't know if that's a promise I can keep. I always get what I want," she says. I laugh as she starts walking away, the two men following behind her. I yell out as she's leaving, "You didn't get Dad." She grinds her teeth again and keeps walking.

Fucking bitch.

64

Liza

"Lizzie, you've got to relax," my dad says as I down the shot of tequila. My father finally found a place up to par for him. I'm pacing back and forth, checking my phone every five seconds.

I haven't talked to Graham all day and it's unsettling. I've called him twice and he hasn't answered. It makes me worry and I'm trying my hardest not to.

"He always answers, Dad. Something's wrong."

"Why don't you try one more time, you've only called twice." I nod my head and try him again. It goes to voicemail. I throw my phone across the floor and plop on the couch.

"Maybe he's still mad at me."

"Remind me, why was he mad at you again?" I sigh and tell my father the whole story of how I all but accused him of cheating. I tell him how stupid I feel and how off we've been since I did it.

"I already apologized; I can't do anything else to fix it." He sits next to me and pulls me into his side.

"Lizzie...if you're going to marry him you have to trust him. There's nothing else you can do about this. He'd never hurt you. It'll all work out."

"He has to answer his phone, Dad. He was supposed to meet with Annika today."

"Who is Annika?"

"His biological mother, she's dangerous." He raises his eyebrow and I nod. "Yup, turns out she's not dead after all."

"This fucking family..."

"I'm going to call Ellis, see if he knows." He answers on the first ring, just like I knew he would. He wasn't happy about me deciding not to take Ralph with me.

"Ms. Crambell, everything alright?"

"Where is he, El?" I hear shuffling and then doors opening. "He's here. He's sleeping." I let out a sigh of relief. "He'll need you; it was a very...disturbing conversation."

"He needs rest. He hasn't slept in two days, El."

"He'll look for you when he wakes up, you know that."

"We both know that if I'm there he won't sleep. Especially if the conversation didn't go well. He probably threatened her, and if I come home, he'll stay up all night to make sure I'm safe. He needs the sleep, El, but watch him, please. I'll be home in the morning."

"Of course, I'll see you in the morning."

"I'm crashing here tonight, Dad." He smiles at me and nods. "So he's ok?"

"Yeah, he's sleeping." I look at the time on my phone. 10:47 *p.m.* I let out a yawn and lay my head back on the couch. "I guess I'm tired, too."

"Working yourself up will do that to you. Get some rest, Lizzie. I'm sure you have a long day ahead tomorrow. Your mom has already sent out tasks to the group chat for tomorrow. I hate to see how she'll be on the wedding day." He kisses my forehead and we both head to bed.

When I climb in bed, I check my phone and sure enough, my mom has sent sixteen messages telling everyone their roles for tomorrow. I type out a message to the group chat.

Liza: *Mom, I just want everyone to have fun. Relax, it's not the wedding.*

Elias is the first one to respond.

Eli: *Yeah, Mom, relax. You're really screwing up my Netflix and chill time with Giselle.*

Liza: *Ew.*

Hogan's message comes in shortly after.

Hogan: *I can tell you right now they are definitely not watching Netflix.*

Mama: *Boys! I am not interested in your sex life! No one can be late tomorrow or I'll have your balls! Love you all, goodnight. Elizabeth, get some rest. No bags under those eyes tomorrow!*

I roll my eyes and shoot Graham a text, hoping it won't wake him.

Liza: *I'll see you in the morning, I love you.*

Moments later I feel sleep pulling me under.

The sound of my phone ringing pulls me out of sleep. I look at the clock on my nightstand. *4:00 a.m.*

"Hello?" I ask in a groggy voice.

"Why aren't you home?" Graham's voice comes through short, clipped and enraged.

"You were finally sleeping."

"I sleep better when you're here."

"Not when you are worried about my safety..." He takes a deep breath and is quiet for a few moments.

"When are you coming home?"

"In the morning, Ralph will be here at seven to pick me up."

"Fine. I'll see you in the morning."

He hangs up before I can respond and I decide right then and there that we are done being mad at each other. We're done being cold with each other. When I get home in the morning, we're going to fix this.

This will be fun.

65

Graham

Our house is full of caterers and florists. My mother insisted on having the engagement party here. She said the backyard was perfect with the fall weather working in our favor. What she did not mention is that the fucking set up was starting at 6:00 a.m.

I opened the door expecting it to be Liza, instead it was my mother, Bethany, and the florists.

"Good morning, honey, I know it's early. You go right back to sleep, you won't even know we're here."

"Mom, the party isn't until 6:00 p.m., that's twelve hours away. What could possibly take eleven hours to do?"

"We have over five hundred lights to hang, we have to turn the backyard into a luxurious place for dinner tonight, and we have to arrange the flowers. Not to mention the chefs will be here at 9:00 a.m. to start the food. Trust me, it'll take the entire eleven hours. But don't you worry, they'll be gone from 12:00 p.m. to 2:00 p.m. for a lunch break." I shake my head and walk back up the stairs, ignoring her calls after me. I shut the door and faceplant back onto the bed.

This is going to be a long fucking day. I must be tired because I find myself drifting back off to sleep moments later.

"Graham...wake up." I pry my eyes open and Liza is sitting on the bed, nudging my shoulder. "Why are there so many people in our house at eight in the morning?"

"Ask our mothers," I say, stretching out. She shakes her head and stands, stripping out of her clothes and climbing into bed.

"I'm still tired. I snuck in; I don't want them putting me to work yet." I chuckle at her and pull her into me. I inhale her scent, I missed her. This is the first time we've laid together entangled. We've been...off since I left for New York and I want to fix it. But there's no way I'm letting a house full of strangers hear her moans. They are strictly for me.

"Sleep. I'll fight the wolves off for an hour, but then you're coming to save me." I kiss her forehead and climb out of the bed.

* * *

My mother was right—it did take eleven hours to do this shit. We're thirty minutes away from when people will start arriving and all of the women in this house are running around, barking last minute orders at everyone. Liza didn't get that hour I promised her. Her mom saw her sneak in and all but practically dragged her out of bed.

"Ok, honey, last thing then you can go get dressed. Where do you want these loose flowers? The florist was thinking of adding them around the trees outside in between the lights."

"That sounds fine, Mom. Can you please let me get dressed

now?" Liza asks, heading towards the stairs. I chuckle at them both and she glares at me. Elias laughs. We're all already dressed, it's just her and Selle who are not. To their defense, every time they tried to sneak away, my mother or Bethany would have another task for them.

"So, I heard you met your bio mom," Eli says. I nod my head and lean back on the couch.

"I did. It was a shit show."

"Yeah? Is she someone we should be worried about? Selle was pretty shaken up that night. Said she's dangerous and tried to kill you."

"Yeah, seems like that's the only kind of people I attract." We both laugh and Hogan brings over a bottle of whiskey with three glasses.

"Well, here's to you not dying...again," Hogan says. We throw back our whiskey and my mother comes barreling around the corner.

"Absolutely not. You three *will not* be drunk before the party even starts."

"Mother, relax," I say, pouring us all another one. She snatches the bottle out of my hand.

"You better enjoy that one." I smirk at her and throw it back again, looking at the time.

I stand to head upstairs when I see *her* walking down them. I stop in my tracks because fuck, she's beautiful. She's wearing a short, white sweetheart dress that should be fucking illegal with the way it hugs every inch of her body. Her long hair tumbles over her shoulders.

"Do I look ok?" she asks, stopping in front of me as she looks over herself. She goes to fix her hair and I stop her. "You look perfect, leave it." She smirks and joins her brother on the couch.

Two hours later our house is full of people and we're being bombarded with congratulations every ten seconds. I haven't had a chance to have Liza to myself all day, and after our fight, I'm craving it. She's still being distant and I don't like it.

"Hey, G," Selle says, bumping shoulders with me. I wrap my arm around her and tuck her into me.

"Hey, sis." I catch a glimpse of Liza with Hogan and Eli dancing. She's laughing; it's been too long since I heard that sound. It makes me happy to see her smiling again.

"You two are weird today. What happened?"

"We're fine…"

"Tell me."

"Madison. She sent Liza pictures of her leaving my building. Let's just say how she looked in the pictures weren't exactly *put together*." I watch Liza while I tell Selle what happened. Out of the corner of my eye Selle shakes her head and turns to me.

"She knows you'd never cheat on her. She was probably shocked, overwhelmed. Even though I know Elias would never cheat on me, if I got pictures like that and his ex looked like she had just been fucked, I would've had the same reaction. She probably thinks you're still mad at her…just go fix it. I'll cover for you." She shoves me away and I smile at her, giving her a quick kiss on her cheek.

66

Liza

Graham looks so good tonight, and every time I'm watching him, he's watching me. We haven't had time to talk since the fight, other than him telling me we're fine that night. We haven't touched each other, besides be getting fucked in the tub, which feels foreign and just not right. Last night he hung up without telling me he loved me, which he never does. Maybe I'm thinking too much into it. He told me I was perfect today and he was happy to see me this morning.

"Gentlemen, I need my fiancée for a moment." I look up and Graham is raising his eyebrow at me, waiting for me to take his hand. I hold back my smirk and place my hand in his.

"Make sure to keep it down if you're going to do what I think you're going to do," Eli says. I elbow him as I walk past and he laughs.

He guides me upstairs and shoves me into the bathroom of our room. "I'm tired of not feeling close to you today." He crushes his lips on mine and I groan in response, at the first sign of true emotional connection again. *Finally.* "This little act of you being mad at me, I'm done with it." He sits me on top of the counter and yanks my dress up, pulling my panties to the side.

"Graham, we have people..." I say like I truly care, but I don't. I need this. I need to feel like we're normal, like we're us.

"I don't care, I need you." He unzips his pants, and a second later, he's thrusting inside of me.

"I'd *never* use you for just sex." He sounds broken.

I wrap my arms around him as he thrusts harder and deeper into me.

"I'd *never* cheat on you." He thrusts again and I moan, pushing my hand into his hair.

"I know, I'm sorry." I say, my voice breaking.

"You're my fucking world, Elizabeth." He starts pumping in and out of me, faster and faster. He lifts me and I wrap my legs around his waist as he pushes my back against the wall. He wraps his hand around my neck before impaling himself in me again. "Only you."

"Graham..." Tears well in my eyes and I feel stupid. How could I ever doubt this man? How could I ever think he'd do something to ruin this, to ruin us? He fucks me harder and I moan louder, not caring who may hear us. My body starts to shake and I know I'm right there. Graham's speed increases and he digs his nails into my throat. I can't breathe and it's intoxicating. I'm coming so hard I think I'll pass out. I can feel the warmth of his cum inside of me before he releases my neck. I suck in a breath as he pulls out of me. He steadies me before grabbing a washcloth and cleaning me.

"You ok?" he asks, pushing a piece of my hair behind my ear. I nod, giving him a small smile. He cups my face and kisses me. "I'm not mad at you, angel. I'm sorry, too." The tears spill over my face and I bury my face into his chest, finally feeling like we're us again. "Hey, no tears. You know I hate it."

"We're ok?" I ask through blurry eyes.

"Of course, we're ok." He kisses my nose and smiles at me. "But, we won't be if our mothers find out that we're missing, though."

"I need to fix myself, I look like I've just been fucked." I turn to the mirror and he wraps his arms around my waist.

"You look beautiful. Let's go"

When we get back to the party, I stop at who I see next to the bar. I look up at Graham and he spots her immediately. He grinds his teeth and I know he's pissed. Selle is in front of her and I know she's probably giving her complete hell.

I'm moving before I realize it. "What the fuck are you doing here?" I ask Madison. She smirks at me and finishes the rest of her champagne.

"What do you mean? I'm just here to give my congratulations to the happy couple. After all, that's what your fiancé here told me I had to do. Or he'd 'ruin my miserable little life.'" I move Selle back and stand face to face with Madison. She's a bit taller, but I stand my ground.

"Listen, you crazy fucking bitch. It won't be him that ruins your life, it'll be *me*. Get your shit and get the hell out of my house." She steps closer to me, narrowing her eyes at me.

"Or what?" she taunts.

I snap. My fist flies at her face and I can't stop it even if I wanted to. Blood splatters out of her nose and her head jerks back as I send another blow to her face. I bend down to her face and yank her hair, bringing us face to face. I hear my mother in the back, yelling my name.

"I promise you, I'm crazier than you think. Stay the fuck away from us." I stand up and smooth my dress down. "Mom, don't give yourself a heart attack. Madison here was just letting herself out." Graham has a smirk on his face and places his hand on my lower back, guiding me to the backyard with the rest of our guests.

"That was fucking hot," he whispers in my ear. I roll my eyes at him and shake out my hand. *Fuck, that hurt.*

"Need ice for that hand, slugger?" Eli asks, handing me an ice pack. Graham puts it on my hand and Eli laughs. "I didn't know you had it in you, sis."

"Yeah, well, she should've done it sooner," Selle says, slipping her arms around Eli's waist.

We're all dancing when we hear yelling from the kitchen. El and Ralph are moving faster than any of us can. Graham grabs my hand and I look around. Who's missing?

Madeline, where is Madeline?

67

Graham

I walk to the kitchen to see Annika holding a knife to my mom's throat. I push Liza behind me and train my eyes on Annika.

"How did you get in here?" I growl out. Madison rounds the corner with dried blood and a smirk on her face. She stands next to Annika and scowls at me.

"I told you that you'd regret it," she sneers.

I step forward and Annika presses the knife further into my mom's neck.

"Graham, don't," my mom says. El is already moving closer to the kitchen through the hallway. Annika can't see him, but I sure as fuck can. I turn to Liza and Selle, expecting them to be scared, but instead I'm looking at eyes seething in anger.

"Keep everyone outside, don't let anyone come in. Go." They both shake their heads. I look at Elias and he nods, pulling them both outside with him.

"Annika, I thought you were smarter than this. Even if you manage to kill my mom, I'm still going to kill you. Then I'm going to make good on my promise and ruin your little henchmen's life." Madison rolls her eyes and lifts herself onto the counter. "I'm just here for the money."

"Of course. How much?"

"Well, she's giving me five hundred thousand for tracking you down, giving her your address, and for luring your mom into the kitchen."

"I'll give you a million to walk away now and never let me see your fucking face again." She stops picking her nails and I know she's considering it.

"Lies," Annika says. She pulls a gun out of her jacket and points it at me. Ralph, and it looks like Axel, decide to join the fun, too. Annika starts moving my mom towards the hallway. Bad idea.

Madison climbs down off the counter and looks at Annika before looking back at me. She raises her eyebrow and smirks. "How do I know you aren't bluffing?"

"Because I'd pay anything to never have to see you again in my life." Annika grows anxious and starts yelling at me.

"I'll kill her right now! You're focused on the wrong fucking person."

"Fuck off. If you were going to kill her, you'd have done it already," I growl, walking closer to her.

"I want a million, Graham. Don't fucking play with me." I nod and Annika turns her gun on Madison, shooting her in the stomach. She screams and clutches her torso as she falls to the ground.

"She talks too fucking much. How did you ever deal with her?" Annika asks, blowing her hair out of her face. She puts the gun back on me and I focus on my mom.

"You're going to be ok, Mom." She has tears in her eyes, and before I know it, she rears her head back into Annika's. It's enough to slip out of her hold.

Annika starts firing her gun in my mom's direction. El yanks my mom into the hallway and I pull out my gun, shooting Annika.

I walk over to her and kick the gun out of her reach. Leaning down, I watch the blood pool out of her body. "I guess you really don't do threats," she coughs out. I raise my eyebrow.

"No, *Mother*, I don't. I guess I got that from Dad." She smirks at me and I sit next to her. I grab her hand and hold it. I rub her hair out of her face, waiting for her to take her last breath. I don't know why I do it, but I do. Moments later she's gone and I drop her hand.

"We have to stop making this a habit," Axel says, walking over to Madison. He feels her pulse and looks at me. "She has a pulse. It's faint, but it's there." Liza walks in and runs to me.

"What the fuck happened? Where is your mom?" I jump up, realizing neither my mom nor El have come from the hallway.

"Mom! Mom!" I yell. When I get to the hallway, I see El with his hand over her side. I run to her side and stare at her.

"I'm ok, honey, I'm ok." I look at El and his eyes are swelled with tears.

"Look at me, baby. The ambulance is on their way. You look at me, alright?" El says to her. She smiles and focuses on him. I rub her head and Liza rubs my back while we wait.

* * *

Mom was in surgery for an hour. The bullet went straight through which was a good thing. They told her it wasn't a serious injury and sent her home a week later. Madison also made it. When they told me that I transferred a million dollars to her account. I also found out that the pictures sent to Liza were from the door man that I fired. They were in fact old photos that Annika sent to him. She threatened his family if he did not send them to Liza and let Madison up to see me.

I reinstated his job and gave him a pay raise for the inconvenience. I also gave Ellis two weeks off to spend with my mom. He was a fucking mess the entire time she was in the hospital. He needed time with her and she needed to heal. Something told me that they'd help each other in that department.

Our house is currently a crime scene, so we're staying at the lake house. It's been nice, being away from the chaos and the news reporters.

Liza is stretched out on the couch, reading a book as I watch her from the doorway. She looks over her book and raises her eyebrow.

"Yes?"

"What time do you have to leave?"

"The dress fitting is at four, so maybe in an hour or so."

"I can make do with that." I stalk over to her and swing her over my shoulder, carrying her upstairs. She laughs and I swat her ass before throwing her on the bed. "You have an hour to come as many times as you can. Ready?"

68

Liza

I, in fact, was not ready. He made me come six times in an hour. As I drive to his mother's house, my legs feel like noodles and I still can't catch my breath. It's been two weeks since the shitshow at our engagement party. I told Madeline she didn't have to come to the dress fitting, but she insisted. She said she was tired of Ellis treating her like she was dead.

Once we got her, my mom, Madeline, Selle, and Emily in the car, we headed to the boutique.

"Who's my bride?!" my consultant asks. I smile and raise my hand. "Oh, perfect! Ok, so I hear that this wedding is in two months now?" I scrunch my face up at the time frame and nod. "Lucky for you, I'm a miracle worker. Let's get you in some dresses."

The first dress she has me try on is a princess ball gown and I absolutely hate it.

"I don't want to show them this," I say, looking at myself in the mirror. She giggles.

"Just for fun?" she asks.

I shrug "Fine."

"Holy hell, you look ridiculous," Em says, choking on her champagne. Selle is laughing so hard she is crying and my mom refuses to look anywhere besides the floor.

"Mom, you can laugh. It's fine, I hate it, too." She sighs in relief while her and Madeline laughs. "Please, the next one," I say to the consultant, Brittany.

The next dress she puts me in takes my breath away. It has a low back with specs of lace throughout the front. The deep V-neckline fits perfectly around my breasts and the bottom is mermaid that flares out. There's shimmer throughout with hidden diamonds on the train. Tears are in my eyes as I stare at myself in the mirror.

Graham would love this.

"Shall we show them?" I wipe my face and smile at her.

"Yes." She helps me out of the dressing room. Selle is the first to see me and her eyes widen.

She whispers, "That's it."

I stand on the podium and face them. My mom is holding back tears and Madeline is smiling so hard I think she might break her face. Emily is staring at me and I smile at her.

"I think this is the one, Liza. You look so damn beautiful; he won't know what hit him," Em says. I wipe the tears from my face and they all nod in agreement. Brittany comes over and puts a veil on my head, turning me to the mirror.

I gasp at the reflection I see. "Oh my God." It hits me right then that I'm getting married. I'm marrying Graham in two months!

"This is it," I say to Brittany. She smiles. "Are you sure?" she asks. I nod. "Very well, you look stunning in it! It just so happens that this is your size. You can take the dress home today and we'll have two more fittings closer to the date."

I change into my normal clothes when my phone rings.

"Hi, baby," I say, zipping up my pants and sliding my heels on.

"Did you find a dress, angel?"

"Yes, I did."

"Good. Because how pissed would you be if I said I wanted to move the wedding up?"

"I'd say you've lost your mind, but I'd do it anyway because I can't wait to marry you." He chuckles and I laugh. "Please don't tell me that's what you're going to say, though," I check.

"No, I just wanted to check if you're as impatient as I am. Hurry home."

"Love you."

"Love you, angel."

As I come out my mom and Madeline are fighting over who's paying for the dress. I shake my head and get in between them.

"How about I pay for my own dress? Problem solved."

"No, absolutely not. Ma'am, are you able to split the payment?" Madeline asks. Brittany laughs.

"Yes ma'am, I can." She takes both of their cards and Selle laughs at them, walking over to me. She pulls me into a hug. "Graham's going to lose his shit when he sees you in that dress."

Emily butts in, "You mean when he gets her out of it." I swat her arm and we all laugh. Our life is finally coming back together.

The rest of the day was nice spending time with the girls and our moms. We did a little shopping and then got a nice lunch before we all headed back home.

"Finally," Graham says, pulling me the rest of the way through the front door.

"Can I see it?" he asks, looking over my shoulder.

"Yeah...in two months. It's at your mom's, I'm not risking you trying to peek." I pour myself a glass of wine and he pulls me into his arms, kissing my cheek. "How was your day?" I ask.

"Travis and your brothers just left. There's a lot of bachelor party talk going on these days. They're tired of me shooting down every idea they have."

"Are you being a groomzilla?" I turn in his arms and kiss his neck. He chuckles and lifts me, sitting me down on the oversized island. He lifts my shirt over my head and yanks his off after.

"I've been thinking about this since this morning." He unclasps my bra and pulls one of my breasts in his mouth, tugging on it. I push my hands through his hair and he plays with my other breast with his free hand. He tugs on the waistband of my pants. "Up," he commands. I raise up and he slides them off, taking my panties with. "It's been too long since I've worshiped this body of yours." He licks the side of my neck and I let out a moan. Then he licks me behind my ear before pulling it in his teeth and biting down.

"Graham..."

"Hmm?"

"Don't tease..." He chuckles and continues kissing down my body. He stops at my pussy and gives it a long, slow, tortuous lick. I pull his hair and he licks deeper, pushing his fingers in along with his tongue. I'm crumbling almost immediately; he always finds that sensitive spot. He tongue fucks me until I'm begging him to fuck me with his cock instead. He adds another finger as he laps his tongue up and down my folds, sucking as hard as he can. As he moves his fingers in and out of me, I clamp down on him, coming immediately. He continues sucking my juices as they pour out of me and I moan uncontrollably.

"Graham...fuck me."

"Not yet." I groan in response, my body feeling weak. He pulls his fingers out of me and shoves them into his mouth. "Such a good girl," he praises. He licks his lips and I wrap my legs around him, yanking him into me. "Impatient today, are we?" he asks.

"Shut up and fuck me."

"Careful what you ask for." I arch my eyebrow and he wraps his hand around my throat, cutting off my air. "You know, the first time I choked you, you came so hard I thought you were going to pass out on me. You enjoy being choked, angel? You enjoy having me in control of your breathing?" He tightens his hold as he thrusts inside of me in one swift motion.

I try to moan, but I can't with his grip around my neck. He pumps in and out of me and I want the release more than I want to breathe. My vision is blurry and I feel dizzy, but the viciousness of how he's fucking me feels too good, too real. I don't want it to end. "Breathe, baby," he whispers as he lets go of my throat. I gasp for a breath and he continues pumping in and out of me as I wrap my legs around him. His hand skates around my neck and he cuts off my air again. I'm so full of him and it's not enough. He adds a finger in as he fucks me. It pushes me so far over the edge I'm sure I'm passed out by the time my body convulses.

Fuck I can't wait to marry this man.

69

Graham

Liza is asleep in my arms and I'm playing in her hair when the phone rings. She groans and I reach over her, answering it.

"Salando."

"Mr. Salando, this is Detective Briggs. I'm just calling to let you know that you and your fiancé can return to your home now. The case has been closed." I let out a sigh of relief. Regardless of it being self-defense, I still killed Annika. I wasn't sure if my connections would be able to get me out of this one. The police force wasn't happy that they lost two of their officers during the shoot-out with Luke's guys to begin with. I guess their loyalty is better than I thought.

"Thank you, detective." Liza opens her eyes as I hang up and raises her eyebrows. "Wanna go home?" I ask. She smiles and nods. I kiss her forehead and call Ralph.

Three hours later we're pulling up to our house with Liza smiling as we park. The backyard is still decorated with the twinkle lights, but everything else is clean as a whistle. My mother told me she had a cleaning crew come while we were on the way here.

"It's so clean," Liza says, looking around. She stops in the kitchen and looks at the spot where Annika was. I wrap my arms around her and kiss her cheek. "You'd never know what happened here." She turns in my arms and kisses my nose, something that seems to be becoming our thing. "You ok?" she asks.

"More than ok."

"You sure?" I nod and kiss her. "Ready for work tomorrow?" she asks.

"Not the slightest. Speaking of, I need to show you something tomorrow," I say.

"Show me now." I chuckle and tuck a strand of her hair behind her ear.

"It's 9:00 p.m., angel. Tomorrow." She huffs and pulls away from me, pouting. I shake my head and grab my keys. "You have fifteen seconds to get your ass into the car before I change my mind." She laughs and shoots past me, grabbing her coat and purse. I laugh as I hear the car door open and shut. Damn, she's fast.

The last two weeks I'd been working on this surprise for Liza. I knew she wanted her own office and I knew how important it was to her to be her own boss, to have her own rules. So, I opened an office in my building for her.

When we get to my office building, she frowns. "My surprise is here?" I nod and round the car to open her door. I intertwine our fingers together and I kiss her hand as I walk us into the building. I have twenty-four hour security in my building, something that I instilled after the accident happened. I'm glad that I did, because I don't want to have to worry about her safety in here.

When we get to the elevator, I gesture for her to use her hand on the pad. "You added me?" she asks.

"I did." She places her palm on the scanner and the elevator closes. I hit level fourteen and she arches her eyebrow.

"What are you up to?" she asks. I smirk and the elevator dings a moment later. We step out and she gasps. The frosted window says *Elizabeth Salando* with *Licensed Psychologist* under it. I wrap my arms around her as she stares at the door. Her eyes are filled with tears and I dangle the keys in front of her.

"Wanna see your new office?" She turns and looks at me, nodding her head. I push her towards the door and she unlocks it, stepping inside. Her office is directly under mine, the end office with a killer view of the city. It's huge—she has a leather couch on the wall closest to the bathroom and a grey desk in the middle. She rounds the desk, sliding her fingers over it. She stops and looks at the photo I put on her desk of us. It was the photo the photographer took of us at my birthday party.

"Graham..." I lean against the door and watch her look around. She comes over to me. "Thank you, this is amazing."

"You'll need to hire some more people, you have the entire floor." Her eyes widen and I chuckle. "Don't worry, I already put ads out for two more psychologists and a few assistants."

"You really thought of everything."

"I just want you happy. Whether that's here or New York, you have options."

"You didn't..." she says, nudging me away. I pull her closer to me and wrap her in my arms.

"Your office is also waiting for you in New York." She kisses me hard and I kiss her back.

"I love you."

"I love you more."

"Not possible."

"Don't care," I growl in her ear. "Now how about we christen this office of yours?" I pick her up and throw her on the couch.

Fuck, am I lucky.

70

Liza

Two months later

Two months flies by when you're planning a wedding, starting a new job, and trying your best to fight off a fiancé who can't seem to stay away from you while you're supposed to be working.

When I started working, the positions for my floor filled quickly. My office was thriving, both in Seattle and New York. We went to New York one week out of the month so I could see clients there and still bond with the staff. I didn't want to be a hands-off boss and I didn't want them to feel like I was never around. I had an open-door policy which seemed to be working great.

Graham and I alternated days for lunch; one day he'd come to my office and the next I'd come to his. Most of the time it seemed like lunch turned into a fuck fest in our office, which was fine, except it always left me starving from skipping lunch.

Today is the last day of work for both of us before our wedding and I can't believe it's here already. I look at the clock and start shutting down my computer when he appears at my door in that fucking charcoal suit that I want to rip off him.

"Ready?" he asks. I smile at him and grab my things. He plants a kiss on my lips and leads me out.

"Happy wedding week, you two!" my assistant, Carrie, says as we pass her.

"See you Saturday, Car," I say to her as Graham nods at her. He's still learning to trust people around me, even though he did extensive background checks on all the staff before hiring.

El is waiting for us in his usual spot outside of the building, his gold wedding band shining on his finger. Him and Madeline eloped almost a month ago. Graham tried firing him twice already so that he could enjoy being married, but he refused to leave. I've never seen him so happy. He smiles more and I even got him to call me Liza for about a week before he went back to calling me Ms. Crambell.

"Ms. Crambell," he says, opening the door for me. I squint my eyes at him. Graham chuckles and pushes me in.

"When will he stop calling me that! He knows I hate it." I hear El do a low chuckle before closing the door. "Anyway, are you ready for your bachelor party?"

"No, I don't trust Travis or your brothers."

"It'll be fun."

"You ready for yours?"

"Ehh, I was thinking I'll just crash yours." He pulls me on top of him and kisses me.

"Four more days until you're Mrs. Salando." I run my fingers through his hair and kiss his nose.

"Can't wait."

The moment we get home Em and Travis pull us away from each other.

"Say your goodbyes, you'll see each other in three days."

"What?! No, this was a one-night thing, not a three-day thing!" I shriek. Graham glares at Travis.

"I told you they'd freak," Travis says. Graham pulls me to him and kisses me.

"Behave, baby." I bite his lip and he deepens the kiss. Em yanks me away.

"Enough, enough. We've gotta go!"

She stuffs me into the car and we're zipping off to fucking God knows where.

"Ok, the limo is picking us up at Selle's. You can change there and then we're fucking out of hereeee!"

I shake my head at her, climbing out of the car and heading toward Selle and Eli's apartment.

"About time. Here, take a shot! It's your bachelorette party! Go put this on." I hold it up and frown. It's a short, white dress that literally looks like it'll stop at my ass. I shake my head.

"Fuck no." She laughs and hands me another dress.

"I knew you'd say that, try this one!" It's white and still short, but longer than the other one. It's strapless and the material is oddly soft. I quickly change and stuff my feet into the red bottom pumps I have. The girls whistle at me when I come out of the room and Em throws a sash over my body that says *I'm getting married.*

"Ok, so we have a lot of ground to cover tonight."

And boy did we really.

The bachelorette party ended up in Las Vegas. I have no idea how they planned this so quickly, but by the end of the night I was wasted. I picked up my phone to call Graham.

"Angel."

"Hi, baby," I slur. We walk down the Las Vegas strip when I see another bride. She points at me and yells, "We're getting married!!!"

"Woohoo!!!!!" I yell back at her. Graham laughs on the other end.

"Is my girl drunk?" I nod and giggle. "What's so funny?" he asks.

"I'm nodding but you can't see me."

"Who says I can't see you?" I stop and look around. Selle and Em are smiling from ear to ear and I frown. A second later, I hear his voice in my other ear. "I can always see you, pretty girl." He kisses my cheek and I smile.

"What are you doing here?"

"You think we're stupid enough to keep you two apart from each other for more than twelve hours? Let's go party!" Travis says, lifting Em up and throwing her over his shoulder as she squeals. Graham wraps his arms around me as we follow.

71

Graham

The headache I have should be illegal. We spent the next two days in Vegas and every night I let Travis and Hogan talk Eli and I into drinking ourselves fucking crazy.

Liza groans next to me and I kiss her forehead, rolling over to grab her some aspirin and water.

"Thank you," she says, taking it. She snuggles up to me and I run my hands up and down her back. "What time do we leave?" she asks. I check my phone and groan.

"In an hour." Our rehearsal dinner is tonight, then tomorrow I finally get to marry the love of life. She sits up and stretches, her ring shining on her finger.

"I feel you staring," she says.

"I can't stare?" She looks at me and throws the pillow at me, heading to the shower.

"Let's go, we have a rehearsal dinner to get to!" she yells. I chuckle and follow after her.

I walk into the shower and she pulls me to her, devouring my mouth. She had been so needy these last few days. She hasn't been feeling all that great since the first day we were here, then the next thing I know she can't keep her hands off me. She wants sex every fucking second. I'm not complaining, though.

I push her against the shower and force myself inside of her. She moans as I enter her and she wraps her legs around me.

"Harder," she cries. I oblige, fucking her harder and harder until she digs her fingers into my back. "Yes, ahh fuck, right there." I push myself deeper, yanking her by her hair to look up at me. I pull her lip into my mouth and bite down.

"You have ten seconds to come, angel. Better hurry." She groans and I pick up my speed, fucking her hard and fast. She matches my thrust, pushing her pussy against me. I feel her tightening around my dick and I explode inside of her, letting every drop spill inside of her. I sit her down and clean her up. "Time to go get married, angel."

The plane ride was full of everyone taking turns vomiting in the bathroom. Well, everyone except Em.

"You all are a bunch of pussies. We didn't even drink that much," she keeps saying, which is a goddamn lie. We drank entirely too much. Liza couldn't even remember the initial night; she woke up confused on how I was in bed with her. I wasn't too happy about that and happily punished her for it.

"Alright, alright. Give me my bride and groom!" Our wedding planner, Javi, snaps his fingers. "Everyone get their shit together!" he yells as noone moves fast enough for him. Liza laughs as Em and Travis make their way up the altar. I asked Travis to be my best man and Liza asked Em to be her maid of honor. They definitely take their jobs seriously. Once they make it to their sides, Javi smiles at me. "Now once these two are done walking, eyes on the prize, Graham, because the star of the show will be walking towards you."

Liza decided that she would have Brant and Axel walk her down the aisle. Brant will walk her to the middle and then Axel will wait to walk her the rest of the way to me. She smirks at me when Javi holds his hands up. "Ok, now, Dad, you'll give her away to this handsome man of hers then you'll shoo fly." Axel shakes his head and takes his seat next to Brant and Bethany. "Then you two will say those magnificent vows, that I hope to fuck you didn't wait last minute to do, and then we'll live happily ever after...damn, I'm good!"

My mom laughs and claps her hands as I dip Liza down for a kiss. "Tomorrow, Crambell."

"Tomorrow. Don't be late."

"Wouldn't dream of it."

* * *

"Remind me again why we can't stay together?" I ask, packing my clothes. All of the girls are staying here at our house with Liza and the guys are staying at Travis'.

"Because tradition says it's bad luck." I roll my eyes and throw the last piece of clothing in my suitcase. "Do you have everything?"

"No, I'm missing an extremely important part." I pull her to me and she wraps her arms around me. "I don't like it."

"Me either, but it's just one night. Then we will be off for our two-week honeymoon."

"Mmm, right. I guess that's a fair trade." I bring her in for a kiss and our door flies open.

"Alright, time to go! She needs her beauty rest, G!" Selle yells.

"What would you have done if we were fucking?" She turns her nose up and fake gags while I chuckle, grabbing my suitcase.

"Fine, fine, I'm out." I kiss Liza again, realizing this is the last time I'll be kissing her as my fiancée. "Mmm... the next time I kiss you, it'll be as my wife."

"I can't wait." Selle smirks at us and leans on the doorway with her arms crossed. I peek at her and she raises her eyebrow.

"It's 10:00 p.m., G. All you need to do is go to sleep and when you wake up you'll have her back, safe and sound. Promise!" She pulls me by my arm and practically pushes me down the stairs.

"Get some rest, honey, we'll take care of her! We'll see you tomorrow! Love you." My mom kisses my cheek and they send me on my way.

Fuck, is it tomorrow yet?

72

Liza

It's my wedding day and I can't stop vomiting. I didn't drink much last night because I didn't want to be hungover for my wedding. But fuck, maybe I should've.

"Here, take some Zofran." Selle hands me a dissolvable tablet and I place it in my mouth. "It's just nerves, you'll be ok in a few minutes."

"Or she's pregnant," Em says, drowning her champagne.

"I am not pregnant." She shrugs her shoulders and pours herself another.

"You two fuck like rabbits, sorry Selle...but you do. It wouldn't surprise me if you were," Em says. I bite my lip and secretly try to calculate how late my period is. There's no way I am. I mean, I missed some pills from the chaos of our lives, but still. I don't feel pregnant.

"Ok, let's get you in this dress!" Javi says. Selle and Em squeal and I smile as he pulls it out of the bag.

Ten minutes later I'm ready to walk down the aisle. It must have been nerves because I'm no longer feeling sick. Instead, I'm feeling anxious. I want to see Graham; I miss him and it's barely been twenty-four hours. Eli walks into the room with a box and a note in his hand. He stops when he sees me and I'm surprised when I see tears in his eyes.

"Hey, stop that. I don't want to cry!" I say. He runs his hand over my cheek and kisses it.

"You look beautiful, Lizzie." I smile at him and he hands me the box with the letter. "It's from Graham. I had to make Travis and Hogan sit on him, he wanted to bring it himself. Something about *fuck tradition*." My mom walks by and smacks Eli on the back.

"Language," she says. He laughs. "Well, I'll see you out there. Good luck, sis. I'm so happy for you."

I go into the bridal room and shut the door, reading the card.
Something new...can't wait to marry you.
-Your husband

I open the box and gasp at the diamond necklace that's inside. It goes perfectly with my dress. There's a knock on the door and it's Selle, giving me a knowing smirk.

"Now I know why he wouldn't let me get a necklace for the dress." She turns me around and clasps it around my neck for me.

"You are a vision; he's going to fall to his knees when he sees you...now let's go get married."

The music starts and they all file out of the room. I down a glass of champagne and then instantly feel bad for doing so. *What if I am pregnant?*

I push the thoughts to the back of my mind and Brant walks over to me.

"Ready to do this?"

"So ready." I smile and he wipes his tears.

"I'm so proud of you, princess." Javi peeks his head in the

curtain.

"Ok, you're up! Knock them dead, and if he doesn't cry looking at how gorgeous you are, run away!" I laugh at him and we head toward the aisle.

Brant offers me his arm and I take it. "He's right, we're leaving if he doesn't cry." I elbow him and he chuckles as the curtains open. I take a deep breath and we walk forward.

Graham is standing at the end in a charcoal gray Armani suit and all I see is him. The look on his face when he sees me is what keeps me moving. I know that I'm walking towards my future and I can't seem to get there fast enough. Brant kisses my cheek as he hands me over to my father. My mother and Madeline are smiling from ear to ear as we make the rest of the way down the aisle.

"I couldn't have picked a better man for you, Lizzie," my dad whispers to me. He kisses my cheek and takes his seat. Ellis is sitting next to Madeline; we actually got him to agree to not work during the wedding and to just be a part of the memories this time. He fought us tooth and nail, but eventually gave in when Madeline asked him.

Graham holds out his hand and beams up at me, tears in his eyes. "You are beautiful," he whispers as he rubs my cheek.

The priest moves quicker than I've ever seen a priest at a wedding and I laugh inside, knowing Graham probably had something to do with that. "Do you, Graham, take this woman from this day forward, to be your wedded wife, to live together in the sacred state of matrimony? Do you promise to love her, comfort her, honor and cherish her, in sickness and health, 'til death do you part?"

He rubs my finger and smiles at me "I do." He slides the ring on my finger and the tears start falling. "And do you, Elizabeth, take this man from this day forward to be your wedded husband, to live together in the sacred state of matrimony? Do you promise to love him, comfort him, honor and cherish him, in sickness and health, 'til death do you part?"

"I do." I slide the custom ring on to his finger, it's perfect for him. Silver titanium, with an outline of diamonds, and a engravement inside that says *I love you more.*

"Graham and Elizabeth have also prepared personalized vows. Graham?"

He grabs my hands into his and looks me in my tear-filled eyes. "Elizabeth...you once asked me why I called you angel and I figured today was the perfect day to tell you. It's because my entire life I felt this darkness around me. I lacked sleep, direction, confidence, and purpose. But when I met you, I found sleep to be peaceful, I found a purpose, I felt confident, and *you* were my direction. You chose me when I didn't choose myself. Our journey has been more than eventful, our love story like no other, but I promise to always put you first, to always make you feel seen, heard, and loved. Even in death I'll find a way to still love you. You are my reason for life, angel. You are my reason for never letting bad circumstances ruin me. I love you today more than yesterday and less than tomorrow. A lifetime isn't enough."

He wipes the tears that are streaming down my face and tightens his hold on my hand.

"Graham, from the moment I met you I knew I had to know you. I wanted to be around you even if it was hard for me to admit. You never shied away from the obstacles I threw at you and you never ran when you saw the damage I had. Instead, you showed me every day how beautiful life could be.

You showed me how someone should be loved, how someone should be worshiped and taken care of. Loving you was the best decision of my life. You always say it's *you* that doesn't deserve me, but it's me. I'm going to spend the rest of my life, honoring you, supporting you, listening to you, and loving you. You are my reason for life, and a lifetime isn't long enough. I love you more than words can explain and I can't wait to show you that love as your *wife*."

"Graham, you may—" He grabs me and kisses me as whistling breaks out all around. The priest shakes his head and smiles at us. Graham dips me and kisses me deeper before bringing me back up.

"You're my wife," he whispers. "You're my husband," I say back. He kisses me again as the priest announces us.

"Ladies and gentlemen, I present to you for the first time, Mr. and Mrs. Graham Salando!" He scoops me up in his arms and I throw my head back in laughter as Travis and Em follow behind us.

We're finally married and damn, it feels good.

73

Graham

For our honeymoon we're back in Rome. Liza loved it so much she begged me to bring her back sooner rather than later.

"Are you sure you're feeling ok? We have two weeks here, maybe we should stay in and you should rest. It's been a long two days, angel." She's been vomiting all fucking morning and it's starting to worry me. She keeps saying she's just tired, but being tired doesn't make you vomit five times in an hour.

"I'm fine, I promise. I just took a Zofran, we're all good now. Let's go to the beach." She pulls me out the door and I follow behind my suddenly not sick wife.

"Mrs. Salando," El says, opening the door. She looks at him and smirks. "Well, I guess you stopped calling me Ms. Crambell, after all." He chuckles at her and shuts the door.

"Can we stop by the market first? I need to grab something," she says, drinking a bottle of water.

"Of course, pretty girl." I tell El to make a pit stop and he nods, pulling us out into the road.

I pat my lap and she climbs over, straddling me. "Hi, husband."

"Hi, wife."

I tuck a strand of hair behind her ear and kiss her. She deepens the kiss and I know what she wants. I push her dress up and rip her panties off. She tugs on my belt until my cock springs free and quickly seats herself on my cock. I let out a groan as she rides me like she's a fucking bull rider.

"Fuck, angel..." She speeds up, bouncing on my cock faster and faster. I run my fingers through her hair and yank her to me. I match her force, fucking her hard and deep. She bites my neck and I wrap my hand around her throat, just how she likes it.

"Mmm, fuck me," she moans as I run my tongue up her neck. I feel her pussy suffocating my cock and I know she's close, so I add a finger to send her over the edge.

"I'm coming..." she moans as I continue my assault. "Ah-hhh, fuck." Her body shakes as she comes and I follow behind her. I kiss her and she catches her breath. I push her hair out of her face and she curls into my arms.

God, I'm a lucky son of a bitch.

74

Liza

I'm staring at the two lines on the test. *Pregnant.* I'm fucking pregnant. When I think about it, I should have known. All the signs were there, but I didn't want to believe it. When we stopped by the market I bought three tests and right now all three of them are staring back at me with two lines, even a digital one that says *pregnant.* I figured I should take one before we had any alcohol. I managed to dodge the drink during our wedding reception by saying I didn't feel that well. But I won't be able to keep Graham out of the dark much longer; he was already talking about taking me to the doctor to be checked out. He knocks on the door and I freeze.

Fuck. Fuck. Fuck. Does he want this now? We just got married. What if he doesn't want to share me yet? What if he changed his mind and doesn't want kids at all? Fucking hell.

"Angel, you ok? You've been in there for a while." I take a deep breath and put the tests in the trash. I have to tell him. We promised no secrets, especially one this big. I open the door and he puts his hand on my head. "Do you still feel sick?" I shake my head.

"No…" I bite my lip and look down, my signature telltale sign that I'm hiding something. He lifts my face up to his and tilts his head. "What is it?"

"I was just thinking, how soon do you want kids?" He arches his eyebrow and looks at my stomach.

"You're pregnant?" I look away again, unable to face him. I can't handle the disappointment I know I'll see. He pulls my face to his again and tears fill my eyes. "Answer me. Are you pregnant?"

"Yes." He stares at me for a while, not saying a word. The silence is killing me. "I'm sorry. I missed a few pills when—" He crushes my lips with his.

"I don't care about that. We're having a baby." He smiles at me and picks me up, spinning me around. I laugh as he set me back on my feet.

"You're happy?"

"Fuck yes, I'm happy. I'm going to be a Dad!" He drops to his knees, putting his hands on my stomach. "Hi, little baby, I'm your Daddy." He looks up at me and kisses my belly. "Ease up on your mom here, we're trying to enjoy our honeymoon."

"I thought you'd be mad at me…"

"Angel, we never use protection and we have a lot of sex. I'm surprised you weren't pregnant sooner, especially since I've been hiding your pills from you for the last few months." He wraps his arms around me and kisses me again.

"I knew it!"

"Now, we have two weeks to ourselves. Let's go get into some trouble."

75

Graham

9 months later

"Graham! Faster!" I'm bobbing and weaving through traffic. Her contractions are every three minutes and she's screaming so loud I think my ear drums will burst.

"We're almost there, baby." Moments later we pull into the hospital. Everything moves so quickly, and the next thing I know, they have her hooked up to cuffs and her feet in stirrups. She doesn't have time for an epidural and that alone fucking scares me. We're having twins—that was a surprise to us. A boy and girl. The best of both worlds.

"Alright, Elizabeth, I want you to give me a big push on the next contraction. I can see the first baby's head." I hold her hand and she breathes before she starts pushing again.

"Come on, angel, push. You got this." The sound of tiny screams fills the room and my eyes water.

"Another push, Elizabeth, your baby boy is right there!" She pushes again and again, then there's another tiny scream. The nurse lays my son and daughter on Liza's chest and I'm in awe. In awe of their tiny faces, tiny noses, and tiny hands. I stare blankly at them.

"Look at them, Graham, they're beautiful." I kiss her head and lean my forehead against hers.

"You did so good, baby." She kisses the top of each of their little heads and turns towards me.

"Want to hold your son and daughter, *Daddy*?"

Daddy. I'm a fucking Dad.

Thank God I don't have a *Daddy* kink.

76

Epilogue

I'm watching my wife and our twins run around the yard.

"Daddy! Catch me!" Celeste squeaks, running towards me. I scoop her up and spin her around as she laughs. Joseph wraps himself around my leg and I fall to the ground as he climbs me.

"You got me!" I say, covering myself. The little fucker loves hitting me in the balls these days. Liza sits next to us and pulls Leste into her lap.

"Ok, you two, go get your suitcases. Your grandma will be here soon to pick you up." She kisses our daughter on her forehead and they both run into the house where Abby and Marco are waiting for them.

They moved here to Seattle and I hired them to work for me at our Seattle home. We still split our time between here and New York, not being sure where we want to stay for good. Liza loves Seattle, but she's grown to love being in New York, too.

The doorbell rings and she kisses my cheek before going inside to let her mom in. The kids run to her and she scoops them up in her arms!

"Grandma!" they yell and she cringes. "Aht, aht, I'm too young for that, remember? You call me *Glama*!" Liza rolls her eyes and grabs the kids' suitcases.

"Hi, Mama," she says. Bethany kisses her cheek and then mine. "Don't forget, we'll be in New York a week from today."

Bethany flew in to get the kids and to see Eli and Hogan. She comes here at least twice a month, so much that she's having a house built here for her and Brant to *vacation*, as she says. Eli and Selle haven't bit each other's head off yet, which is funny because Hogan still lives with them. That's a situation I'm not fucking touching with a ten-foot-pole—I know I won't like the answer I find.

"I know, I know. I don't understand why I can't just keep them for two weeks and bring them back with me for the ball. You two deserve a break; all you do is work and parent."

"Mama."

"Angel, it's just another week, they'll be fine. Let her have some time with them." She rolls her lips in her mouth and picks her finger. She hasn't been away from the twins for longer than two days and even that was hard for her.

"Fine. Ok, *fine*."

It's our anniversary and we're going to the mountains to celebrate. If I have it my way, she'll be pregnant with baby number three by the time we leave.

"Bye, Daddy!" the twins say, running to me. I hug and kiss them both. "Give your grandma hell, ok?" Joseph smirks and nods while Celeste frowns, sticking her finger in my face. "That's not a nice word, Daddy!" I kiss her nose and she giggles, running to her mom.

"Mommy! Daddy said a bad word." I gasp in surprise at my little girl telling on me.

"Mommy loves you both! Be good and have so much fun!" She leans down and whispers in Leste's ear, "Don't worry, baby, Mommy's going to get Daddy for that."

"Mmm, Daddy hopes so," I say, briskly walk past her, smacking her ass. I scoop up Celeste in one arm and Joseph in my other.

"Jesus Christ, we're still here," Bethany says with a sly grin on her face. "Let's go, my little babies. We're going to have so much fun! Uncle Eli and Uncle Hogan are coming to visit, too! And I even think they're going to bring your Auntie Selly!!

"Oh yay!!!" the twins shout in unison as I scrunch my eyes close.

"You two are going to burst Daddy's eardrums!" I say, squeezing them closer as they squeal.

We walk them outside and I put them in their car seats, kissing both of their noses.

"Daddy loves you both."

"Love you more!" Leste screams.

"Not possible," Liza says, bending her head down into the car to kiss them.

"Don't care!" Joseph screams even louder.

My eyes burn with unshed tears as my heart triples in size. I'm staring at three pieces of my heart outside of my body and I don't think I'll ever get used to it.

Liza sighs as the car pulls off and I grab her hand.

"Two weeks, baby. Two weeks with just us. Two weeks of me making you remember who makes the rules, who makes you come, who makes you scream, and who makes you beg," I say, pushing her against the door frame.

"Animal," she whispers before I kiss her and she jets inside.

I grab her by her waist and she laughs as I drop us onto the couch. She crawls on top of me and wraps her arms around me.

"Hi, Mr. Salando."

"Hi, Mrs. Salando."

"Still happy you married me?" she asks, raking her fingers through my hair.

"No, I'm mad I didn't do it sooner." I kiss her nose.

"We have our whole lives."

"Baby, a lifetime isn't enough." I kiss her and she moans into my mouth.

"Upstairs, now." She takes off running for the stairs and I'm quick on her heels. I catch her at the top and spin her to face me. I cup her face and she smiles.

"I love you," I say, resting my forehead on hers.

"I love you more."

"Not possible."

"Don't care."

Again, I'm a lucky son of a bitch.

Acknowledgments

Writing acknowledgments for my second book blows my mind. I am filled with so much gratitude and love for you all. To my readers, this could never be possible without you, thank you for sticking it out with me during this journey. To my editor, Hannah, you are my girl! 4am and I'm having a meltdown? No problem, Hannah calls me. Like, what? Who do you know will ever be that invested? I am tremendously grateful and can't thank you and your brilliant mind enough. Olivia, my, PA, girl. You do SO much, from graphics to quotes, to emails, to talking sense into me when I'm being crazy. You are truly a blessing; thank you and I love you and all your crazy antics! To my ARC team, your feedback has been insane, the imposter syndrome is real. Thank you all for your love and sweet responses! Alexis, this cover!! I could not think of a better cover for this book. The detail is insane, you are the best. To Bri, you almost gave me a heart attack but thank you for helping me through this process! Your suggestions, your help in my blurb (which was bomb!), I can't thank you enough. To my husband, thank you again, for believing in me and pushing me to write and do what I love. To my parents, specifically my dad, if you're seeing this—ROLL DAWG! I wish I could tell you the language is better in this one, but it's not. Mama, I love you girl! To everyone that has cheered me on, my friends and my family; I love you all so much. Let's write another!

About the Author

Hi, my new friends! I'm so excited that you're here! I'm a country girl who loves writing and reading in my free time. I'm a mama of two and married to a man who makes my world spin. I live in Oklahoma (Boomer Sooner!) and love traveling and making memories with my friends and family. Food is seriously the way to my heart. I can be a bit of a firecracker sometimes, especially if I'm hangry, but can't we all? I love baseball, good beer, and great vibes!

I started writing when I was about 15 years old; my imagination should have gotten me in trouble long ago. I have so many ideas for different books, and I truly cannot wait for you all to experience them with me!

Thank you for trusting me to give you the book fill you need!

You can connect with me on:
    Instagram: @alainatlee_author
    Facebook: @Alaina T. Lee Author
    Facebook group: Alaina T. Lee Reader's group
    TikTok: @alainatlee_author

Also by Alaina T. Lee

If you loved this duology, THANK YOU. It has been such a journey and I am not ready to say goodbye to Graham and Liza.

I'd be lying if I said I wasn't seriously entertaining the idea of furthering this series with the side characters. I mean come on, aren't you DYING to know if Selle ever finds out her father was a piece of shit? Aren't you on the edge of your seat wondering what Travis and Emily have been doing while they travel, and especially now that they're moving to New York? And don't tell me you aren't wondering if Hogan is banging it out with Eli and Selle.

I bet you are now huh? Haha, little book slut. I love you.

Xoxo,
Alaina T. Lee

Oh! Don't forget to write your review on Amazon!

9 798330 363186